THREADS OF SILK

THREADS OF SILK

ROBERTA GRIEVE

LARGE PRINT
Oxford

First published in Great Britain 2010
by
Robert Hale Limited

Published in Large Print 2011 by ISIS Publishing Ltd.,
7 Centremead, Osney Mead, Oxford OX2 0ES
by arrangement with
Robert Hale Limited

British Library Cataloguing in Publication Data
Grieve, Roberta.
    Threads of silk.
    1. Young women - - England - - London - - Fiction.
    2. Young women - - England - - Essex - - Fiction.
    3. Family violence - - Fiction.
    4. Mills and mill-work - - England - - Essex - -
    Fiction.
    5. Love stories.
    6. Large type books.
    I. Title
    823.9'2–dc22

        ISBN 978–0–7531–5261–4 (hb)
        ISBN 978–0–7531–5262–1 (pb)

Printed and bound in Great Britain by
T. J. International Ltd., Padstow, Cornwall

CHAPTER
ONE

Ellie Tyler reached the corner of the narrow terraced street and looked back to see that Gran was still standing at her back door.

"See you next week," she called, waving. She waited until her grandmother had gone back into the house before ducking through a gap in the dilapidated fence surrounding the rubble-filled site that had been cleared to make way for a new block of flats.

She ran across the uneven ground, her shiny nut-brown curls bouncing on her shoulders. She couldn't wait to get home and tackle Mum about what Gran had just told her.

She should have been thinking about the exams next week. If she didn't pass she'd never get a good job or go to college. She didn't want to end up working at the Riverside Club like her sister. Not that she really thought Dad would let her go to art college even if she won the scholarship. She was lucky he'd agreed to her staying on the extra year to take the GCE exams.

She reached the main road leading past the market, jumped over the strand of wire, all that remained of the fence on this side, and then started as a meaty hand descended on her shoulder and a loud voice said, "Wotcher, Ellie. 'Eard from your 'Arry lately?"

She turned to face the big man with his even bigger grin. "Oh, Mr Varney, it's you."

"'Oo d'yer think it was then? The Lord Mayor of London?" The laugh boomed out and Ellie couldn't help smiling, despite her preoccupation with her grandmother's recent revelations about the family history.

"I had a letter from him the other day. He's still in Germany," she said.

"Well, when you write, tell 'im I miss him down the market. All the old dears do too. I reckon I don't sell 'alf as much veg since 'e's bin gone."

"I'll tell him, Mr Varney." Her smile faded. "I miss him too."

"Well, he's only got a couple more months to do. You tell 'im, love — there'll be a job waiting for 'im when 'e's finished 'is National Service."

A couple of months, Ellie thought as she said goodbye to the stallholder, her steps dragging as she turned off the busy Roman Road into Kendall Street. It seemed a lifetime to her. Ever since she was a little girl she'd worshipped Harry, the boy she'd been brought up to think of as her brother all these years. He'd always been there, sharing his sweet ration, sorting out the bullies who jeered at her in her grammar school uniform, and most of all shielding her from her father's temper. When he'd left to do his National Service, she knew he'd had no choice, but it felt as if he'd deserted her.

She reached the tall shabby building on the corner where their landlord, Mr Solomons, had his second-hand furniture shop. The shutters were up and she realized it must be later than she thought. As she ran up the steep stairs to their flat, her mother appeared in the doorway of the back room which served the family as combined kitchen and living room.

"Where've you been, Ellie? I've been worried to death. It's gone six." She didn't sound angry, just tired.

All thoughts of the conversation with Gran and the questions she wanted to ask flew out of Ellie's head, as her mother gripped the doorframe, knuckles white, eyes red-rimmed in her pale face.

Ellie hung her satchel over the banister and took her mother's arm, leading her into the kitchen and guiding her into the armchair beside the range. She poked the fire into life and pushed the kettle over the flames.

"What is it this time?" she asked in a resigned voice, for what else could it be but her father having one of his paddies again? The slightest thing could set him off, especially when he'd been drinking.

"It's Sheila." Tears spilled over and ran down Mary's cheeks.

Ellie looked on helplessly before busying herself making a pot of tea. As she got the cups out and warmed the teapot, she wondered what had happened. Her half-sister had started work at the Riverside Club when she left school four years ago, despite her mother's protests that it wasn't a respectable place for a fifteen-year-old.

Sheila had defied her, egged on by Bert and his promises that his mate Tommy Green would pay her twice as much as she could earn behind the counter in Woolies.

"What's wrong with being a waitress?" she'd asked and Mary had reluctantly given in.

When she'd matured into the long-legged, bosomy beauty she now was, Tommy raised her salary and moved her into the nightclub. A hostess, she called herself now and Ellie knew her mother wasn't happy about it.

"What's she been up to?"

Mary shook her head. "She's only been carrying on with that hoodlum — and him a married man." She began to cry again.

Ellie shivered at the thought of Sheila carrying on with Tommy Green. She couldn't stand her father's boss who owned several clubs and gyms in the neighbourhood. Everyone knew they were a cover for his criminal activities but he was very well off and that would be the attraction for Sheila. She'd always wanted the things that money could buy.

Mary gave a sarcastic laugh. "Your Dad's furious — only threatening to beat Tommy up, if you please."

Ellie couldn't help smiling too. The ex-boxer could make mincemeat of Bert if he chose, and he had the back-up of the gang of thugs who hung around the club. But that was her Dad all over, shouting and carrying on with no thought of the consequences, especially when he had a few drinks inside him.

4

"Don't worry, Mum. He won't do anything. Too scared of losing his job," Ellie said.

But that wasn't why Mum was so upset, she realized. It was the thought of her daughter carrying on with a man more than twice her age, and married at that. She'd tried so hard to bring her children up to be respectable, despite their poverty and terrible living conditions — not to mention her husband's shady dealings. Harry and Ellie hadn't disappointed her, but it had always been a losing battle as far as the headstrong Sheila was concerned.

"Where's Dad now?" Ellie asked.

"He went looking for Sheila, threatening all sorts if he catches up with her."

The slam of the front door shook the house, its echoes reaching up the stairwell and both Ellie and her mother jumped, straining towards the door as footsteps sounded on the uncarpeted stairs.

Mary gave Ellie a little push. "Best get up to your room, love. Get on with your homework. I'll come up before I go to work."

Ellie didn't need telling twice. She darted out of the room, grabbed her satchel off the banister and crept up to the attic room she shared with Sheila. She took her books out of her bag and sat at the table in front of the window. Although it was supposed to be almost summer, the mist from the river seeping through the cracks in the badly fitting window frame made it feel cold.

She fetched the eiderdown from the bed and wrapped it round her, pulling it up around her ears to keep out the draughts as well as the sound of shouting from downstairs. Not Dad's voice, thank goodness. This time it was Sheila having a go.

Ellie got up and wedged a chair under the doorknob, just in case Dad came back. Sometimes she got so engrossed in her homework, especially if it was English or history, that she didn't hear him coming.

It was English tonight, but she couldn't really concentrate. She put down her Shaeffer fountain pen, a present from Harry for passing the scholarship exam, and glanced across at the door, reassuring herself that the chair was still in place. There was no privacy in the Tyler household and even the wedged chair wasn't always proof against Bert's more determined efforts. But she was safe for a while. Mum hadn't gone to work yet and he never came to her room while Mum was still there.

She sighed. If only Mum didn't work nights at the hospital, she thought, picking up her exercise book and reading through her composition. She wasn't really satisfied with it but she replaced the book in her satchel and got out her pad to write to Harry. Usually she had no trouble filling several pages with family news and gossip. She got as far as telling him she'd met Mr Varney but then she got stuck. She couldn't mention what Sheila had been up to and, as for what Gran had told her earlier, she thought she'd better wait till she'd talked to her mother.

She chewed the end of her pen, thinking that perhaps she should have gone round to Judith's after school. At least she'd have someone to talk to. But, she was fed up with her friend's teasing every time she mentioned Harry.

"Anyone would think he was your boyfriend, the way you go on about him," she'd said and Ellie had been unable to prevent the hot red tide flooding her face, which of course only made Judith tease all the more.

She stood up and lifted the curtain, gazing out at the twinkling lights of the city. The fog had lifted now. It had only been a light mist from the river, not like the pea-soupers in the winter, when all the fires of the close-packed houses were belching out their thick coal smoke.

She remembered a few years ago when it had been so bad that people were told to stay indoors. Mum had kept her off school for a couple of days and she'd missed her art lesson that week. Gran had been ill too, with a bad chest, and her cough had never really cleared up.

Ellie leaned on the window sill. She loved the city at night. The tall blocks of flats that were going up to replace the wartime bombsites, seemed like fairytale castles when they were all lit up. She would often sit here, watching the trains rattling over the bridge at the end of the road by the market, listening to the distant hooting of ships on the Thames, and daydreaming about a different world far removed from the drab one she'd known all her life. She often longed to get away from it, especially when her father was making life miserable for her. But here, under the cloak of darkness, London seemed a magical place and she couldn't imagine living anywhere else.

The doorknob rattled and Ellie started, relaxing as she heard Sheila's whisper. "It's only me, let me in."

Ellie removed the chair and opened the door a crack. "Where's Dad?"

"Still out."

"Has Mum gone to work yet?"

"Not yet — she's just getting ready."

"She's really upset."

"I know. She called me a trollop." Sheila gave a short laugh when she saw her sister's expression. "It's not like that. Tommy loves me, he said so. He's going to get me a flat."

Ellie's eyes widened. "But Sheila, he's already married."

"So what? I don't care — not when he gives me such lovely presents." Sheila grinned, fingering the gold bangle which encircled her wrist. "Well, where do you think I got the clothes, the jewellery?"

"I thought you bought them yourself — out of your wages."

"Don't make me laugh. You know I give most of it to Mum. She needs it with Harry gone. Gawd knows she gets little enough from Bert after he's had a few drinks."

Ellie sat down on the edge of the bed. To be honest, she wasn't really surprised that Sheila accepted gifts from her boss in return for "being nice to him" as she put it. Her sister had always liked pretty things and had vowed that one way or another she would have them. But to be nice to Tommy Green, with his piggy eyes and black greasy hair, his stomach hanging over his

8

trousers, albeit half-hidden by his silk waistcoat and expensively-cut jacket? He was old enough to be Sheila's father. She voiced the thought aloud and her sister turned on her.

"Well at least he's good to me. Anyway, it's no different to doing it with 'im." She jerked her head towards the door. "And at least I get something out of it."

Ellie didn't reply and Sheila sank down on the bed beside her, putting her arm round the younger girl. "Don't look so shocked, love. You must've known. Why do you think he got me the job at the club and stood up for me when Mum tried to stop me working there? I threatened to tell her what was going on. 'E nearly wet 'isself. He knows I'm not scared of 'im any more."

Ellie wasn't shocked in the sense of being surprised. She'd always shared a room with her sister, so she could hardly avoid knowing what her father got up to. The surprise had come when he'd started on her. After all, she wasn't pretty like Sheila and when he was in a bad mood he'd call her horrid names like "skinny little runt" and "know-it-all brat". She'd put his attentions down to the fact that, once Sheila started work, she wasn't available, so he had to make do with her. At first, because she'd been used to him coming to their room at night, she'd accepted it as normal, although she didn't like it, even when he stroked her hair and called her his little angel. It was only when she'd cried out and Bert had threatened her, promising far worse if her mother ever got to hear of it, that she'd realized his behaviour was wrong.

Now she tried to talk to Sheila about it, but her sister just brushed her off. "You'll get used to it. I had to."

When Ellie started to cry, she softened a little, putting her arm round her shoulders and giving her a hug. "There's nothing we can do about it, kid," she said harshly. "If Harry knew, he'd kill the bastard — come to that, I've often thought of it myself. But he's not worth swinging for." She turned to Ellie, pinching her chin in her fists and looking into her eyes. "Promise me, you won't say anything to anyone. You wouldn't want to get either of us into trouble, would you?"

Ellie nodded silently, sniffing and wiping her hand across her nose, watching as Sheila banged around slamming drawers and muttering to herself; "I never thought he'd do it to his own kid. I'd like to get my 'ands on 'im."

When she pulled an old suitcase down from the top of the cupboard and started throwing things into it, Ellie suddenly realized what she was doing. "Where are you going?"

"Tommy's waiting for me round the corner in his posh car. 'E's got a Jag. Real leather seats, goes like a bomb." Her voice lost its chirpy tone and she said, "Look, Ellie, you've gotta understand. I can't stay here after what Mum said. She told me I was no daughter of hers. Besides, I was leaving anyway."

"Well, I can understand Mum being upset. You know she's always going on about us being a respectable family."

Sheila laughed. "Respectable! Then why did she marry Bert after my dad was killed? She must've known what he was like. And letting me work for Tommy, of all people. I knew his reputation before I ever got the job."

"So why did you agree to work there then?" Ellie asked.

"It was the only way I could see of getting out of this dump. I meet a lot of blokes — blokes with money — at the club." She laughed again. "Never thought I'd hit it off with the boss though."

She picked up her case and went to the door. "Look after yourself, kid. Don't let the old man get you down." She gave that bitter little laugh again. "It ain't so bad, once you get used to it."

Ellie nodded but she didn't believe her, and she didn't think Sheila believed it either. She's just trying to make me feel better, she thought.

Sheila dropped the case and gave her a hug. "Just try to keep out of his way. If Mum goes to work and leaves you by yourself, go down and sit with Solly. You'll be safe with him." Then she was gone.

Ellie sat on the bed for a long time, listening to the silence. Mum would be off to her night shift at the hospital soon and she would be alone, really alone. Harry had gone and now Sheila had deserted her. None of them really cared, she thought as the tears rolled down her cheeks.

When Mary called up the stairs a little later she managed to reply in what she hoped was a normal voice.

She replaced the chair under the doorknob but she knew that if Bert really wanted to get in, nothing would stop him. She slowly undressed, folding her white school blouse and navy gymslip and hanging them neatly over the back of the chair. Her maroon blazer went on a hanger behind the door. Then she realized she had to go downstairs to clean her teeth and go to the toilet.

Best get it over with, she thought, pulling an old cardigan over her thin nightdress. She crept to the top of the stairs and peered down into the darkness. She made it past her parents' room and the kitchen, down to the ground floor where Mr Solomons had his living quarters behind the shop. The bathroom and toilet they shared with their landlord was at the end of a long dark passage.

Ellie hated it, especially when everyone was out. Still it was better than having to go outside like Gran, she thought, as she crept along, her hand on the wall feeling her way. As she grasped the knob of the bathroom door the sound of the toilet flushing made her stomach leap and her heartbeat quickened. It's only Solly, she reassured herself, but she ran back to the foot of the stairs, clinging to the newel post and chewing her fingernails.

The door opened, spilling light out into the passage, and her father staggered out, dragging his bad leg and mumbling to himself. He was drunk and Ellie hoped that he'd pass out before he realized she was alone in the house.

She crept up the stairs and crouched at the bottom of the next flight, listening to his mumbled obscenities. "Abused my trust, 'e did. My old mate Tommy, carrying on like that. Would never 'ave let 'er work there if I'd er known." He stumbled as he reached the landing and Ellie shrank back into the darkness. "Still, she prob'ly led 'im on. Always was a little tart. Well, it's good riddance to 'er. I've still got my little angel."

He pulled himself up, clutching the newel post and calling out in a wheedling voice. "Angel, where are you, pet? Come and give Daddy a goodnight kiss."

Ellie shuffled up one more stair on her bottom, hoping he wouldn't spot the movement, but he looked up.

"Oh there you are, Angel. Waiting for Daddy to come 'ome, were yer?"

His shadowy form loomed over her and she could smell the beer and cigarettes on his breath. Even in the darkness she knew he'd be wearing that glazed smile he always had when he wanted her to be "nice" to him.

If she ran up to her room and put the chair against the door, she'd be OK. He could hardly stand. Surely he wouldn't be able to get upstairs without falling. But she knew that, despite his old war injury, he could sometimes move with surprising speed. She inched herself up, back against the wall, and had been ready to turn and run when his hand shot out and grasped her ankle.

She struggled to escape but he held on with determined strength, dragging her along the passage. Her head banged on the floor and when it cleared she found herself on the kitchen floor with Bert looming over her. As his body covered hers and his hands fumbled with her nightdress, she turned her head away from the sour taste of his breath. She bit her lip, the metallic taste of blood overwhelming the smell of his beery breath in her face.

A coal shifted in the grate nearby and flared up, throwing Bert's shadow on to the wall behind him. Ellie looked away, trying to shut out the sounds and images, and most of all the sick shameful feeling of what he was doing to her. Her cheek rested against the rough rag rug Mary had made from the family's old coats and jumpers, and from the corner of her eye she could see the little wooden stool Harry had made in woodwork lessons.

Bert's hands were all over her and she scrabbled around trying to find something to hit him with. But as her fingers closed over the coal shovel, he gave a sigh and passed out, pinning her to the floor with his body.

CHAPTER
TWO

The rattling of the curtains on their brass rings brought Ellie awake. Wind-blown rain rattled against the window.

"Come on, sleepy-head," her mother said. "You'll be late for school."

Ellie tried to sit up, her bruised body protesting against the movement, and memory flooded back. She closed her eyes as Mary approached the bed and asked, "Are you all right, love? You look a bit flushed."

"I don't feel well," Ellie said. It wasn't a lie. Her head ached and she felt bruised and sore all over.

Her mother gave a short laugh. "If it was your sister staying in bed on a school day, I'd think she was swinging the lead. But you wouldn't miss school for anything." She sat down on the edge of the bed and felt Ellie's forehead. "You are poorly, love. Have you got a tummy-ache as well?" Ellie nodded "I'll fetch you up a drink and hot water bottle. Try and go back to sleep."

After she'd gone, closing the door quietly behind her, Ellie forced herself to think back to last night. She hardly remembered crawling into bed. Thank goodness Dad had passed out before she hit him. She could imagine his rage if she had dared to fight back. When she was little she had tried to protest and he told her it was his way of showing that he loved her. She was his little "Angel", wasn't she? But recently things had been different. And now that Sheila was gone, she was more afraid than ever.

Sometimes she wondered whether it was her fault. Mum had told her off loads of times for walking around the house in her nightie. Respectable girls didn't show off their bodies when there were men around, she said. That must be it then. Dad didn't think she was a respectable girl, so he could do what he liked. Perhaps he didn't love her any more.

She choked back a sob. She'd tried so hard to be good, determined to make the most of her chance at grammar school and make something of her life. But what was the use of trying? She'd just end up like Sheila, working at that awful club and having to be nice to horrible old men.

Her mother's footsteps clattered up the stairs and she slid further down in the bed, pulling the blanket up over her ears.

"Here's your drink, Ellie. And the hottie. I'm just popping down the market but I won't be long."

Ellie kept her eyes closed as Mary tucked the hot-water bottle under the blanket and leaned over, brushing her cheek with her lips. When she heard the door close, she sat up and took a sip of the tea, which her mother had placed on a chair by the bed.

The hot drink helped a little but what she really wanted was a bath. As well as being bruised and battered, she felt unclean. But she couldn't bring herself to get out of bed and make her way down the two flights of stairs. And she couldn't face the battle with the big gas geyser on the wall which didn't always work properly, sometimes gushing out boiling water, sometimes just a trickle of cold. Harry could always fix it though. He seemed to have a knack with mechanical things. Despite her misery, Ellie felt a smile beginning — as it always did when she thought of her brother.

The smile disappeared as memory flooded back. Not her brother; not even a stepbrother or cousin, as she'd always thought. If she'd got it right, Harry was no relation at all. The thought brought a funny feeling in her stomach and she remembered the way he had kissed her goodbye after his last leave. Since then, she'd found herself thinking about him all the time. She wasn't interested in boys — not like some of the girls at school, always whispering in corners. But since Gran's revelations she had dared to think that, maybe, Harry looked on her as more than a sister. The knot in her stomach grew as she realized that, if he knew what had happened last night, he would never love her.

She lay with her face to the wall, thinking about the day before. Since calling in to see Gran on her way home from school yesterday, she'd almost forgotten their talk, what with the row and Sheila storming out. Then her father coming home drunk and . . .

Ellie's mind sheered away from the thought. But she was determined it wouldn't happen again. It might have been her own fault this time; she still wasn't sure about that. But if he did try it on again, she'd run away, go and live with Gran. With Sheila and Harry gone, there was nothing to keep her here. Only Mum. But she didn't really care. Why else would she work at nights, leaving her alone with Dad? It wasn't as if they really needed the money. Dad had been in work for years now.

With a guilty start, she thought of her mother's tired, careworn face, the tender touch as she'd tucked her in bed only a little while ago. Of course Mum cared. She just didn't know what was going on, that's all. And how could she add to her worries? Not to mention her father's anger if she told.

Ellie sighed. Did all families have these problems, she wondered?

Wherever her agitated thoughts went they always came back to Harry — her big brother and champion ever since she could remember. She'd never questioned his relationship to the rest of the family. After all, Sheila was her sister and her surname was the same as Harry's. Mum's first husband, Jim Scott, had been killed at Dunkirk, leaving her with two children to bring up. Less than a year later she'd married Bert Tyler and Ellie was born soon after — too soon, Auntie Vi often said with a sniff.

It was Judith's teasing that had prompted Ellie's curiosity. On the way home from school yesterday her friend had said carelessly, "I know you think of him as your brother, but you're not really related are you?"

"Of course we are. My mum's first husband was killed in the war. That's why Sheila and Harry are called Scott."

"Perhaps I've got it wrong then," Judith said.

Of course she'd got it wrong, Ellie thought. But she tackled Gran about it all the same. It was no good talking to her mother. But Gran needed no excuse to get out the old photograph album and start reminiscing about "before the war".

The old lady had been sitting in her armchair in front of the gas fire. She looked tired but she greeted Ellie with a warm smile. "If you want a cup of tea, love, you'll have to make it. My old legs are playing up something cruel these days."

As she went through to the scullery out the back and put the kettle on, Ellie thought perhaps she shouldn't bring the subject up if her grandmother wasn't feeling well.

But when she went through with the tea tray, Gran was sitting up and looking more wide-awake. "It's good to see you, Ellie love. Where have you been hiding yourself lately?" she asked.

Ellie told her about Miss Evans, the art mistress, picking her to help paint and design the scenery for the school play.

Gran smiled. "You always did like your painting and drawing, didn't you?" She pointed to the mantelpiece, where a brightly painted picture of a fairground hung. "I'll always keep it. Looks good in the frame our 'Arry made, don't it?"

"I did one for Harry too," Ellie said. "To thank him for taking me to the fair."

"Well, you're a good little artist — I will say that. Though what good it'll be to yer when you leave school, I don't know. The things they teach yer at this school of your'n."

"Miss Evans says I'm good enough to go to art college," Ellie said proudly. "She's put me in for a scholarship."

"I wouldn't get yer 'eart set on it, love. You can guess what your dad'll have to say about that." Gran took a noisy slurp of her tea.

Ellie didn't answer. She knew in her heart that Gran was right. But it didn't hurt to dream, did it? She changed the subject, asking if any jobs needed doing.

"No thanks, love. Your mum was round earlier." She started coughing and Ellie hurried to get her medicine. "What with this chest and me legs," she wheezed, trying to smile. "Don't worry, girl. I'll be all right."

Ellie poured out more tea, wondering how to bring up the subject that had filled her mind recently. Gran was stroking Buster, the cat, who'd jumped up on her lap and was now purring loudly. He was getting old too, and spent most of his time dozing — just like Gran, Ellie thought, as the old lady's head started nodding.

She got up, intending to creep out quietly. But she couldn't leave without finding answers to the questions Judith's remarks had prompted. She was almost sixteen. She ought to know about her family. She went over to the sideboard and took out the old photo album. She carried it to the table near the window.

She paged through until she came to the pictures of her mother's wedding to Jim Scott. There was Mary, small and dark, smiling up at Jim. Ellie recognized him from the photo Harry had kept beside his bed. Her mother's friend Anne stood beside her and on the other side was the best man, Jim's brother. What was his name? Frank, that was it — the one Gran didn't like to talk about. He would be Sheila and Harry's uncle. Ellie wondered what had happened to him. Did he die in the war too?

She turned to ask but a muffled snore from the armchair stopped her. She looked again at the pictures of Jim and his brother, remembering Sid Varney's tales of growing up with her father and the Scott brothers. What was it he'd said? *"Like as two peas in a pod, they were."* Ellie held the album up to the window. Yes, they were alike, tall and fair — just like Harry and Sheila.

She felt a thrill of excitement as she realized what this meant. If only Gran would wake up so that she could ask her. She turned the pages quickly, but that was the only picture with both the young men in it. A little further on was a snapshot of a young woman holding a baby, a toddler by her side. She thought it was Anne, but it was too blurred to be really sure.

As she put the album down, Gran gave a little snort and opened her eyes. Buster stretched lazily and jumped down from her lap.

Gran stretched and yawned. "Oh dear, I've let the tea go cold. You should've woken me, love."

"I'll make some fresh," Ellie offered, jumping up and taking the tray.

When she came back a few minutes later, Gran was poring over the album. "You always did like looking at the old pictures," she said, looking up with a smile. "I only get to see them when you're here."

"I wish you'd tell me about the people in the photos, Gran. I know you don't like talking about the war, but they're my family too — even if I never knew most of them."

"You're right, Ellie love. I forget how quickly you're growing up." She sighed. "Sometimes it all seems like only yesterday. I've been thinking about it a lot lately. I suppose it's knowing I've got to move soon that's brought it all back to me."

Gran shifted in her chair and took a sip of tea. "I remember that night like yesterday. We were all down the shelter — but others weren't so lucky."

Her eyes misted and Ellie said quickly. "Don't talk about it, Gran, if it upsets you."

"No. It was a long time ago. Well, you know your mum was married to Jim Scott. And her best friend Anne married his twin brother, Frank. Nice boys . . ."

"Mr Varney told me they were all in the army together — Dad as well," Ellie said.

"That's right — they couldn't wait to join up when the war started. Anne had a little boy and your mum was expecting too. But they didn't think about that, did they?" The old lady's voice trailed away again.

"What happened?" Ellie asked, willing Gran to finish the story. She wanted to know what had happened to Anne and her little boy, although she'd already guessed the answer.

Gran sighed again and went on, "Things were pretty quiet at first. But they made the women take the children to the country because they knew there'd be bombing. The older kids went on their own but toddlers had their mums with them." She shifted in her chair. "There weren't any bombs, so after a bit they came back — your mum and Anne. They hated the quiet of the country and they missed their friends and families."

Ellie leaned closer to catch her grandmother's next words. "The blitz — the bloody blitz started, didn't it? Night after night. But Mary insisted on staying here with me. I begged them to go back to the country."

Gran's eyes filled with tears and Ellie took her hand, rubbing the cold fingers. "Don't get upset, Gran. You don't have to talk about it, you know. I'm sorry I reminded you."

But the old lady was determined to finish the story now. "I'm reminded of it every time I look out of my window," she said bitterly, gesturing towards the patch of weed-ridden waste ground beyond the net curtains. "That's where the big one fell, right where Anne's house was. My Bill — your grandad — was a warden. He had to help dig them out. The whole family — killed in one go. He never forgot it — was never the same man after that. Poor Bill."

Ellie patted Gran's hand. She didn't know what to say. Until now, "during the war" and "before the war" had just been stories. She could hardly remember it. She'd been just a toddler when the doodlebugs came.

"Well, it was all a long time ago," Gran said with a sigh. She straightened in the chair. "One good thing happened though. It was sheer fluke, they said. But they rescued the little boy . . ."

"It was Harry, wasn't it?" Ellie said eagerly. "He was Anne's little boy."

"That's right, love. Didn't you know?"

"No one ever told me. I've only just realized — something Judith said."

"I thought you knew. Anyway, your mum looked after him — said she would treat him like her own until Jim and Frank got back from the war. Then Jim was killed and Frank — poor Frank."

Gran's voice trailed away again and Ellie couldn't bring herself to ask what had happened. Instead she asked if her mother had adopted Harry.

"Not officially," Gran said. "And when she married Bert, he wanted her to give him up — put him in a home. But she wouldn't. It's the only time I've known her to stand up for herself. Bert couldn't budge her. She said she'd promised Anne and that was that."

Good for Mum, Ellie thought.

"Of course, she'd have had to give him up if Frank had come home," Gran said. "Poor Frank — he was worse off than the ones who were killed, if you ask me. Bad enough being wounded, but his mind went, poor lad. He was in one of them special hospitals. Your mum went down there once to let him know how Harry was. But he didn't even know her. Kept asking for Anne."

"Is he still there?" Ellie asked.

"No, he died a few years ago."

"And does Harry know all this?"

"Of course. Your mum never hid anything from him."

Poor Harry. No wonder no one spoke about it. Gran had called it a hospital but Ellie knew how the kids round their way would have taunted him if they'd known his dad was in the "loony bin".

"So Judith was right," Ellie murmured. "He's not my real brother. Why was it kept a secret then?" she asked.

"It wasn't a secret, love," Gran exclaimed with a throaty laugh. "Everyone around here knew. I suppose it never occurred to us that you didn't know as well. Besides, people want to get on with their lives, not keep talking about the war."

"I'm glad you told me," Ellie said. She looked up at her grandmother. "Is that why Dad doesn't like Harry? He's always picked on him as long as I can remember."

"Probably a bit of jealousy there if you ask me," Gran said.

"I can't get over it — Harry not being my brother, I mean."

Gran laughed. "What's the difference? He's still our 'Arry, aint' he?" She closed the album and said, "It's all water under the bridge now, love. Put it away and let's have another cup of tea."

Ellie hugged the hot-water bottle to her stomach as she replayed the conversation with Gran in her mind. Everything now seemed so much clearer. That strange feeling she'd had when Harry had kissed her goodbye at the station didn't matter any more.

He'd looked down at her, a twinkle in his blue eyes, his fair hair flopping over his forehead, despite the army's efforts to tame it.

"You're growing up, Ellie love," he'd said. "I won't know you when I come home again."

"I wish you didn't have to go," she said.

"You won't have time to miss me." He laughed. "I expect those grammar school boys have got their eye on you. You'll forget all about me."

She'd tried to protest but he'd given her a quick hug, before getting on the train. She'd stood waving, long after the train had pulled out from Waterloo.

Now, she brushed away a tear. It would be ages before he came home again. And when he did, would he still want to know her, once he knew what Bert had done?

CHAPTER
THREE

Ellie looked up from her porridge as Mary came into the room, smiling and holding a letter.

"It's from Harry," she said.

Usually Ellie would grab it before her mother had a chance to open it. But, still confused about her feelings for him, she listened half-heartedly as Mary read the letter aloud. "Thank goodness he's still in Germany. I thought they might send him out to Cyprus with all that trouble out there," she said.

"Best place for 'im," Bert muttered.

Another row was brewing and Ellie didn't wait to hear any more. She pushed her dish away, grabbing her blazer off the back of the chair. "Mustn't be late — exams today," she said.

"Don't know why you're bothering. I've already told you there's a job waiting for you when you finish school," Bert said.

Mary turned from the stove, about to speak, but Ellie couldn't face another row. She picked up her school satchel and ran down the stairs.

The high wooden gate into the back yard was ajar and she went to close it. Not like Solly to leave it open — there was some valuable furniture stored there. Her hand was on the latch when she noticed a pile of boxes in the corner. Some had words on the side in red. "Pye" it said. Others had "Bush" stamped on the side. She smiled. Maybe Solly was fed up with secondhand furniture and was branching out into televisions and radios.

But as she hurried towards the bus stop, another possibility struck her and her legs began to tremble. Dad had been extra flush with money lately. Was this the reason?

Ellie leaned against the bus stop and took a deep breath. Should she tell Solly or her mother what she suspected or would it just cause more trouble? If only Harry were here, she thought. He'd know what to do. Besides, he was the only one capable of standing up to Bert.

She shook her head. No, it was a good thing Harry was still away. She still wasn't ready to face him. Would she ever be able to look him in the eye again? There had been a time when she could have told him anything. Now she felt ashamed and confused, wondering whether everything was somehow her fault. After that dreadful night, she'd been listless for days, hardly answering when anyone spoke to her. Mum thought she had the flu and wanted her to stay off school a bit longer, but she'd insisted on going. She couldn't let those years of study go to waste by missing her exams.

To her surprise, the English exam went well despite her preoccupation. She still had the art exams to look forward to — saving the best till last, she thought, as she got off the bus and started up the road. They'd been let off early, as soon as the exam finished, and she thought about popping in to see Gran.

Then she remembered the letter from Harry. She'd been in such a state that she hadn't waited to hear his news that morning.

Mum had just got up and was combing her hair in the mirror over the fireplace when Ellie came in. "You're early, love. I was just going to sit down with a cuppa before starting on the tea," she said.

"I'll do it, Mum." Ellie poured water into the brown earthenware teapot and got cups off the dresser. She glanced at her mother, who was leaning back in the chair, her eyes closed, noticing the blue shadows under them. "You all right, Mum?" she asked.

"Just tired, love. This night work is getting to me."

"Why don't you ask to change then?"

"More money on nights." Mary sighed and took the cup, taking a grateful sip. She drained her tea and stood up. "Better get on with the cooking," she said. "Dad'll be home soon."

"I'll answer Harry's letter then — unless you want me to help."

Mary shook her head. "That's all right, love. You write this time. I don't know what to say to him after the shock he gave me."

Ellie grabbed the letter from behind the clock. "What's happened? Are they sending him to Cyprus?"

"He's getting married."

Ellie's stomach churned and she sat down, crumpling the envelope in her fist. "Did you say married? He can't be." She swallowed the sob that threatened to burst from her. No one must know how she felt.

"He's met some German girl and got her into trouble." Mary's voice was flat and her lips tightened. She turned away and began to chop the carrots.

Ellie slowly withdrew the single sheet of paper from the envelope. The letters danced in front of her eyes and she had to blink to make out the words. Even after reading it again she still didn't want to believe it. That last goodbye kiss had meant nothing, then. How naïve she'd been to think it had.

Harry looked across the crowded bar, peering through the thick smoke which made the dark beer cellar even darker. The place was crowded — mostly with British soldiers and young German girls. The men were only too pleased to buy drinks and offer their cheap cigarettes in exchange for an evening of feminine company. But Harry was beginning to regret his nights out with the boys and their inevitable outcome as he waited for Gerda.

Gerda Meyer, with her blonde curls and saucy look, reminded him of his cousin Sheila. And she spoke excellent English too, which made it easier to have a conversation. Not that they talked much that first night — the bar was too noisy. But they'd met again and walked by the river, where he found himself telling her about his family and his plans for the future. He had no intention of going back to Bethnal Green and working on Sid's vegetable stall. He'd signed up for the army's course in motor mechanics and maintenance and now helped keep the jeeps and lorries in good repair. When he got home, he planned to get a job in a garage and eventually to have his own business. Harry could see the day coming when everyone would have a car — not just those who were well-off. There'd be plenty of work for him in the future.

Gerda had listened patiently, seeming to recognize his need to escape from his background. She too had struggled, though in her case the war was more to blame than poverty. Her father had been in the navy, a stoker who'd gone down with his ship, and her mother had worked in a grocery store. But they'd lost everything in the punishing bombing raids of 1944 and 1945. The store, their home and Gerda's school had vanished in a pile of rubble.

She and her mother had been forced to scratch a living among the ruins — might even have starved if Mrs Meyer hadn't taken up with an American GI when the allies entered the stricken city. Gerda showed no shame when she told Harry.

"I was still a child only. To me the food he brought was the most important thing. You understand, Harry?" she'd said in her charming accent.

At least her mother's past had made it easier for Gerda to invite the young Englishman to her home. Mrs Meyer wasn't in a position to disapprove, although Harry knew that he and his mates were not always welcomed so warmly by their former enemies.

But he hadn't intended things to go so far. He'd just been grateful for the company — and he had to admit

Gerda's open admiration had turned his head a bit. But that was in the early days. She was attractive and fun to be with and an evening with her was better than poring over engineering manuals back at the barracks.

Then one night he'd had a drop too much to drink and she'd been all over him. The inevitable had happened. He didn't regret it but he should have known she'd read more into it than he was prepared to give. After all, she seemed like a nice girl — not one of those who gave her favours in return for a pair of nylons or a few drinks. And when she'd told him she was pregnant, of course he'd asked her to marry him. But it had meant the end of his dreams and ambitions. How could he do a garage apprenticeship and support a wife and baby?

He gazed gloomily into his tankard, looked up and scanned the crowded room again. There she was, biting her lip as she fought her way through the crowd. In that second, despite the blonde curls and the make-up, she reminded him of Ellie and something happened to him in the pit of his stomach. This time it was impossible to ignore the feeling. How could he have been so blind to what had been staring him in the face since his last leave?

As Gerda approached the table, her blue eyes lighting up as she spotted him, Harry forced himself to smile back. But inside he was cursing his stupidity. He would do the right thing — but it was the hardest thing he'd ever had to do in his life.

Writing to his family had been hard too. But he had to break the news some time. He could just see Bert's knowing smirk when he learned that Gerda was pregnant. Mary wouldn't be happy about it either, but she would realize he was trying to put matters right by marrying the girl. It was Ellie he was most concerned about, and he didn't know how he was going to face her. He just knew it wouldn't be possible to carry on acting as if she were still his little sister. Maybe it would be best if he never went back to London at all.

CHAPTER
FOUR

Ellie hadn't been able to eat the fried liver and bacon her mother had prepared. Just the thought of food made her feel sick. She had pushed her plate away and stood up when the door at the foot of the stairs banged open. Muttered swearing and heavy steps on the stairs heralded Bert's homecoming and, as he lurched into the room, she sidled towards the door, hoping to get up to her room before he said anything.

But he anticipated her, smiling glassily. "So, my angel's been doing her exams today. That means no homework, so you can come and sit with me while I eat my dinner. Tell me all about it."

It was rare for him to show any interest in her studies and she couldn't help the little glow of pleasure when he praised her for doing so well at school. The shock of Harry's news eased a little as she started to tell her father about the composition she'd written for the English exam.

His mood changed instantly. "What they teaching you all that nonsense for?" he asked. "Fat lot of good that'll do you when it comes time to leave school and get a job." He banged his knife and fork on the table for emphasis.

"Well, if I pass all the exams, it'll help me to get a better job," Ellie ventured timidly. She didn't think this was the right time to bring up the art scholarship.

"I already told you there's a job waitin' for yer," Bert said, leaning over and touching her cheek.

Ellie glanced anxiously at her mother. Surely she'd speak up. But Mary avoided her eyes. "At least you won't be waiting at tables," she said.

Bert laughed. "Too right — can't have you wastin' all that education."

"What's this job then?" Ellie was intrigued in spite of herself.

Her father tapped his nose. "You'll soon find out. I'll let you know when the boss is ready to talk to yer about it." He got up from the table and went to slump in his armchair by the fire.

Ellie glanced at her mother but Mary still refused to look at her. She poured her husband a cup of tea and took his empty plate to the sink.

What's the use, Ellie thought? Hadn't she always known in her heart that college — especially art college — was just a dream? Was it really worth another row, especially with Mum looking so poorly these days? Quickly she gathered her books together and moved towards the door. She wasn't quick enough. As she reached for the door handle, Bert caught her hand. "Come and give us a goodnight kiss then, Angel."

Reluctantly she gave him a quick peck on the cheek, trying not to flinch as the beery smell wafted towards her. He pulled her against him, kissing her and stroking her hair. "My little girl's growing up," he murmured.

The sound of a plate crashing on to the draining board made Ellie jump and Bert's hand fell away. Ellie seized the opportunity to move out of reach. "Goodnight Dad, 'night Mum," she said and quickly left the room.

Upstairs she put her school books down and sank on to the bed. Her knees trembled and her heart was thudding. It seemed that all her life she had lived with tension in her family. As she did every night now, she wedged the chair against the door — a futile gesture, she knew.

By the time she was undressed the trembling had stopped. But her mind was still downstairs, trying to make sense of the undercurrents which ebbed and flowed around the members of her family.

Mum had been in a funny mood earlier that evening and it wasn't just her obvious disquiet about Harry's shocking news. Dad hadn't done anything to upset her either — other than being late for dinner.

Ellie chewed at her thumbnail. No. It must be something she'd done. Had she guessed about what had happened with Dad? Ellie had grown up a lot lately, especially since Sheila had left home. She'd listened to the whispered conversations of the older girls at school, asking questions, not caring if they laughed at her, always careful not to reveal the reason for her curiosity. She had to have answers to the problems that had puzzled her for years.

Now she knew that what her father had done was wrong, despite what Sheila had said about having to put up with it. But a new worry had taken its place —

her feelings for Harry. Childish hero-worship had given way to a new emotion. Her recent discovery that she was in no way related to him had made her feel better. There was nothing wrong or abnormal in feeling this way. But now he was getting married. How stupid and naïve she had been to dream that he might no longer think of her as his little sister.

Sunlight streamed through the thin curtains and Ellie screwed up her eyes against the ache which throbbed in her head. At least Dad had left her alone last night, probably too drunk to get up the stairs. She turned towards the wall, reluctant to face another day of family squabbles and tensions. She had to get up though. It was the art exam today.

Downstairs, Mum had just got home from her shift at the hospital. She looked even more tired than usual, but she still bustled around, doing the chores. She would wait until Dad was up before allowing herself to fall into bed.

Ellie made some toast and poured a cup of tea for herself and her mother. She sat down at the table, fiddling with the teaspoon before plucking up courage to ask. "What's this job Dad's on about?" She tried to keep her voice bright and interested but Mum must have sensed how she really felt.

Mary sat down opposite and reached across the table for her hand. "Oh, love. I'm so sorry. I know you'd got your heart set on college but you must have known . . ." Her voice trailed away.

"It was just a dream, wasn't it, Mum?"

A bitter smile twisted Mary's lips. "Can't live on dreams, love."

But you could, Ellie thought. Dreams had sustained her through so many bad times — dreams of being a real artist one day, of Harry and a life with him. A little sob escaped her.

Mum squeezed her hand. "You'll still have your painting. You mustn't give that up. Who knows, maybe one day . . .?"

"One day! So — the job, Mum."

"Did you hear Tommy Green's opening a new nightclub — up West?" Mary asked.

At first Ellie thought her mother was trying to change the subject. Surely Dad didn't expect her to work for Tommy Green?

"It's a real posh place apparently. All on the level. I was a bit worried at first but your dad told me Tommy wants to go straight. You know he hasn't always been exactly legit."

"What sort of club is it?"

"Somewhere posh people can meet for a drink, have a game of cards — that sort of thing," Mary said. "You'll have to ask Dad when he gets up. Besides, you'll be late for school if you don't get a move on."

Ellie didn't see the point of taking the art exam now. But deep down there was always the hope that if she won the scholarship to art school they'd let her take it up. It was a forlorn hope and Ellie consoled herself with the thought that if she started earning, her mother wouldn't have to work so hard.

"You need a rest, Mum. I'll finish clearing up. My exam's not till later."

"I must admit I've been feeling a bit down lately — so tired all the time." Mary sighed.

Ellie finished her toast and took the plates to the sink. "I bet Sheila's pleased Tommy's going straight," she said.

"Don't mention her name," Mary snapped, biting back a sob. "I couldn't believe it. After threatening to beat Tommy up only a few weeks ago, your dad's completely changed his tune. He said Tommy's treating her OK and she's fallen on her feet."

Ellie had hoped her mother would have forgiven Sheila by now. But Mary had strong principles and it would be a long time before Sheila was allowed to set foot in the flat. "It's all Bert's fault, letting her work there in the first place." Mary started to cry. "And now, you'll be in the same boat."

"Don't get upset, Mum. I'll be all right. Anyway, you've still got me — and Harry," Ellie said.

Mary cried even harder.

Ellie's footsteps dragged as she went towards the bus stop, wondering whether all these exams were a waste of time like her father said. She'd always been determined to have a real career and not be dependent on some man for the luxuries in life — like her sister. When she thought about it logically she had to admit she'd been deluding herself. She'd known ever since she started at the grammar school how Bert felt about education — especially for girls. The fact that he'd allowed her to stay on past the legal leaving age was a miracle, only brought about by her mother's insistence. Auntie Vi agreed with Bert — about the only thing they did see eye to eye on, Ellie thought.

"What's it all in aid of?" Vi had said. "She'll only end up getting married and having a load of kids — like most of them round here."

Gran tried to stand up for her. "Our Ellie's got a brain in her head. She deserves a chance."

But Vi had pursed her lips and folded her arms, refusing to change her views.

The opposition only fuelled Ellie's determination. She'd show them, she thought now, as the examiner rang the bell for them to begin. She'd always loved drawing and painting but it wasn't until Miss Evans had taken the class to the Victoria and Albert Museum during a half-term holiday that she'd really considered art as a career. The visit had been an inspiration. She'd been enchanted by the display of eighteenth- and ninetenth-century costumes. But for her, the highlight of the school trip was the textiles: the bed hangings and wall coverings of silk, richly embroidered or woven in intricate patterns. How she wished she'd been allowed to take them out of their glass cases, to feel the smoothness of the silk, the rich textures of the brocades.

She'd had to be content with the coloured postcards she'd bought as well as the sketch-book she'd filled with drawings of the designs she'd seen. One day she'd be designing her own materials.

The time flew as she became absorbed and the bell marking the end of the exam made her jump.

Judith was waiting for her in the corridor. "Was it that bad? You love art — why so glum?"

"I'm just thinking it was all a waste of time. It doesn't matter how well I do, they won't let me go to college.

"They'll have to if you get the scholarship."

Ellie didn't answer. It was impossible to make her friend understand.

At home, all was quiet. Mary had left a note propped on the mantelpiece saying she was round at Gran's and that Dad wouldn't be home till late. Good, Ellie thought, I can do some more painting. Might as well, while she had the chance. She wouldn't have time once she started work. Since the exam her mind was buzzing and she had an idea for another design. She sat down at the kitchen table with her box of paints and a selection of brushes. Soon she was lost in a world of colour and beauty. The delicate combination of scrolls and ribbons, with tiny butterflies interwoven, was based on a Chinese silk hanging she'd seen in the museum.

As she worked, using a fine brush to paint in the gossamer wings of the butterflies, she imagined the finished painting reproduced many times over. It would look equally nice on material or wallpaper, she thought. She pictured her bedroom done out in the shades of turquoise and mauve she'd used in the painting, with matching curtains and bedspread.

The idea excited her. That was where Dad and Auntie Vi were wrong. They said art was a waste of time, just painting pretty pictures. She could understand why they thought she wouldn't earn a living from that. But if she showed this to them, explained how it could be used in a practical way, perhaps they'd stop their carping. Harry would understand, she thought, wishing he was here. Then the realization hit her with a jolt. She'd been so absorbed in her work that for a few hours the memory of his devastating news had faded into the background.

Another dream shattered, she thought, as she washed her brushes and cleaned her paintbox. Despite her desperate hope that Harry wouldn't go through with the marriage, she knew she was deluding herself. She'd have to get on with her life and make the best of things. If only she'd be allowed to follow that other dream of a career in art, she might feel better, she told herself.

She studied the finished painting — the best she'd ever done. She couldn't waste her talent. Squaring her shoulders, she decided to pluck up her courage and tell Mum about the art scholarship. Perhaps she could talk Dad round, especially if she explained it wouldn't cost too much with the grant she'd receive.

She was so engrossed in her thoughts that she didn't hear her father come in.

She jumped when he said, "Where's your mother?"

"She's round Gran's. I'll get your tea, Dad." With relief she saw that, for a change, he didn't look as if he'd been drinking. Instead of getting angry, he smiled.

"No rush, Angel." He came over to the table and looked at her painting. "What you bin up to, then?"

Ellie smiled back uncertainly as Bert picked up the painting. "What's it meant to be?" he asked.

"It's a design — for wallpaper," she said. Hope flared. He was showing an interest for a change. Perhaps now would be a good time to mention the art scholarship.

He turned the paper round in his hand and looked at it again. "Oh, I see," he said flatly and put it back on the table. "What you wasting your time with this rubbish for? Won't be any use to you when you're working." His voice had hardened, heralding one of his swift changes of mood.

Ellie reached for the painting but Bert screwed it into a ball and threw it across the room. It hit the wall and landed in front of the kitchen range.

She made a small sound of protest but he pulled her towards him. "Your mother tells me your teachers are very pleased with you," he said.

She nodded and smiled tentatively, nervous at the change in tone, realizing from the glint in his eyes that he hadn't finished with her. "All these exams. What's the point?"

Ellie had asked herself the same question.

"You don't need exams. You're starting work soon. And don't argue. I'll not have you letting my old mate down." With each sentence, he gave her a little shake.

"But, Dad, Miss Evans said —" Ellie began.

"Miss Evans — good 'eavens!" There was no humour in Bert's voice. "That's all I 'ear about lately." He pushed her away roughly so that she was forced to clutch the edge of the table for support. "I know she's been feeding you ideas about college and all." He banged the table. "Why is it that some stuck-up vinegary old spinster of a schoolteacher thinks she knows better than your own father?"

As Ellie nerved herself to speak, his eyes narrowed and a spiteful smile creased his thin lips. His hands gripped her arms and he shook her roughly. "You're getting too big for your boots, my girl."

The door opened and Bert's hands dropped to his sides.

Ellie rushed to take the shopping bags that were weighing her mother down. "You all right, Mum?"

Mary looked from one to the other. "I'm fine. What's going on here?"

"Nothing, Mum. I was just telling Dad about the art exam."

"Stupid kid's on about college again." He smiled and put on his wheedling tone. "Angel, you know sending you to college costs money. You haven't thought of that, have you? We're not Rothschilds, you know."

Ellie was about to mention the grant but her mother said, "Oh, Ellie, we've been over it so many times. I thought you'd accepted it."

Mary sounded so dejected that Ellie was sorry she'd upset her. She bent to pick up the screwed-up painting. Might as well throw it on the fire, she thought. But something made her hang on to it.

As she turned to leave the room, her father reached out and pulled her towards him. "Look, Angel. Maybe we made a mistake letting you go to that posh school in the first place. But your mum persuaded me you should have your chance." He squeezed her waist and she stiffened. "Look at it this way. You're all we've got. With his lordship off in the army and that sister of yours up to gawd knows what, it would break your poor mum's heart if you left us to go away to college."

Ellie looked across at her mother, who had sat down at the table. She still looked pale but she gave a small tight smile and Ellie tried to smile back. Mum had done her best, despite Dad's opposition to her going to the grammar school. He'd thought she was getting ideas above her station, thinking she was too good for them all, even starting to speak differently. No matter how hard she tried to explain, he'd never understand.

Bert seemed to sense that the fight had gone out of her and he reached out and touched her hair. "You know it makes sense, love. Besides, you'll like working at the club, you know. Meet lots of posh people, film stars even."

Ellie felt the anger stir again. As if that would make up for everything. She managed to swallow her feelings. He stroked her arm and she was glad she was wearing a long-sleeved blouse. To an onlooker the gesture would probably seem innocent enough, but her knees were starting to shake. And he had that funny look in his eyes again. He wouldn't do anything while her mother was there but she still felt nervous being so close to him.

She swallowed hard as he pulled her towards him and kissed her cheek. "You're a good girl, Ellie, love. Not like that sister of yours."

Mary stood up abruptly, pushing her chair back. "Don't talk about Sheila like that," she said. "I know I was upset at first and I can't deny it sickens me to think of her with that thug. But she seems happy enough and now that they're going to get married —"

Bert gave a little laugh. "Married? He's got to get his divorce yet. Let's hope it's all sorted before the baby comes."

Mary's face paled. "Baby?" she whispered, sinking into a chair. "You mean I'm going to be a grandmother?" A smile slowly spread over her face. "Grandma," she said.

"Changed your tune, ain't yer?" Bert sneered.

"I'm still her mother, ain't I?" Mary snapped. She picked up her purse and turned to Ellie. "I've just remembered. I promised to get your gran some cough medicine. Run down to the chemist for me, love."

Ellie took the money and moved towards the door, the screwed-up painting still clutched in her hand. Before leaving the house she ran upstairs. In her attic room, she smoothed the paper out and put it under a pile of books. If that didn't work maybe she'd try ironing it. The design was one of the best things she'd done so far and she wanted to keep it for her college portfolio. She gave a little sob. She wasn't going to college, was she? Even with the scholarship that Miss Evans was so sure she'd win — the scholarship she hadn't dared mention tonight — they'd never let her go.

CHAPTER
FIVE

It was pouring with rain the next day and Ellie pulled the hood of her raincoat up, forcing it over the brimmed velour hat, which they had to wear whenever they were in school uniform. It was a fate worse than death — a visit to the headmistress — for anyone seen in public without their hat.

"At least I won't have to wear this horrible old thing any more," she said to Judith, cramming the hat down on her head.

"So, you're definitely not coming back next term?" her friend asked.

"My dad says I've got to go out to work — he's even found me a job."

Judith was about to ask where but Ellie said, "I don't mind — really. I know I wanted to go to college but they can't afford it."

"What about the art scholarship, though?"

"Even with that it would still be hard for them."

Judith looked as if she wanted to ask more questions but the bus came along. It was crowded and, to Ellie's relief, they couldn't find seats together. She just didn't feel like satisfying her friend's curiosity today.

She stared out at the rain streaming down the window, wondering how she was going to achieve her ambitions when her family seemed determined to stop her. She would just have to work hard and save her money until she could leave home and do what she wanted.

As they so often did, her thoughts turned to Harry. He'd be home soon, bringing his German bride. All the more reason to leave home, she thought. But first, she had to face Miss Evans and tell her not to bother about putting her in for scholarship.

As she left the art room, Miss Evans said, "Are you really sure?"

Ellie nodded.

"I don't understand. Is it because you're nervous — you don't think you stand a chance?"

"Something like that," Ellie agreed.

Miss Evans smiled. "Nonsense, child. I wouldn't be recommending you unless I was confident of your success. And you must be confident too."

The bell went and Ellie seized the opportunity to escape. The art mistress meant well, she knew, encouraging her talent and giving her the confidence to develop it. But kind as she was, there was no way Ellie could ever confide in her the problems of her home life and the difficulties of getting her parents — especially her father — to agree that a career in art was a valid choice.

Dad kept on about how much she could earn working for Tommy Green and had even managed to convince her mother that the new club was a respectable place where Ellie would be mixing with a better class of people.

It was easier to give in, to let her parents think she'd accepted the situation. Besides, in some ways, she didn't care. Since receiving Harry's letter with its devastating news, Ellie felt that life couldn't hold any more disappointments. She tried hard to tell herself she was happy for him — if he was happy, so was she. But deep down, the hurt remained.

She was worried about her grandmother too. With the exams, she hadn't visited the old lady as often as she'd have liked and Mum had said she wasn't well.

It had stopped raining and Ellie decided to go round to Gascoigne Terrace. She cut across the bombsite as usual, pushing her way along the overgrown path between the clumps of rosebay willow herb and bright yellow ragwort. Clouds of insects and the occasional small butterfly rose in front of her, and she thought of Judith, off to spend the summer holidays with relatives in the country. If only she could go with her, she thought.

But she had to start work, although she was determined it wouldn't be for ever. Daft as it seemed, she couldn't quite quell the hope that, when her exam results came through, Dad would see that she deserved her chance at college.

Gran was in her tiny patch of garden. Most of the houses in the terrace only had paved yards, but Grandad, who'd died when Ellie was just a baby, had built raised beds round the edge of the yard. During the war he'd grown tomatoes and runner beans, a few cabbages and carrots.

Now, the garden was aglow with nasturtiums, pansies, and pinks, which Gran grew from seeds bought for a few pence in the market.

"It looks lovely, Gran," Ellie said as her grandmother straightened painfully, rubbing the small of her back.

"Yeah, but it's all getting a bit too much for me, love. Still, I can't let it all go to pot. I don't know where the weeds come from." She waved her hand at the bombsite beyond the fence. "Perhaps when they get rid of that lot, it'll be a bit better."

"You should've waited for me. I'll do the weeding for you — and the watering," Ellie offered.

"I don't mind. I like to keep busy — you know that. But my knees are playing up something shocking." Gran bent over and plucked another weed from the soil.

"Leave it, Gran. I said I'd do it."

"All right, all right — I heard yer." Gran laughed and the laugh turned into a cough.

Ellie turned to her in concern. "Let's go inside. I'll make you a cup of tea."

"Fetch a couple of chairs out here, love. Might as well make the most of this sunshine," Gran said.

Ellie settled her grandmother in one of the chairs and went back inside to fetch the tray. She balanced it on the low wall and poured out two cups. As she sat down opposite the old lady, she apologized for not coming more often.

"You don't want to worry about that. Your mum comes round a couple of times a week and Vi pops in. I'm not lonely. Besides, you've got better things to do than spend time with an old woman — what with all your school work and all." She took a sip of her tea and put the cup down. "How did you get on with your exams, Ellie?"

"I won't know till the results come in." Ellie managed a smile. "Anyway, school's finished now. I've got a job."

"Work? I thought you were set on going to college?"

"Didn't Mum tell you? They can't afford to let me stay on so I've got a job at Tommy's new club."

Gran pulled a face. "What's your mum thinking of, letting you work in a place like that?"

"Dad says it's not like the Riverside. This is a posh place up West. I'm going to be a receptionist."

"Let's hope it's as legit as he claims."

Ellie didn't answer and Gran patted her hand. "Don't mind me, love. I'm sure it'll be all right. But I know how much you were banking on going to college."

"It was just a dream, Gran." She stood up and picked up the watering-can. "Anyway, I thought I'd come round to help with the garden."

Lou Bowman glanced round at the riot of colour which filled the tiny yard. "I don't know why I'm bothering really. Looks like I won't have a garden for much longer."

"What do you mean?"

"I'll be moving out soon. They haven't given us a date yet, but I'll be going into a council flat."

"Oh, Gran. They can't make you move, can they?" Ellie was horrified. She knew how much her grandmother loved the little house and garden, and its convenient position close to the shops and the market. And all her friends were here. She'd lived all her life in this street, moving only a few doors away from her parents when she'd married Fred Bowman.

Lou waved her hand at the little row of houses. "It's all going — the whole terrace. The end ones are empty already — all boarded up. As soon as there's a place vacant, I'll be off." Her voice caught as she went on, "It was that big bomb that did it. Brought down the whole of Hope Street, as well as part of this terrace. It undermined the foundations, they say, and now it's too late to fix it. The whole lot's got to come down."

Ellie patted her grandmother's hand sympathetically, reminded of the story Gran had told her about Harry's family, trapped in the rubble. It had all happened so long ago, before she was born, but for Gran the memories would always be there. Maybe it would be better for her to move away from the constant reminders. But would she be happy in one of those new multistorey blocks of flats with no garden and no neighbours to chat to over the wall?

Not knowing what to say, Ellie went indoors to fill the watering-can. When she came out again, Gran was sitting with her eyes closed, her face turned up to the sun, her dark print dress pulled up above her knees to expose the thick white legs, knotted with blue veins like rivers on a map.

As Ellie started to water the plants, Gran opened her eyes. "Take no notice of me, duck. I'm just feeling a bit sorry for meself. I daresay one of these new flats will suit me fine — they've got a lift, and a nice bathroom and indoor lav. What more could I ask for at my time of life?"

"And I'll still come and see you," Ellie promised.

"Vi's moving too," Gran said. Her sister still lived in the house a few doors along where the sisters had been brought up. "With a bit of luck she'll get a flat in a different block." Gran gave her throaty chuckle and continued, "but knowing my luck, the council will put her right next door."

Ellie laughed too. The sisters were close but she knew Auntie Vi sometimes got on Gran's nerves with her bossiness and constant criticism of everything and everybody.

When she left her grandmother's house Ellie felt a lot more cheerful. Gran had seemed much better, resigned to the move and grateful for Ellie's promised help with the packing and sorting out of the accumulated debris of a lifetime.

Ellie stepped over the broken wire fence and, instead of turning into Kendall Street, she decided to go and see Mr Varney. She couldn't face going home yet.

As she neared the Roman Road market she scarcely took in the raucous shouts that had formed a background to her life for as long as she could remember. She could hear Sid Varney's voice above them all. He hadn't taken on a new assistant after Harry left, promising to keep his job open until he'd finished his national service. Maybe he'd take her on, Ellie thought, at least until Harry came back. If she had to leave school and start earning she'd rather work for Sid than for Tommy Green.

Most of the stalls were family businesses, run by parents and children who all mucked in with unloading the vans, stacking the stalls and clearing up at the end of the day. Sid had taken over the fruit and vegetable stall from his father and, as he'd never married, there were no sons to carry on the business. And he had no brothers and sisters either.

She spotted Sid, standing on a box and shouting his wares. As he extolled the virtues of the huge Jaffa oranges — "only sixpence apiece, ladies" — he juggled two or three of them in the air. A laughing crowd surrounded him and, as he stepped off the box, having finished his spiel, hands stretched towards him, eager for the fruit which, even so long after the war, was still something of a treat.

A rare treat for those with little money to spare for extras, Ellie thought, feeling in her pocket for the few coppers Gran had pressed into her hand as she left. No sixpence though. She'd have to ask Sid if he had any "specks", damaged fruit that he'd be willing to almost give away at the end of the day.

Sid was on his own so Ellie slipped round the back of the stall. The big man smiled down at her as, without a word, she started serving, wrapping cabbages in newspaper, shooting dusty potatoes straight off the scale and into the worn shopping bags held open by the customers. She'd watched Harry do it hundreds of times and was amazed at how easily it came to her — even adding up the prices in her head without any trouble.

When the crowd thinned out, Sid turned to her gratefully. "You're a natural, Ellie girl. 'Arry better watch out or he won't have a job to come back to when he gets home."

Ellie laughed. "Thanks for the compliment, Mr Varney. But I won't be taking Harry's job away from him."

"Oh, I forgot. I'm talking to an educated young lady, aren't I? You'll be setting your sights a bit higher than a market stall, I bet."

"Much, much higher, Mr Varney," Ellie said, laughing. When Sid said things like that, she knew he was just teasing. There was no malice in his voice — not like the sneering tones her father used.

"So you're turning down my offer of employment, then?"

Ellie's face fell. She wasn't sure whether Sid was serious but she knew Dad would never agree to her working on a market stall. "I can't, Mr Varney. I've already got a job."

"Thought you were goin' to college."

"I wish." Ellie forced a smile. "It's all right, Mr Varney. I always knew it wasn't going to happen. Mum says we can't afford it. So I start work as a receptionist next Monday."

"Receptionist, eh. Some posh hotel up West is it?"

Fortunately, a rush of customers saved her having to reply and Sid did not return to the subject.

When she got home, after helping Sid pack up the stall and load all the leftover produce into the back of his van, she was tired, but well satisfied with the few shillings he'd paid her. He'd also given her a bag full of "specks", a few potatoes and a large cabbage, stuff he swore he wouldn't be able to sell the next day.

She bounded up the stairs, anticipating her mother's pleasure when she handed them over.

But as she entered the flat, her father leapt up from his chair. "Where the 'ell have you been? Your mother's been worried sick," he yelled.

Ellie flinched at the unexpected attack. She'd thought he would still be out. And where was Mum?

Before she could say anything, Bert was shouting again. "You know you should come straight home and help your mum instead of leaving it all to her."

"But I've been to see Gran — Mum knew I was going. And I've been working — helping Mr Varney on the stall." She threw the money down on the table and plonked the bag of vegetables down beside it, then turned to go out of the room.

But Bert wasn't going to let her go so easily. "Working, is it? I never thought Miss 'Igh and Mighty Grammar School Girl would lower 'erself to work in the market."

The scorn in his voice was almost too much for Ellie. But she took a deep breath and turned to face him. She wouldn't let him see how near to tears she was, or how nervous she was of standing up to him.

"I don't consider it lowering myself to work for Mr Varney — no more than working for Tommy Green."

Bert climbed down. He usually did when Ellie spoke up for herself — as she was learning to do more and more these days. She'd been frightened of his temper all her life, while at the same time wanting to please him and gain his approval. Since that last brutal assault she'd ceased to care, her only aim being to keep the peace.

Now, she noted with satisfaction how he refused to meet her eye. "I only got cross cause I was worried, Angel," he said, in that whining tone she hated. "And Mum likes to know where you are as well."

"Where is she?" Ellie had expected her mother home ages ago.

"She's doing an extra shift at the hospital — so you'll have to get the tea ready tonight," Bert said.

Ellie gave an inward shiver. She'd be alone in the flat with him — the first time for weeks. But he hadn't been drinking. Surely she'd be safe for a while. "What time will she be home?" she asked.

"About ten."

"Will you be going out?" Ellie tried to disguise the eagerness in her voice and her sigh of relief when he nodded.

She put the vegetables in the cupboard under the sink and piled the fruit into a china bowl which she placed in the middle of the table. Then she prepared beans on toast and made a pot of strong tea — making sure that everything was exactly as her father liked it. He was quite capable of throwing something at her if the meal wasn't to his satisfaction. She had learned to cope with his outbursts — when she was younger she'd even told herself she deserved it. What she found harder to deal with were his maudlin expressions of remorse afterwards, which inevitably led to the fondling she hated. How could she have believed that the things he did were expressions of love?

Bert finished his meal and pushed his plate away. He picked up his mug and took a long slurp of tea, wiping his mouth with the back of his hand. As he stood up, Ellie took the plates over to the sink. She ran cold water on them, then turned to lift the kettle of hot water from the back of the range.

As she did so, her father shrugged himself into his jacket and took his cap from the peg on the back of the door. Ellie sighed with relief. He really was going out. With a bit of luck Mum would be home before he returned.

Her relief was short-lived. He came over to her and put his hands on her shoulders. "I wish we didn't have ter fight, love." He ran his hand down her arm and grabbed her hand, pulling it towards him. "You seem to be avoiding me, lately. I've missed yer, Angel." Ellie stood her ground, looking him steadfastly in the eye. His hand dropped to his side. "What 'appened to that sweet little girl who always tried to please 'er daddy?" he whined.

"She grew up," Ellie snapped.

His eyes hardened and she steeled herself for a blow. But he moved away from her and a spasm of hatred crossed his face. "Yeah. Grown up into a right little tease. I bet it'd be a different story if it was golden boy touchin' yer up. I've seen the way yer look at 'im, big cows' eyes."

She felt her face growing hot. She couldn't deny it. Such thoughts had crossed her mind. But, since the news of his marriage, she'd tried hard to suppress them. She turned away, trying to hide her confusion and self-disgust. She shouldn't be admitting it, even to herself.

Bert gave a short laugh. "So that's the way the wind blows, is it? Well, 'e won't be showin' 'is face round 'ere any more. He's decided to stay on in the army. Besides, I won't 'ave him here, now he's got some tart up the duff." His hand shot out and sent the dish of fruit crashing to the floor. "I've got to go out now. I'll deal with you later," he said as he left the room.

Ellie's hand shook as she returned the kettle to the range. She stood quite still, her shoulders hunched until the slam of the street door told her he'd gone. She wouldn't cry, she told herself. It was a good thing Harry wasn't coming home. She'd been dreading facing him and his new wife.

CHAPTER
SIX

Ellie pulled the blankets over her ears to stifle her sobs. She'd tried telling herself it was for the best, that at least she wouldn't have to face Harry's new wife just yet. But it was no good.

Loud voices penetrated the fog of misery that had engulfed her and she sat up as her father shouted up the stairs. "Ellie, get down 'ere now."

The doorknob rattled and she was glad she'd wedged the chair under it. But when her mother called softly, begging her to answer, she swung her legs to the floor.

"Your dad wants to talk to you. Come down, love. He's in a right paddy," Mary whispered as Ellie opened the door a crack.

Downstairs, Bert paced the kitchen, his face livid. "You can get down the market early tomorrer and tell Sid Varney you won't be helping 'im out no more."

Ellie started to protest.

"No arguments, girl. You're not working for him for coppers. I told you, it's all arranged. You'll be earning real money."

"But, Dad. I can't let Mr Varney down."

"You've got a proper job now. And don't you worry about Sid. I'll sort him out." A spasm of hatred flashed across his face. "It's time he saw I can look after my own family — don't need 'im interfering."

Ellie looked to her mother for support but Mary gripped the edge of the sink, avoiding her eyes. Hating to see her mother upset, she nodded. "All right, Dad."

Bert grinned, his mood changing, as it usually did once he'd got his own way. "That's my angel. You don't want to waste that education on a market stall, do you?"

Back in bed, Ellie wished she'd had the courage to say that, education or not, she'd rather work for Sid Varney than Tommy Green. She remembered Sheila's tales of what went on behind the scenes. The waitresses and hostesses were employed more for their pretty faces and shapely figures than for their brains.

Her sister hadn't minded and she seemed happy enough with the way things had turned out — living with the boss in a big posh house and soon to have a baby. Being a kept woman didn't seem to bother her, but it wasn't the sort of life Ellie wanted.

She tried to console herself with the thought that the place up West was different — her mother seemed to believe Dad's assurance that Tommy Green wanted to become respectable.

Ellie couldn't sleep, wondering why her father hated Sid Varney so much. She knew they'd been friends as children and had been in the army together during the war. Perhaps it was because Sid had his own business, albeit only a market stall, while Bert had been unable to find regular employment until Tommy Green had taken him on.

★　★　★

Next morning, Ellie went down to find her mother sitting by the fire, cradling a cup of tea in her hands.

"You're going to be late for work," Ellie said, helping herself from the pot.

"They've put me back on nights, now that the nurse I was covering for is back on duty," Mary said. "It was only temporary and, besides, I prefer night duty — it's not so hectic. And if I'm off in the daytime I can pop round to your gran's — make sure she's all right."

Ellie bit her lip. She couldn't tell her mother that the thought of being left alone in the house at night terrified her.

Mary stared into the glowing bars of the kitchen range, apparently lost in thought. She looked up suddenly. "I'm sorry about you having to take that job," she said.

Ellie refilled their cups, putting the pot down slowly as she turned to her mother. Maybe it was a good moment to mention the scholarship. But her mother went on, "You know once your dad makes his mind up, you can't budge him. If you defy him, he'll make your life a misery."

As if it isn't already, Ellie thought, hearing the defeat in her mother's voice. "I know, Mum," she said with a catch in her voice. "It's all right. I won't make a fuss."

"Good girl." Mary sighed and ran her fingers through her uncombed hair. "I must get washed and dressed. I can't sit around all day."

"You stay there for a bit, Mum. I'll do you some toast, then I'll go down the market and see Mr Varney, tell him I haven't got time to help out. Don't worry, I won't tell him what Dad said. I can get the shopping while I'm out, then I'll clean up. You need a rest if you're going to be working tonight."

Mary relaxed gratefully into her chair and Ellie bustled round the kitchen, anxious now to get out of the house before her father got up.

When she reached the market Sid was busy with the early morning rush. He interrupted his banter with a customer and grinned. "Thanks for coming, love," he said. There was no chance to explain so she shrugged and turned to one of the women, who was testing the tomatoes for firmness.

Half an hour later the crowd had thinned out and Sid sighed and mopped his forehead. "Goin' ter be a hot one today, Ellie. Better go and get us a cuppa before the rush starts again," he said, giving her a handful of coppers.

She couldn't bring herself to say that she couldn't stay. If Dad saw her, it was too bad. She'd claim she was shopping for Mum.

She hurried over to Bob's Café on the corner and came back, carefully balancing a large mug of strong tea and a bottle of Vimto with a straw poking out of it. The bottle had been in the fridge and, as Ellie walked along, she licked at the cold droplets which had formed on the side of the bottle. She glanced round at the busy market, breathing in the familiar smells, enjoying the hot sun on her bare arms. If only she could work for Sid all the time, she wouldn't mind having to leave school.

When she got back to Sid's stall he was sitting on an upturned orange box. He reached out for the tea gratefully. "Park yer bum, love," he said. "Make the most of it while we're quiet."

Ellie pulled up another box and, without giving herself time to think, told Sid that, after today, she wouldn't be able to help out any more. "As I told you, I start work soon. My dad's already got me job you see, Mr Varney," she apologized.

"Well, I'm sorry too, love." Sid sighed and Ellie thought he really did look disappointed. She hated upsetting him. He'd always been nice to her and she knew Harry thought a lot of him too.

Sid turned to serve a customer before she could reply. When he sat down again he was quiet for a while, drinking his tea. Suddenly he turned to her. "Thank God he's not making you work at that club." He gave a short laugh. "Don't mind me — I know your mother wouldn't hear of it."

"She let Sheila," Ellie said.

"Well — yes — and we all know what 'appened to 'er."

A steady trickle of customers prevented any further conversation for a while but when they had time to talk again, Sid turned to Ellie and ran his fingers through the sparse remains of his hair. He gave an embarrassed cough, then blurted out, "Sorry, love. Shouldn't have said that about your sister."

"It's all right, Mr Varney. Everyone knows — that's why Mum was so upset."

"At least they're talking now though."

Ellie nodded and told him that Sheila was expecting a baby.

Sid smiled. "I heard. A grandchild is a great peacemaker, you know."

Ellie smiled back. Mr Varney was such a kind man and he wasn't like the other grown-ups. He talked to her like she was an adult too. Maybe he would explain something that had been puzzling her.

"I will be working for Mr Green," she confessed. "But he's opening a new place — very posh — up West. He wants me to be his receptionist."

"You sure that's all it is?"

"Well, Mum seems to believe it. Everyone says Mr Green wants to go straight."

Sid gave a snort of disbelief, then sighed. "Could be true. Perhaps that's why he wants you — educated, nicely spoken. What could look more legit than having a girl like you as receptionist?"

Ellie felt herself blushing. "I don't really want to but Dad says I must." She finished her lemonade and turned to Sid. "Why is he so keen to keep in with Mr Green? They fell out when there was all that trouble over Sheila. Now they seem to be mates again."

"Well, I did hear that Tommy 'ad some sort of hold over your dad. I 'eard that Bert 'ad done something a bit silly and Tommy got to hear of it. He needed a man for a dodgy caper and roped Bert in — in exchange for keeping shtum about the other job."

Ellie nodded slowly. She was sure now that the "dodgy caper" Sid referred to had something to do with those boxes she'd seen stacked in Solly's yard. It still didn't explain Tommy offering her a job though.

"You know your dad," Sid said with a laugh. "'E likes to think he's well in with the big boys. 'E probably asked Tommy to take you on and now that they're mates again he was glad to oblige."

Ellie was anxious to change the subject. "Did you know Harry was staying on in the army?" she asked.

"It's a good career. I'd like him to work for me but don't think I could pay him enough to support a wife and child." Sid didn't seem to notice the shadow that passed over Ellie's face and went on, "Your Harry's ambitious. He wrote me that he's training to be a vehicle mechanic. If he's still set on it when he gets home, I might be able to get him a job with an old mate of mine out Essex way." Sid threw the dregs of his tea on the ground and stood up. "Can't sit around nattering — gonna get busy again in a minute."

Ellie took his mug and the bottle. "I'll take these back to Bob's, then I've got to go down the shops for Mum."

"You run along, gel. Don't want you getting into trouble with Mum — or Dad," Sid told her. He slipped a few coins into her hand. "Thanks a lot — you've been a big help."

"I'll try and come again — if I have time. Don't know what hours I'll be working yet," Ellie said.

As she left the noise of the market behind, she felt a lot happier. Her talk with Mr Varney had cleared her mind. He hadn't seemed too worried when she told him about the club. Like Mum, he seemed to think the new Paradise Club would be more respectable than the Riverside. Maybe it wouldn't be so bad after all. She wasn't quite so happy about the other thing Sid had told her. She'd always pictured Harry coming back to Bethnal Green when he left the army. She didn't like the idea of him going to work in Essex. But perhaps it was just as well, she thought. She wouldn't have to face seeing him — and his wife — every day.

Sid watched her go, smiling. Not for the first time he thought that if things had been different he could have had a daughter like Ellie. But he'd never married. Despite his big laugh, the cheery backchat, Sid was a shy man, hiding his real feelings behind his seemingly extrovert manner.

He'd only ever cared for one woman. But his lack of confidence had held him back and he'd let her slip through his fingers — not once, but twice. Mary Bowman, as he still thought of her, had been one of the most popular girls in their little gang — vivacious, sparkling, small and quick with laughing brown eyes. He'd understood when she'd fallen for Jim Scott — all the girls were after him or his twin brother Frank. Why would she look at him, fat, balding even in his early twenties and with no prospects beyond taking over the stall from his father?

When she got married he'd been pleased for her — and his mate. Jim was a good sort and Sid knew he'd make Mary happy. Once he'd become resigned to the fact that she'd never look on him as anything more than a friend, he just got on with his life. But he still lived for the sight of her, the warmth of her smile when she and her friend Anne shopped in the market — which they did nearly every day.

The pain faded after a while and he was able to take pleasure in seeing her happiness when Sheila was born and in being an unofficial uncle to the little girl and her cousin Harry. Despite everything, those years before the war had been good years.

As Sid watched Ellie threading her way between the market stalls, stopping to wave or call out a greeting, he thought how like her mother she was — bright, ambitious, full of life. His smile faded as he pictured Mary now — thin and careworn. And he could see Ellie ending up the same way. It worried him when he saw the purple shadows under her eyes, the droop of her shoulders. But, like her mother, she could always manage a smile for him.

Sid snapped out of his reverie as a sharp voice said, "Well, are you gonna serve me or not, Sid Varney? I ain't got all day you know." It was Vi Thomas, Ellie's great-aunt.

"Sorry, Vi — got a lot on me mind," he said, weighing out carrots and picking an especially hearty cauliflower for her to make up for his lack of attention.

She handed over the money, tightening her lips as he passed her the change. "Mooning over some woman I expect," she said. "Time you got married, Sid Varney — if you can find anyone who'll 'ave yer." She gave her cackling laugh.

Sid replied with a weak smile, his usual repartee deserting him for the moment.

It had started to rain and the market was almost deserted. He might as well pack up and go home. But the thought of the dismal two rooms above the newsagent's where he lived alone had no attraction for him.

His thoughts turned to Mary again. He was sure she had no idea how he felt about her. In a way he hoped she never would. After all, she was a married woman and there was nothing he could do about it. And if Bert ever got so much as an inkling there'd be hell to pay.

Not that Sid was frightened of that weedy little toerag. But Bert had a powerful friend in Tommy Green. He wasn't afraid for himself, though he'd heard tales of beatings down dark alleys when someone had upset Tommy or any of his mates. Sid's concern was for Mary and Ellie. And now, with young Harry gone, they were even more vulnerable.

Not for the first time Sid wondered why on earth Mary had married Bert Tyler. After all, Jim had only been dead a few months when she took up with him. But she'd been struggling to bring up two children, having taken on responsibility for Harry when Anne was killed. And Bert could be charming when he put himself out — until he got what he wanted, that was. He'd always been jealous of the Scott brothers' popularity and Sid suspected he'd seen a way of getting back at them.

And Mary, soft-hearted as ever, had admitted to Sid that she felt sorry for Bert, wounded at Dunkirk and knowing he would walk with a limp for the rest of his life. What Sid had never told her was that Bert's wound was not the result of enemy action. His leg had been crushed between boat and breakwater as he'd fought for a place on one of the little ships. Sid, supporting the wounded Frank Scott, had been pushed aside as Bert forced his way to the front of the queue.

He sighed, knowing he would never tell her the whole story now. Let her carry on thinking Bert was a wounded hero if it helped her to put up with him.

"Cheer up, Sid. It might never 'appen," Maisie Jones shouted across from her second-hand clothes stall.

"It already has," he said, pointing upwards. The rain had increased to a downpour and the awning was sagging under the weight of water.

"Yeah. Wouldn't send a dog out on a day like this. I'm packing up — won't do no more trade today." Maisie started folding her goods and packing them into boxes.

"I've had enough as well," Sid said.

"What say we go for a cuppa and a bite to eat at Bob's Café," Maisie said, "then you can tell me all your troubles."

"I might do that." Sid laughed. But he'd never tell her what was on his mind. Maisie was a good sort, but she did love a gossip. Sid's unrequited love would be all round the market by next morning.

Ellie would have lingered over the shopping but her father had insisted she should go to see Mr Green about the receptionist's job. Her feet started to drag as she neared Kendall Street and she felt that familiar churning in her stomach as she mounted the stairs.

Although Bert had more or less left her alone since that terrible night, she was still wary of him. He'd never referred to it directly but on several occasions when he'd been drinking he had made a grab for her, gripping her shoulders or running his hands up and down her body. All the while, he would mutter under his breath — comments on her growing up to be a lovely young woman, phrases such as "what do you expect, I'm only human after all?" Worst of all, he would tell her over and over that she was still his little angel and he couldn't help loving her.

With her mother near by, or if she was round at Gran's, she could tell herself that she wasn't to blame — and she almost believed it. But when her father talked like that and especially when he made insinuations about her feelings for Harry, she would begin to doubt herself.

Upstairs, she would look in the mirror, hunching her shoulders to flatten her bosom, pulling her skirt down over her knees and scraping her hair back from her face. As her reflection looked back at her, she would flush with shame and throw herself on the bed to let the tears come.

She was crying for the child she had been and the loss of that uncomplicated love she'd felt for the boy who had been her "big brother". But she was crying for the future as well as the past. She could never let Harry know that the love she'd always felt for him had changed into a completely different emotion.

No, he deserved someone better, a respectable girl. Not someone like her — the sort of girl who could tempt even her own father to such unspeakable acts.

Locked in her misery, she forgot the way Bert had treated Sheila, not to mention the times as a very small child when she'd heard the sound of blows and his snarling voice demanding his rights, followed later by her mother's stifled sobs.

In the depths of her hurt and shame she managed to rationalize Bert's behaviour. Sheila, as her mother had so often said, was no better than she should be, she'd been "asking for it". And as for her mother's sufferings, Ellie unconsciously mimicked Auntie Vi's opinion: "*she knew what he was like. She should never have married him.*"

CHAPTER
SEVEN

Ellie gazed around her, awestruck at the size of the wood-panelled room with its rich blue carpet, soft and thick underfoot, the desk of polished walnut behind which Tommy Green sat. In one corner was a small bar with soft lights glinting off the bottles ranged on the shelves behind.

Her father caught her eye and, with a satisfied grin, leaned back in the deep leather chair, puffing contentedly on the cigar that Mr Green had offered him.

"Well, Ellen — or can I call you Ellie, seeing as you're gonna be my sister-in-law before too long?" Mr Green said, his eyes almost disappearing in the flesh of his perspiring face as he smiled at her.

Ellie nodded, wondering what her sister saw in him — apart from his wealth, of course.

"I think you're just the sort of girl I need as a receptionist." He leaned forward. "What do you say — would you like to work here?"

Ellie glanced at her father but he was gazing up at the wreaths of blue smoke drifting in the air, a self-satisfied smirk on his face. Emboldened by his apparent lack of interest in the conversation she tried to protest.

"But, Mr Green . . ."

"Call me Tommy, please."

She couldn't, she just couldn't. "Mr Green, I don't think I'm the type of person you're looking for, really I don't."

The big man's eyes narrowed. "And why's that then?"

"Well, working in a club — I'm not like Sheila, you see."

To her surprise he burst out laughing. "I should say you're not. But that's why I want yer. This new place I'm openin' is nothin' like the Riverside. It's gonna be real posh, up West. I want someone who looks the part, someone who talks nice, not too plummy but proper English — like you do."

"But what would I have to do?" Ellie still wasn't convinced.

"I told yer — call me Tommy." He waved his cigar. "It's simple — just answer the phone, take bookings for tables. Be there ter greet the guests."

"Is that all?" Ellie smiled. He hadn't said anything about having to "be nice" to the guests. Her relief was short-lived.

"'Course, you'd have to look right — dress up a bit, get yer 'air done, make-up an' all. Gotta impress the punters. But don't worry — we'll get yer rigged out before yer start."

"Mum doesn't like me wearing make-up," she said tentatively.

Bert spoke up. "I'll speak to yer mother."

Tommy nodded. "She must realize yer growin' up now — into a very attractive young lady if I might say so."

Ellie squirmed as he went on, "I know you're only sixteen but, with the right clothes, you'll pass for eighteen." He paused, then continued, "Oh, I don't mean I want yer all dolled up like a tart. I want a bit of class — you'll fit in a treat." He smiled again and wagged his finger at her. "Who knows, if yer play yer cards right, yer could end up married ter some posh geezer with loadsa dough — maybe even a title."

Bert nodded. "That's what I've bin tellin' her. It's waste a time all this talk of paintin' and drawin'. With her looks and brains, she's got it made already."

Tommy stared hard at Bert and gave a short laugh. "Don't know where she gets it from — must be 'er mother."

A flicker of anger crossed Bert's face, quickly followed by a forced laugh. "Well, you know my Mary," he said, leaning forward to grind the cigar out in the crystal ashtray.

"Well, that's all settled then. The decorators and fitters 'ave nearly finished and we're just waitin' on the delivery of the furniture. We should be ready by the twentieth — that's a Saturday night — for the grand opening. Better come along early afternoon and I can go through things with yer."

He stood up and handed an envelope to Bert. "I think you'll find there's enough there to cover getting her all rigged out — and a bit over fer your expenses."

Bert put the envelope inside his jacket. "Come on then. We've taken up enough of Tommy's time," he said.

On the bus back to Kendall Street, Bert was in an expansive mood but Ellie hardly said a word. If only Mum had stuck up for her just this once. But Mary, once she'd been assured that there wouldn't be any "funny business", had seemed to accept the situation. Until Bert took the envelope out of his pocket and she saw how much money there was.

"What's that for?" she asked, her lips coming together in that familiar thin line.

"Clothes and things for our Ellie. Tommy wants her to look good when she starts work."

"We don't need his money," Mary said. "Does he think we can't take care of our own? I've got money put by."

Bert laughed. "You're too proud, you are. We're doin' him a favour, letting our Ellie work fer him. There's not many girls round 'ere with her education who look the part. Tommy's goin' upmarket. He wants to be respected, not just an ex-boxer who's made a bit of money wheeling and dealing."

Mary didn't reply. She picked up the bundle of notes and reached for her handbag. When Bert held out his hand, she peeled a few notes off and gave them to him. He gave her a hard look but she ignored him and calmly tucked the rest of the money into her purse.

"We'll need to go up West for her clothes if Tommy wants her to 'look the part'. Can't have our girl letting the side down can we?" Her voice had a sarcastic edge, but as she turned to Ellie, she smiled. "Looks like you and me are going on a shopping spree, love." But Ellie detected a false note behind the gay tone.

Her own feelings were much the same. She should have been excited at the thought of choosing new clothes in the posh West End shops. Judith would have been green with envy but fashion and make-up had never really interested Ellie — only from the point of view of design. She'd often sketched out ideas for dresses and had even briefly considered going into the fashion business — after college of course. But her real interest was in textiles and soft furnishings.

She sighed. No good thinking about that. She smiled at her mother and, like her, pretended enthusiasm for the proposed shopping trip.

Bert gave a self-satisfied grin and put his arm round her. "I'm proud of yer, Angel. I told yer everything would work out all right if yer listened to yer dad. Tommy'll see yer right, you'll see." He kissed her cheek and gave her a squeeze, his hand brushing lightly against her breast. She tried not to flinch and instead stared hard at him, wishing she had the nerve to speak up and tell him that she'd do what he wanted if he agreed to leave her alone.

But he seemed to get the message and he averted his eyes. "I'm off," he said to Mary. "Don't bother saving my dinner. I'll eat out."

When they'd finished their sausages and mash and washed the dishes afterwards, Ellie and her mother sat down on opposite sides of the range, enjoying the unaccustomed interlude of peace and quiet.

"You're a bit quiet, love," Mary said, as the sound of coals settling in the grate disturbed the silence. She had taken out her knitting, but the needles stilled and she leaned towards Ellie. "I know you're disappointed — but you never really thought he'd let you go to college, did you?"

"I suppose not. But I always hoped he'd change his mind once he saw how hard I'd worked." Ellie stood up with a defeated gesture. "I suppose I ought to write to Miss Evans — thank her for taking an interest in me. She'll be so disappointed . . ." Ellie almost started to cry, but she controlled herself. It was too late for tears. Hadn't she always known it was just an impossible dream?

"It's no good crying, love. You've got to make the best of it," Mary said. Ellie wondered if the words were really intended for her — or if maybe her mother was thinking about her own life.

"Did you have dreams and ambitions, Mum?" she asked suddenly.

"Of course — doesn't everybody? But real life has a way of taking over — as you've just found out." Mary's knitting was still idle in her lap and she stared into the fire.

"What were your dreams, Mum?" Ellie didn't expect a reply.

Mary gave a little laugh. "Oh, the usual silly romantic notions," she said. "And of course, I always wanted to be a nurse but I never got to be sister as I'd planned." She turned to Ellie, smiling. "But I didn't mind, you see, because I married Jim and we had Sheila. I was so happy — then the war started . . ." Her voice trailed away.

"Gran told me about the bomb — and how you took Harry in after his mother was killed."

"Yes, well, Anne and me were close, like sisters. I couldn't do anything else really. I've never regretted it. Harry's been like a real son to me."

Ellie didn't want to talk about Harry. The shock of his sudden marriage was still too painful. But she didn't want her mother to stop. It was so rare for her to speak about the past and even rarer for her to exchange confidences with her daughter. It was a moment to treasure. She seized the moment to ask, "Why don't Dad and Harry get on?"

"Difficult to explain really. As you know, Dad and Frank — Harry's father — were friends before the war. When we decided to get married, I assumed he'd be only too pleased to take on Frank's boy. After all, he accepted Sheila. He told me he liked the idea of being a family man — and of course you were on the way too."

Ellie looked up, startled. She'd worked out for herself that her parents had married in haste — that was why she'd found it hard to understand her mother's anger and disappointment when first Sheila, then Harry, had made the same mistake. But Mary had never openly spoken of it.

Her mother coloured and looked away. "We tend to blame everything on the war and I suppose it's hard for you to understand how things were. We felt our lives were being destroyed; we'd lost our homes, our loved ones — it was only natural to live for the moment."

Ellie didn't understand. If the person she loved most in the world had been killed, she was sure she'd never want someone to take his place — let alone only a few months later.

Mary seemed to sense her confusion. "I'm not making excuses, love. I was almost demented when I got the news about Jim. Me and Anne had been evacuated to Norfolk with our children. But when we heard, we came back to London — couldn't stand being away from our parents and family. Besides, Frank was in hospital in Kent and Anne wanted to be able to visit him. But she never did get there — the bomb got her first."

She got up abruptly and poked the fire, pulling the kettle over the flames.

Ellie held her breath. Don't stop now, she thought. It was the first time her mother had ever spoken of those far-off days. Most of what she knew of her family background had been gleaned from eavesdropping on Gran and Auntie Vi or when poring through Gran's family albums.

Mary sat down again, took up her knitting and went on: "I went down to see Frank — but he didn't know me. He kept asking for Anne — couldn't seem to take in that she was dead."

She sighed. "That's when I promised him I'd look after Harry — and I was determined to keep that promise. I don't think your dad ever really forgave me for sticking to it. He felt I had enough to do with Sheila, and you on the way."

"So how come you and Dad got married then? He was in the army wasn't he?"

"Yes, but he'd been wounded and was later invalided out. I met him at the hospital when I went to see Frank. I knew him before — we all grew up together. Used to go over Victoria Park on Sundays — swimming in the lido, boating on the lake. But I never took much notice of Bert." She smiled in reminiscence. "Jim was always the one for me."

Ellie smiled too, recalling the photo in Gran's album. Not for the first time she wished he'd been her dad instead of Bert. She just couldn't understand why Mum had fallen in love again so quickly — she'd remarried less than a year later.

"Jim was very good-looking," she remarked now. "I've seen his photo in Gran's album."

"Well, looks aren't everything you know, Ellie," Mum said. "But I was lucky — he was a good man too."

Ellie stood up and got the tea caddy off the shelf, avoiding her mother's eyes. Mary still hadn't told her what she wanted to know, and she couldn't ask. She spooned tea leaves into the pot, poured the boiling water over them, then sat down and waited for the tea to brew.

"I know what you're thinking, Ellie," Mary said sharply.

Ellie made a gesture of protest but she couldn't deny that compared with Jim Scott, her own father left a lot to be desired.

Mary's shoulders slumped. "I can't blame you for the way you feel — Bert hasn't exactly been a good father. But he wasn't always like this, you know — it was the war. Losing his friends, being wounded and not able to work. He turned to the drink when he was in pain and that's what changed him." Mary took a sip of her tea and in a very low voice said, "I felt sorry for him."

And you've been sorry ever since. Ellie only just stopped herself saying the words aloud. It was the sort of thing Auntie Vi would say. She felt ashamed of the thought. Besides, it wasn't Mum's fault. She'd always done her best for her family — even for Bert. He was too selfish to appreciate it but you couldn't blame the war for that.

Mary seemed to sense Ellie's thoughts and she gave a little half-laugh. "Not much of a basis for marriage is it?" She picked up the cups, emptied the teapot and rinsed it while Ellie dried up and put the things away.

Before they sat down again Mary put her arm round Ellie's shoulders in an unaccustomed gesture of affection. "I've had many regrets over the years — but I've never regretted having you, love," she said. "I just hope your sister feels the same in years to come."

"Mr Green told me they're getting married. Will you go to the wedding?" Ellie asked.

"If I'm invited. She's still my daughter when all's said and done," Mary said. "She should have waited though. It'll be a long time before people round here let her live it down."

Ellie thought Mary was more concerned about the gossip than Sheila was. She sighed and stood up, bent and kissed her mother on the cheek. When Mary smiled and patted her hand, Ellie felt a lightening of her heart. She wished they could always be this close.

As she climbed into bed, she decided that as soon as possible she would go and see Sheila and make sure her mother got an invitation to the wedding.

CHAPTER
EIGHT

Dad was still in bed, sleeping off a night on the booze, when Mary called Ellie to get up. She had just come home from her shift at the hospital and looked even more tired than usual.

"You should get some rest, Mum," Ellie said, coming into the kitchen to see her leaning against the sink.

"I'll have a lie down when your dad gets up," Mary said. "I need to get a few jobs done first."

"I'll help," Ellie said.

"No, love. You pop round to Gran's and give her a hand with her packing."

Ellie insisted on making some toast for her mother before grabbing her cardigan off the back of a chair.

"I won't be too long," she called, running down the stairs and out of the side door.

Although she was somewhat anxious about what Gran would think of her working for Tommy Green, Ellie was feeling a bit better about it now. Mum wouldn't let her take the job unless she was sure it was a respectable place.

As she turned the corner, intending to cut across the waste ground, she stopped short. The fence had been mended and beyond it bulldozers were busy churning up the rubble that had been her playground for as long as she could remember. She supposed that before long one of those giant blocks, ten or twelve storeys high, would be casting its gigantic shadow over her grandmother's sunny back garden.

Then she remembered, with a pang, that Gran wouldn't be there to mind. Her house would also be fodder for the jaws of the bulldozers before long. Ellie wished they could have waited till her grandmother had moved out before starting work. It must be hard to see the destruction of the place you'd lived all your life and where you had such happy memories, for Gran often said that despite the war and the bombs, there had been good times.

Ellie called a cheerful greeting as she opened the back door, expecting that the old lady would need cheering up. She was standing by the kitchen window watching the workmen. But to Ellie's surprise she didn't seem at all upset.

"About time they did something about that eyesore," she said, turning as Ellie came in.

"Are they building flats?"

"I hope so. There's so many people needing homes. Flo — her what lives next door to Vi — well, she's got her daughter living with her and four kids, not to mention her own two boys just back from doing their National Service. And there's Dot's boy — wants to get married but says he won't start married life with his in-laws. Been on the council list three years, he has."

Ellie busied herself with kettle and teapot while her grandmother rambled on about friends and acquaintances.

She had to admit that she hadn't thought about things from that point of view, although people often remarked how lucky they were to have the flat above Solly's shop. She was just sorry that the little streets with their shops on every corner were gradually disappearing under a sea of concrete. The thought that Gran's house, her refuge throughout her troubled childhood, wouldn't be there any more was depressing. She'd heard someone say that the planners were doing more damage to the East End of London than all the German bombers during the war, and she'd thought they were right.

Gran, despite her sympathy for the homeless, was angry with the planners too. "It makes me so mad," she said. "Vi and me went to the pictures last night and what were they showing on the newsreels — this street, can you believe? And the bulldozers over the back there. Building a new East End, they said, getting rid of the slums." Gran took an indignant breath. "Calling my 'ouse a slum — how dare they?"

Ellie was sympathetic. She'd heard similar remarks from some of the girls at school. They seemed to think that everyone living east of Tower Bridge lived in the utmost poverty and degradation. They were poor, yes, but not destitute. So what if their houses did have outside toilets and no bathroom? That didn't mean they lived in squalor.

"Have you heard anything definite — about the new flat?" she asked when Gran eventually paused for breath.

"No, not yet. But Auntie Vi's got her letter, so I should hear soon."

"Well, we'd better get on with your packing then, hadn't we, Gran?"

She ran up the stairs, while her grandmother followed more slowly, groaning at the strain on her arthritic knees.

Two hours later she carried the last of the boxes of rubbish downstairs and dumped it by the back door. Old Blakey, the rag-and-bone man, could take them away when he next came by with his horse and cart.

The bits and pieces Gran would be taking to the new flat were now neatly packed into cardboard boxes and stacked in the small back bedroom.

"We'll make a start on the front room tomorrow, Gran," Ellie said as she washed her hands and tidied her hair. It was amazing how much dust you stirred up once you started moving things about, she thought, even in a house as clean and tidy as Gran's always was.

As she got ready to leave she turned to her grandmother. "You're not too sad about leaving are you, Gran?"

"I am a bit, love," Lou admitted. "But it's for the best. No more stairs, not to mention indoor plumbing — what more could I ask at my time of life?"

But as Ellie stepped out into the rain, which was still pelting down, she couldn't help thinking that her grandmother was trying to make the best of things.

Although Mary knew she should get some sleep, she couldn't face getting into bed while Bert was still there.

Usually, after a night shift on the casualty ward, she would fall into oblivion for several hours, waking just before midday. After going down to the shops or the market to get something for dinner she'd have time to clean the flat and get a meal ready. Then, if Bert wasn't home, she could enjoy a couple of hours relaxing with her sewing or knitting until it was time to get ready for work again.

She went into the bedroom intending to wake him, but as she looked down at him, she wrinkled her nose at the blast of beery breath that wafted towards her and her stomach recoiled in disgust at what he'd become.

She turned away. Let him lie there, she thought. Better than having to listen to his whining hard-done-by attitude, his insistence that everything wrong in his life was someone else's fault. How she hated him and his idea that everything could be solved by bullying and violence. True, the war had left its mark on him — though she was beginning to think the shattered leg that had left him with a permanent limp was not the heroic war wound he'd made it out to be.

But then, she thought, everyone she knew had suffered in some way or other. Hadn't she been left a widow with two young children to bring up? And people were still paying even now, years after the war had ended — her mum and Auntie Vi, turned out of their homes, Frank dying in the mental hospital, Jim . . .

Mary choked back a sob. She wouldn't dwell on it — couldn't — otherwise she'd never get through the day. She must make the best of it. Bert was her husband.

No one had forced her to marry him and, if it hadn't turned out the way she'd hoped, there was nothing she could do about it. But since Harry and Sheila had left home, she felt so alone. Ellie was too young to understand.

And Ellie was the one she should be thinking of now. She was a good girl, always willing to give a hand with the chores or run errands.

If only she'd been able to persuade Bert to let her stay on at school. She'd done so well in her exams and she deserved a chance. But proud as she was of her daughter's determination to succeed and her willingness to work for what she wanted, she knew it was no use trying to get Bert to change his mind.

She still wasn't happy about this job though. It was bad enough her husband getting involved with the gangster again, but the thought of Ellie working for Tommy Green worried her. Mary thought it was unlikely that her friends knew of the gangster's new business venture but she still dreaded anyone finding out that her daughter had anything to do with him. Once more she wished she'd had the strength to stand up to Bert and insist that Ellie find another job. Tommy Green had already caused enough trouble in this family. Although she had softened towards Sheila, and was pleased she seemed happy, she felt shame at people knowing her daughter was living with a married man and a criminal at that. It was only the thought of never knowing her grandchild that had softened her attitude. She smiled at the thought that soon she would be a grandmother, but the smile changed to a frown at the thought of the sort of world she or he might grow up in.

Bert grunted, snorting and muttering, and Mary hurried out of the room. If he woke up and saw her he'd be pawing at her and demanding his "rights" and she was in no mood to put up with it today. Not that he did that so often these days and she wondered if he was getting his satisfaction elsewhere. There was a time when she'd been worried that he might be after Sheila — there'd been something in the way he looked at her. But she couldn't bring herself to believe he'd do such a thing.

Ellie was on her way back from her grandmother's when she saw Mary struggling with a heavy bag of shopping. She ran to catch up with her. "Mum, I thought you were going to bed."

"I decided to go down the market first — needed a bit of fresh air."

Ellie took the bag without replying. She thought she knew why Mum had gone out instead of getting her much needed rest. She just hoped Dad had gone out before they got home.

As they turned the corner on their way back from the market, they saw Mr Solomons standing in the doorway of the shop. He was looking rather sombre but his lined old face creased in a smile as he spotted them.

"Everything all right, Solly?" Mary asked.

"Could be worse, Mrs Tyler. Business isn't too good these days — but I get by." He shook his white head.

Ellie smiled. She'd heard Mum saying that Mr Solomons did quite well from his second-hand furniture shop, especially now that more people were moving house these days. It was an opportunity to get rid of the sticks of cheap old stuff they'd started married life with. Solly sold good quality furniture which he bought from posh people who'd fallen on hard times or whose houses were being sold for death duties. But he always acted as if he were on the verge of bankruptcy.

Although he smiled as he chatted, Ellie could see he wasn't his usual cheerful self. Maybe this time there really was something wrong. Her stomach started to churn as she remembered the boxes she'd seen in the yard a few weeks ago. She was sure they were stolen goods and that her father had had something to do with it. Had Solly found out — or worse still, had Dad done it again?

Ellie bit her lip as her mother asked Mr Solomons what was the matter, relaxing as he took a letter from his pocket. It was from the landlord, saying that the building had been sold and that he had until the end of the year to find somewhere else.

"What about us?" Ellie asked.

"You'll get a council place — a nice new house with a garden maybe. You'll like that, won't you — instead of this draughty old place?"

Ellie nodded doubtfully but Mary was smiling. "I'm looking forward to it," she said. "Anyway, what about you? It's about time you retired and took things easy. It can't be good for a man your age, having to lug buckets of coal up and downstairs."

"Ah, that's where I miss young 'Arry," Solly said, with a shake of his head. "He's a good lad — always ready to lend a hand. I expect you miss 'im too."

Mary nodded sadly. "More than I can say. He's always been just like a real son to me. Still, it won't be too long before he's home again."

"Well, when you apply for your council place, don't forget to put him and his wife down as part of the family too — that way you'll get a bigger house," Solly advised.

Ellie flinched at the reminder that when Harry returned to London he'd be bringing his German wife too. Even worse was the thought that they'd be living with them until they could get a place of their own. How could she bear seeing them together?

She sighed and listened impatiently as Solly rambled on.

"I don't want to move at all," he was saying. "Fifty years I've lived 'ere — brought me family up, saw them all go off and make their way in the world — except for my poor Sam." The old man paused and sniffed. His son had been killed in the war.

He wiped his nose and went on, "And when my Ada went, it was only having you and the kids around that kept me going." He put his hand on Ellie's arm. "Take no notice, me dear. I'm just gettin' maudlin in me old age."

Ellie and her mother left the old man and went up to their flat.

"Can they really turn us out?" Ellie asked as she helped to put the shopping away.

"Well, Solly has the house on a lease — they've always renewed it in the past but now the owner wants to sell. We're only sub-tenants so we haven't got a leg to stand on. Goodness knows what your dad'll say, though. He hates the idea of a council flat."

At least he's not here to start a row, Ellie thought, seeing the draining-board littered with dirty crockery. He must have dragged himself out of bed and gone to work.

Mary filled the kettle and lit the gas, then reached up to the mantelpiece for an envelope. "This came while you were out," she said.

Once upon a time Ellie would have snatched any letter from Harry and torn it open. Now, she sat down at the kitchen table with it but did not attempt to read it. "What does it say?" she asked.

Mary gave her a funny look. "Why don't you read it and find out?"

"Mum!"

"He's coming home in a few days, he says." Mary's lips thinned. "I suppose he'll be bringing his wife — that Gerda."

Ellie burst into tears.

"Whatever's the matter with you? I thought you'd be pleased. Our Harry's coming home."

"But he's not our Harry any more, is he? He's Gerda's now."

Mum sighed and patted her shoulder. "You silly girl," she said affectionately.

Ellie shrugged her off. Mum just didn't understand why she felt so wretched. It was jealousy pure and simple. If she truly loved him like a brother she ought to be glad he'd found someone to love. A year ago she would have been.

When had it all changed, she asked herself? Was it when she discovered he wasn't her brother after all? Or when she had kissed him goodbye and he had told her she was special?

She'd dared to hope that that meant he felt the same way, that by the time he came home from the army he would be ready to tell her so. But from his letters she'd begun to realize how wrong she'd been. And now there was no hope for her.

Was it really love she felt for him? How could you tell? People would say she was too young to know for sure. It was like the song said. Every time she heard Nat King Cole on the wireless singing. "*They try to tell us we're too young*", she thought the song might have been written just for her.

As the thoughts churned in her head Ellie stood up, her legs unsteady, and stumbled out of the kitchen. She had to get away from Mum's questioning.

Maybe Gran would understand. But when she got there, Auntie Vi was sitting in the kitchen gossiping.

"What's up with you then?" she asked. "Dad playing up?"

"Harry's coming home — bringing his wife. I hate her," Ellie said.

"Yer must've realized he'd find a girl one day, you soppy thing," Auntie Vi said. She turned to Gran. "I always said it wasn't 'ealthy, the way she mooned after 'im all the time."

"Leave the girl alone, Vi. She's probably only upset because 'Arry's geting married out there in Germany and she couldn't be a bridesmaid," Lou said.

Ellie gave her a grateful smile. She wondered if Gran understood more than she let on and was covering up for her. Anyway, it wouldn't hurt to let Vi think that was why she was upset if it stopped her asking questions.

She didn't stay long, unable to face the two old ladies going on about Harry and his new wife. As she wandered back through the market, she tried to tell herself she didn't care. Her love for Harry was just that of a younger sister for a big brother, wasn't it? She'd been stupid to think it was anything else — stupid, too, to think that he felt anything like the romantic love of her imagination. But to get a girl into trouble and have to get married . . . How could he do it?

Back home she went up to her room and picked up the snapshot of Harry in his army uniform. With a little sob, she thrust it into the drawer, pushing it deep under her spare jumpers. Her lips set in a thin straight line. The people you loved always let you down in the end. But she'd always have her art — and her ambition. From now on, she'd put away those childish thoughts of love and romance.

She'd work hard and save her money. Then, when she was old enough to do what she liked without needing anyone's permission, she'd go to college. Nothing was going to stop her achieving her ambition.

CHAPTER
NINE

When she went downstairs, the inevitable row was going on. Mum looked as if she was about to burst into tears and Dad was prowling about the room clenching and unclenching his fists. His braces hung down over his trousers and a cigarette dangled from his unshaven face. He never bothered when he was at home, though he could look smart enough when he was meeting Tommy Green and his mates.

Ellie paused in the doorway and looked at him, not bothering to hide her disgust. And Mum wondered why she never brought any of her friends home? She tried to slip past, hoping to get out of the house before they noticed her.

But Bert turned in his pacing and spotted her. "I suppose you're going to stick up for 'is nibs an' all," he snarled. "Well, that cocky little bleeder's not coming here expecting a ready-made 'ome for 'imself and that woman." He banged his fist on the table. "I won't 'ave it."

Mary thumped the iron down. "I already told you, Bert. He's no intention of living with us." She gave a short laugh, which quickly turned to a strangled sob. "He couldn't wait to get away, if you must know.

Anyway, he's decided to stay in the army — make a career out of it. He'll only be home for a few days, then he's been posted to Sheerness."

Ellie noticed that her mother didn't mention Gerda. Mum was just as unhappy about Harry's impending marriage as she was — if for different reasons.

Bert gave a little grunt and sat down. "That's good — 'cause I wouldn't 'ave 'im 'ere anyway," he said, determined to have the last word.

But Mary wouldn't let it rest. "Besides, we might not have a home ourselves for long. I told you Solly's been given notice to quit when the lease runs out. So it might be a good idea to get off your backside and start looking for another flat," she said.

Ellie gasped. Mum must be really upset to talk to Dad like that. She stepped forward, heart thumping, as Bert leapt up and raised his bunched fist towards her mother.

He must have seen her quick move of protest and his hand fell to his side. He smiled sheepishly at her. "I keep telling yer mother not ter worry, Angel. I know who's bought this place and they've said we can stay on after Solly goes. Besides, our name's on the council list, so if it comes to the worst, we'll get a place."

Ellie hoped they would get a council flat. She'd been looking forward to moving out of the draughty old house and having a decent kitchen and bathroom. And wouldn't it be smashing if they got a place in the same block as Gran? Then, when things got difficult at home, she could pop in and keep the old lady company.

To her relief, Dad dropped the subject, asking Mary how much longer she'd be ironing his shirt. "I got an important meeting with my business associates," he said, thrusting out his puny chest.

Ellie couldn't help smiling inwardly but the smile soon faded when her father turned to her.

"They've finished work on the new club. Grand opening tomorrer and Tommy wants you there — all dressed up in your new finery. You lookin' forward to it?"

When Ellie hesitated, he reached out and grabbed her wrist. She glanced anxiously at her mother but Mary carried on ironing, all her attention apparently on getting the minutest creases out of Bert's shirt collar.

Bert stroked her hair. "Looks nice like that," he said. "But you don't look like my little girl any more." He pushed her away. "Still, it's a good chance for yer so make the most of it. You'll do all right for yerself — just like Sheila."

The iron thumped down again. Mum always got upset at any mention of Sheila. Getting involved with a married man, and a criminal at that, wasn't what Mary thought of as doing all right. Ellie agreed with her. She resolved that she would just do the job until she could afford to get away — by her own efforts, not the influence of some rich man.

She was about to say so but Mary shook her head, handing the shirt to her husband. He let go of Ellie's wrist and shrugged into it, grabbed his jacket and left the room.

When he'd gone, Mary hugged her daughter wordlessly. Ellie knew Mum was on her side, but she was too frightened of Bert's temper to stand up for either of them. She'd just have to do what she was told — for the time being, that was.

She went back up to her room and opened the wardrobe door, trying to imagine herself all dressed up in the clothes which now hung there — long dresses in black, midnight blue or dark green, with matching stole and gloves, as elegant as anything the guests at the club might wear. The shopping trip "up West" had been a success, although Ellie suspected her mother had enjoyed it more than she had.

Looking in the mirror, Ellie hardly recognized herself. Her hair was shorter now, expertly cut to frame her heart-shaped face, with soft chestnut waves. Dressed up in the long gowns with a little make-up and costume jewellery, no one would question that she was old enough to be working in a sophisticated nightclub. But she still felt more comfortable in her old tartan skirt and maroon school jumper.

Ellie sat on the edge of the bed and sighed. The chores were all done and Dad had gone out. She could get her art things out and do some drawing or painting. But the thought only made her sad. She had put all her sketch pads, paints and pencils in a box on top of the wardrobe, together with the portfolio she'd been compiling for the college scholarship. What was the point of bothering? Maybe Dad and Auntie Vi were right — it was just a childish hobby. Deep down, she wasn't really convinced — but it helped to tell herself so.

She stood up abruptly. She'd go down to the market and talk to Sid. They didn't need any vegetables — she'd already done the shopping that morning. But she needed to see a cheerful face — and if anyone could cheer her up, Sid could.

As always, the comforting familiarity of the market lifted Ellie's mood as soon as she turned the corner. The raucous shouts of the stallholders, together with the salty whiff from Ernie's whelk stall and the warm blast of air laden with a rich meaty aroma as she passed Al's pie shop, always spelt home to Ellie.

As she threaded her way through the crowds towards Sid's stall, waving and calling a greeting to the other market traders, it dawned on her how much she would miss these familiar faces if ever she left this part of London. And with the thought came the realization that, if she'd won the scholarship and gone away to art college, she would have been forced to leave this all behind. She'd been so fixed on her ambitions that she hadn't really thought what it would mean. There was no way she could pursue a career in art here in her native East End. Of course, the job in Tommy Green's new club was up West, but at least she'd be coming home each day and her free time would be spent among friends and family. Maybe it was all for the best after all.

Her mood changed when she got home and Mum started talking about Harry again. "It'll be nice to see him again, won't it, love?" she said.

Ellie nodded, unable to speak. In her dreams she'd almost convinced herself that Harry's marriage had been a mistake and that when he returned to England he would leave Gerda behind. But of course, he couldn't do that. Gerda was having a baby and Harry wouldn't desert his own child. She forced a smile. No one must ever guess how she felt. Her love for Harry was a secret she would bury deep within herself. Despite her youth, she knew that she would never love anyone else like this. Mary glanced at the letter tucked behind the clock and patted Ellie's shoulder. There had been a time when she had been quite worried about her daughter's attachment to her foster brother, but she thought she'd got over it. Not that there was really anything wrong with it — they weren't related, after all. But she'd been inclined to agree with Aunt Vi that such obsessive devotion wasn't healthy. Still, young girls did develop crushes on the most unlikely people.

Maybe now that Harry was married and his wife expecting, she would start thinking of him as a brother again, and enjoy the thought of being an auntie to his baby. And perhaps she'd start going out with friends of her own age and make the most of being young and carefree.

With a sigh, Mary realized that that probably wouldn't happen either, now that Ellie was starting work for Tommy Green. How she wished she'd been assertive enough to stand up to Bert when he suggested it. She told herself that Ellie was sensible enough not to get into any trouble, but she couldn't help worrying that she'd come under the influence of the wrong sort of people. And if her younger daughter ended up the same way as Sheila she would never forgive herself.

Harry was looking forward to returning to England but he was beginning to wish he hadn't been so hasty in agreeing to sign on as a regular. It had seemed the right thing at the time. He'd get a marriage allowance and married quarters and be able to provide for Gerda.

Now it had all gone wrong and he didn't know whether to be relieved or angry. As usual he had arranged to meet Gerda at the beer cellar where they'd originally met. He'd been kept late at the barracks and arrived to find her sitting on someone's lap, laughing and pouring beer down his throat. As he pushed his way through the crowded bar he saw her take a swig from the stein.

She shouldn't be drinking while she was pregnant. He grabbed her arm and she looked round at him, the laughter draining from her face. "Oh, Harry, *liebchen*, I thought you weren't coming." She pouted. She scrambled off the other soldier's lap and put her arms round him. "I thought you had deserted me."

"I couldn't help being late." He bit his lip to stop the angry outburst. He knew Gerda liked to have fun and there was no harm in a little flirtation. After all, it was him she loved — hadn't she said so over and over?

She stroked his cheek and kissed him. "You're not cross with your Gerda?"

He could smell the beer on her breath. "No, of course not. But you shouldn't drink so much. Think about the baby."

She threw back her head and laughed. "No baby. Was a mistake. Silly mistake, Harry."

He felt a churning in his stomach. No baby. The wedding was set for the following week, the arrangements brought forward when his posting came through. Was it too late to back out?

She noticed his expression and frowned. "We still get married, no? You take me to England with you?"

He forced a smile. "Of course. I don't go back on my word."

But as the evening wore on, Gerda drank more and more and she began to flirt with his mates. Harry told himself it was the relief of discovering she wasn't pregnant after all. But he couldn't help wondering whether she was really ready for married life on an army base.

When he returned from getting more drinks she was once more sitting on someone else's lap and he felt another surge of anger. He slammed down the beer steins and pushed his way towards the door. As he turned back at the foot of the stairs leading to the street he saw that she hadn't even noticed he was gone.

Back at the barracks he threw himself down on his bed, cursing himself for a fool. He'd known right from the start that getting involved with Gerda was a mistake. But he wasn't one to shirk his responsibilities and he'd thought he was doing the right thing. She hadn't been too bothered about him leaving so abruptly, but would she feel differently when she sobered up? He hardly dared to think he'd be let off the hook so easily. He sighed. How naïve he'd been, thinking she loved him. Had the supposed pregnancy been just a way to trap him?

As the men who shared his billet returned from their evening out he pretended to be asleep. Some of them had been in the beer cellar and seen Gerda's behaviour. He couldn't put up with their snide remarks.

Thank goodness he'd be away from here soon. He smiled at the thought of a few days' leave before going to his new posting in Kent. Now he could look forward to seeing Ellie with a clear conscience. Would she be as pleased to see him? Or would her head be so full of art college that she hadn't got time for him?

Harry swung his kitbag on to his shoulder and strode down the platform at Liverpool Street station. As he stood on the escalator, breathing in the hot, stale smell of the Underground, he could hardly believe he was back in London. Almost a year had gone by since his embarkation leave but so much had happened. A poster showing the National Gallery and Trafalgar Square reminded him of outings with Ellie and he smiled. When had he felt the first stirrings of love — a different kind of love from the brotherly feelings he'd always had? It had come upon him slowly and it was only when he was leaving that he realized how strong that love was.

Why had he tried to deny it, he asked himself now? He'd been worried that Mary would see it as a betrayal of her trust. But he could have waited until Ellie was older. It should have been easier being away from her. Not for the first time he cursed his stupidity in getting involved with Gerda — and he had been stupid, he realized that. Still he was free of her now. He hadn't even seen her since that night in the beer cellar and one of his mates had told him she'd been seen with one of the officers. Good luck to him, Harry thought.

When he came to his stop he got off and walked up the steep stairs into the comparatively fresh air. He ran towards a bus stop and swung himself aboard a red double-decker. As the bus swayed round a corner and into Roman Road he felt a surge of nostalgia for his old home. It would be good to see Sid and his market friends. But he knew he was just putting off the moment when he'd have to face his family and tell them what a fool he'd been.

In the market it was as if he'd never been away and he was flushed and laughing by the time he'd run the gauntlet of the stallholders and their raucous comments. He stopped for a jaw with Sid, catching up on the gossip, then hefted his kitbag on to his shoulder again.

"Gotta be off. I can't wait to get home. I haven't told them I'm coming today — wasn't sure if I could get on the boat."

At the corner of the street he stopped outside the flat, taking a few deep breaths to calm himself. Would Ellie be there? Perhaps he should go straight down to Kent, write and tell her his marriage was off. Give it a bit of time before he told her how he felt.

He dumped his kitbag in the passage and leapt the stairs two at a time before he could change his mind.

105

Ellie was sitting at the kitchen table flicking through a magazine, her back to him. She didn't look up when he came into the room and he noticed that her shoulders were tense, her knuckles tight on the glossy paper. He'd expected to see her in her school uniform doing her homework.

She turned her head and he caught his breath. The shorter hairstyle suited her heart-shaped face and she was even lovelier than he remembered. His stomach lurched as the spontaneous welcoming grin faded, to be replaced by a cool smile.

"Harry, you should have told us you were coming."

Once she would have leapt up and thrown herself into his arms. Had he been mistaken then, in thinking she shared his feelings? So what if she did — he'd told her he was getting married, that his girlfriend was expecting. Maybe he shouldn't have come.

His hands dropped to his sides and he grinned. "I didn't know meself — got a few days' leave before me new posting."

Ellie looked over his shoulder. "Isn't your wife with you?"

He shuffled his feet and looked embarrassed. "Gerda's stayed behind in Germany. We had a few problems," he said.

"I expect you'll sort it out," Ellie said, going over to the range and pushing the kettle over the coals.

There was an awkward silence, but while she pottered around the kitchen he had time to collect his thoughts. He'd thought she'd be pleased he wasn't getting married after all but perhaps he'd misread the situation. He didn't want to believe that the feelings he'd had on his last leave weren't reciprocated despite the amount of time he'd spent trying to convince himself of it.

He sat down at the table and took a deep breath. He'd give her time to absorb his news. He coughed. "How's Mary?"

Ellie sat down opposite him. "She's tired all the time. I think she's ill but she won't admit it."

"Don't suppose your dad's much help?"

Ellie shrugged but didn't answer. He could see now that she was unhappy although she covered it up well, telling him about her new job and almost convincing him that she was looking forward to it.

Her composure slipped when he asked her if she minded not going to college.

"I didn't have any choice did I? Besides, it was just a dream really." There was a bitter note in her voice as she continued; "That's what growing up means, doesn't it — realizing that real life is nothing like your dreams?"

He looked down at the table, unable to meet her eyes. In the old days he'd have coaxed a smile out of her, reassured her that everything would turn out right. But he couldn't find the right words. He finished his tea in one gulp and stood up abruptly.

"I can't stay — got a train to catch." He didn't have to report for duty till the end of the week but he had to get away.

"Aren't you going to stay and say hello to Mum? She'll be home soon," Ellie said.

"I'm sorry, Ellie. I only popped in for a quick hello. You know what the army's like."

She followed him downstairs and held the door open while he put on his cap and picked up the bag. He looked down at her and smiled. "Remember what I said last time, Ellie — you're special and you can do anything you want to. It doesn't matter about school or college. You'll make something of your life, I know you will."

A tear glistened on her eyelash and he reached out to wipe it away. "God, Ellie, don't cry — please." His voice choked on the words.

Then she was in his arms and he was stroking her hair. She lifted her face to his and he tasted the salt of her tears mingled with the sweetness of her lips. "Oh, Ellie, Ellie," he murmured.

They stood together in the dark passage for what seemed like hours. But it could only have been a minute before Ellie pulled away. She dashed her hand across her eyes and smiled up at him. "I love you, Harry. I always have. But it's too late for us, isn't it?"

"I've been such a fool." He touched her hair. "Can you forgive me?"

She gave a strangled cry and rushed back upstairs. He heard the door slam. She hadn't given him a chance to explain that getting involved with Gerda had been a mistake, that it was Ellie he loved and always would. Should he go after her?

He shrugged. She was so young and at that age everything seemed black and white. She would never understand that homesickness and loneliness could drive a man to act foolishly. He'd just have to give her time.

He picked up his kitbag and walked out of the door.

CHAPTER
TEN

Ellie fastened the glittering rhinestone necklace and clipped on the matching earrings. A final flick of the hairbrush through her thick chestnut waves and she was ready. She bit her lip as she stared at the reflection in the long mirror in her parents' room. Was that really little Ellen Tyler, the tomboy of the bombsites, the earnest grammar-school student? No — this was a different creature altogether and Ellie wasn't sure whether she liked what she saw. Was she just being silly? Most of the girls she'd grown up with would give anything to be able to dress up like this and spend an evening mingling with the rich and famous in the West End of London.

Despite her father's and Mr Green's assurances that the Paradise Club was a very high-class establishment, Ellie still had her doubts. How could someone like Tommy Green, who was well-known as a spiv and wide boy in his native East End, hope to move into respectable business? Did he really want to go "legit" as he'd told Bert — or was this new venture just a cover for yet more shady deals?

Apart from the apprehension natural to anyone starting a new job, Ellie also had a dread of what she was getting mixed up in. But she was only sixteen, too young to take control of her own life. How would she get through the next few years, she wondered as she smoothed down the long satin evening gown and went to show her mother the new Ellen Tyler.

Mary looked up from her sewing with a gasp as Ellie came into the room.

"You look — taller," she said.

It wasn't the reaction Ellie was expecting but she smiled as her mother stood up and gave a little laugh. "No, love, you look gorgeous — but so different."

"It's the high heels," Ellie said, as she twirled round, giggling. But the laugh died in her throat as she saw her father in the doorway, staring at her.

"Who's this then? I thought it was Princess Margaret come to visit," he said with a sneer. "Well, well — our little Ellie's all grown up."

Ellie held her breath and managed not to flinch as he stepped close to her, his face thrust forward. Was he going to spoil things as usual? But he smiled and looked her up and down. "Better not keep Tommy waiting — the car's downstairs."

The car was a sleek black Wolseley, a bit like the ones the Metropolitan police used, Ellie thought, smiling at the irony, as Tommy's driver, Sammy Groves, opened the door for her. She knew Sammy from his market days when he'd run a jewellery and bric-a-brac stall — until he'd been caught selling stolen goods. When he came out of prison, Tommy had given him a job and the little man had been his unwilling slave ever since. Ellie wondered if Tommy had a similar hold over her father as she remembered the unexplained boxes of electrical goods that had been stored in Solly's yard.

"Cor, I 'ardly recognized yer, young Ellie," he said, sweeping his hand back across his greased black hair.

Bert came up behind them and interrupted. "Come on, get a move on. We don't wanna keep the boss waitin'." He got into the back seat beside Ellie and took her hand.

When she tried to pull away, he squeezed her fingers. "No need to be nervous, love. Tommy'll see you all right."

It was a relief when the car pulled up outside the club, jostling for a parking space in the busy street.

Ellie had only been to the club once since her interview with Tommy Green. Then the place had been noisy with carpenters and decorators, the air sharp with the smell of new paint. Tommy had shown her round, waving his cigar expansively, proud that he was going up in the world.

He had shown her the little office behind the reception desk where she would answer the phone and keep the records of bookings. But during the club's opening hours she would be in the foyer, her job to smile and look immaculate as she greeted the guests, signed them in and directed them to the various bars, the restaurant or the legal gaming-tables upstairs.

She followed Bert up the wide steps and through the heavy double doors into the foyer, where Tommy was waiting, surrounded by his minions, some of whom looked distinctly uncomfortable in their smart evening wear. Like fish out of water, just like me, she thought, smiling sympathetically at Sammy, who was running his finger under his collar.

112

Tommy greeted her expansively, introducing her to some of the guests as his future sister-in-law. She smiled nervously and took her place behind the reception counter, until Tommy called her away. "This isn't a normal working night," he told her. "Everyone's here by invitation only, so there's no signing in or anything. I just want you to enjoy yourself, love."

He grabbed a glass from a passing waiter and handed it to her. "Champagne," he said with a grin. "Don't go thinking it's lemonade."

Ellie glanced across at her father, who was talking to a group of his cronies. She knew Mum wouldn't approve of her drinking but Bert probably didn't care one way or the other. Besides, she couldn't say no to Tommy — he was her boss. She decided to sip it slowly and make it last.

The bubbles tickled her nose and she screwed her face up at the unfamiliar taste. But after a couple of sips she decided she liked it. She left the foyer and wandered into the next room. A bar with tall stools placed along its length took up most of one wall. The room was carpeted in thick dark-red plush with matching curtains at the long narrow windows. Small gilt tables were dotted about with comfortable chairs upholstered in gold brocade. Ellie thought it was a bit too lavish but Tommy evidently liked it. He had chosen the décor himself.

As she looked around, taking small sips of the champagne and trying to appear at ease, a voice at her ear startled her.

"Are you sure you're old enough to be drinking that stuff?"

She turned, a slow flush stealing up her neck to her cheeks, stuttering as she recognized the man looking down at her with a sardonic smile. At first she couldn't recall his name although his face was familiar from visits to the cinema with her mother — Philip Devereux, that was it. In his heyday, he'd been one of her mother's favourite actors, although he was seldom seen nowadays.

Ellie took a deep breath and another sip of champagne. Tommy had told her that the rich and famous, even a few of the nobs, were among his clients. She would have to get used to talking to them.

He was waiting for her reply. She smiled up at him. "I wouldn't be here if I wasn't old enough."

He smiled and took her empty glass, placing it on a small table nearby. As he turned away to take a fresh glass from the waiter she thought she heard him mutter, "Pity." He handed the champagne to her with a small bow, then excused himself and moved away.

Ellie watched him go, thinking how excited Mum would be when she told her she'd actually spoken to Philip Devereux. Close up, he wasn't as handsome as he was on the films, and of course, he was a lot older. And there was something in the way he'd looked at her, something that made her feel uncomfortable. Maybe she wouldn't tell Mum after all.

She'd only drunk half her second glass but already her head was feeling a bit swimmy. Trouble was, the room was so hot and it was becoming noisy and crowded as more and more guests arrived. What Ellie really wanted was a drink of cold water.

As she pushed her way through the crowd towards the door, little Sammy Groves stopped her. "Do you know who that was you were talking to?" he asked.

"Yes, it was Philip Devereux, the film star. My mum thinks he's gorgeous." Ellie giggled and put her hand over her mouth. She shouldn't have had that second glass of champagne.

"Well, that's what most people think — people who've only seen 'im on the films," Sammy said. "If your mum knew what 'e was really like, she wouldn't want you talkin' to 'im."

"Why ever not? He seemed quite nice. I was just thinking how jealous Mum will be when I tell her," Ellie said.

Sammy looked round furtively and took hold of her arm, drawing her into the foyer where it was less crowded. "Tommy'll kill me if he finds out I've said anything." He shook his head and looked down at his feet. "You could've knocked me down with a feather when I picked you up at your place. I thought I was giving Bert a lift. What's he doing, letting you work in a place like this?"

"Mr Green told Dad he was going straight, otherwise Mum wouldn't have let me come," Ellie said.

Sammy gave a little snort. "So he convinced her, did he? Well, I bet your 'Arry's not so easily fooled. He'd 'ave something to say if he knew."

The mention of Harry made Ellie's stomach lurch. She'd been trying so hard to get him out of her head.

She hadn't even told her mother about his flying visit. Trying to keep her voice level she said, "But it's a respectable club, isn't it? All the gambling's above board — Mr Green's got his licence and everything,"

Sammy looked worried and lowered his voice. It wasn't hard to believe him when he confided that the club was a front for other things — things he obviously felt uncomfortable discussing with the sixteen-year-old daughter of his old mate Bert. She'd known Sammy since she was a little girl, had gone to school with his children and run errands for him, as she had for the other market traders. But for that one lapse which had cost him a few years in jail, Sammy would still be running his stall alongside Sid and Maisie and all her other childhood friends. So Ellie was prepared to listen when he told her about the private theatre in the basement — a place she hadn't even known existed.

Philip Devereux — one-time matinée idol — had gone into the film business on his own — as a director. And the films he made would not be showing in any High Street cinema.

"That's why I was so worried when I saw you talking to him," Sammy said. "I thought you might fall for that old line about getting you into the movies. He's always on the lookout for new talent — and he likes 'em young, very young. That's why he's not in films any more. The studios were always havin' to hush up the scandal — and he did it once too often. Now no one will employ him."

"I'm glad you told me — I'll be on my guard if he talks to me again," Ellie said. Now she understood the meaning of Devereux's muttered remark. She was obviously too old for his perverted tastes. She suppressed a little shudder, glancing round at the laughing throng, wondering how many were here for the normal pleasures of an evening out — and how many knew of the hidden basement room. The effect of the champagne had worn off and, stone-cold sober, she knew she couldn't spend another moment in this place.

She retrieved her coat from the ladies' cloakroom and went back to the foyer, wondering how she would manage to get away without Tommy or her father noticing. But now the rooms were crowded, the air full of blue smoke and loud champagne-fuelled voices. No one saw her go, except the doorman, a burly ex-boxer, whose crumpled face creased in a lopsided grin when he recognized Ellie.

When he offered to call her a taxi, she declined. "I need some fresh air," she said. "If Dad asks where I am, can you tell him I didn't feel well and I've gone home?"

As she hurried away from the Paradise Club towards the main road, she breathed a sigh of relief. Even this late at night the Soho streets were crowded and noisy, the air filled with the mingled smells of food and alcohol. But the air seemed clean and fresh after the atmosphere she'd left behind.

Stumbling in the unfamiliar high heels, Ellie had covered several streets before the shoes began to rub a blister on her heel. She'd have to get a taxi home.

As she sank back in the seat, she began to shake. When Dad got home, he'd be furious that she'd run away. But what distressed her most was the thought of her sister marrying a man like Tommy Green who would connive at the corruption of young girls. Did Sheila know what he did for a living? Or was she deceived by his protests that he wanted to put his past behind him and become respectable? Of course, Tommy had always been a crook. But black-market dealing, illegal gambling and fixing fights were almost acceptable to many of the people Ellie had grown up with. This was something else and she only hoped that her sister would never find out what sort of a man she had taken up with.

She bit back a sob as it dawned on her that her father must be mixed up in it too. He was close to Tommy — he must know. And yet he'd forced her to work at the club. Why should she be surprised, she thought bitterly? Hadn't he already corrupted first his stepdaughter, then his own child?

As she stepped out of the taxi on the corner of Kendall Street, Ellie took a hankie out of her bag and tried to wipe away all traces of the tears she'd been unable to hold back. She didn't want her mother to see how upset — and angry — she was. As it was, she'd have a job explaining why she'd come home early instead of waiting for her father.

The flat was in darkness. Ellie took off her shoes and crept quietly upstairs to the kitchen, anxious not to disturb her mother. She wanted to bathe her sore feet in salt water before going to bed. But as she reached to pull the kettle over the banked-up coals of the range, she saw the note propped up in front of the clock.

When she read it, her tears started again. Gran had been taken ill and rushed to hospital. *"It's no good you going over there as they won't let you in. So try to get some sleep and I'll wake you when I get back with any news. Mum."*

Ellie had thought things couldn't get any worse but this was the last straw. Her sore feet forgotten, she went up to her attic room and savagely tore off the beautiful gown and jewellery. She would never wear them again, she vowed, as she threw the dress in the corner.

She rummaged in the drawer and retrieved Harry's crumpled photograph. If only he were here, he'd know what to do about Tommy Green. But he was settling down in Sheerness and no doubt Gerda would soon be joining him when things were sorted out. She knew she was being unfair. How could Harry know what she and her mother had to put up with? She'd always tried to make her letters chatty and cheerful and since his brief visit she hadn't written to him at all.

She ought to write and tell him about Gran. Maybe he'd be able to get some leave to visit the old lady. Ellie didn't dare to think that he might be too late. Gran wasn't going to die, she told herself. And when she got better, Ellie would go and live with her and look after her. On her long walk through the streets of Soho that evening she'd already made up her mind there was no way she'd stay under the same roof as Bert Tyler.

She had dried her tears and got out her writing pad and pen, when it occurred to her that she wouldn't be allowed to stay with Gran. The old people's council flats were for single tenants only — if any of them needed looking after, they were transferred to the old people's home. If only Gran were still in her little terraced house. But Gascoigne Terrace no longer existed and Ellie couldn't even walk past the flattened ground where the new tower blocks were going up without feeling sad.

Her tears started again and she tried in vain to think of someone who would take her in — someone who could be trusted not to tell her father where she was. But there wasn't anybody. Mum's brother, Uncle Jack, had moved to Glasgow with his Scottish wife when he'd been demobbed after the war and they hardly heard from him these days. Where could she go? There was only Harry — the one person she knew she could rely on. Of course he'd take her in — but she couldn't face the thought of seeing him with his wife. And it would be even worse when the baby came. She'd never be able to hide her feelings.

Still, she'd write to him. It would pass the time till her mother got back from the hospital.

She finished the letter and read it through, knowing she'd never send it. Once she'd started writing it had all come out — not just Gran's illness, or her disillusionment with the job her father had forced her into. She also told him of her bitter disappointment at not being allowed to pursue her ambitions, and then, without really thinking, she'd poured out her true feelings, pleading with him to tell her he felt the same way, to admit that marrying Gerda was a mistake.

120

With a little sob, she screwed up the sheets of paper. She'd have to burn the letter. It wouldn't do for anyone else to read it. In a strange way, though, she felt better. Spilling it all out had eased the pain — if only a little. Besides, she'd lived with hurt and disillusionment for most of her life — this was just one more thing to be buried in the recesses of her heart while she got on with her life.

As she started downstairs, she gave herself a firm telling-off for her selfishness. How could she have indulged in such a bout of self-pity when her dearly loved grandmother was lying in hospital seriously ill?

She shivered in her thin petticoat as a cold draught crept up the staircase and she wished she'd put a cardigan on. She would shove the letter into the range and make sure it was well alight, then she'd get to bed. She was exhausted and Mum had promised to wake her if there was any news.

A light showed under the kitchen door and Ellie held the letter behind her back as she pushed it open. Mum must be back from the hospital.

"How's Gran?" The words were out before she realized it was her father, one hand supporting himself on the edge of the kitchen table, the other holding Mum's note.

"What's this then — where's your mother?"

"Like it says — she's gone to the hospital. Gran's been taken ill," Ellie said. At least he hadn't shouted at her for leaving the club early, she thought. But her relief was short-lived.

"And what do yer think you were playin' at — runnin' off like that? Made me look a right Charlie."

The words were spoken quietly and Ellie began to think he wasn't too angry. "I didn't feel well. It was so hot and I came over giddy. Didn't the doorman tell you? I asked him to let you know," she said.

"No one said a word to me. Felt a right fool, didn't I, when Tommy asked where you were." He swayed and sat down abruptly in the armchair, his head nodding, his words trailing off into mumbling incoherence.

Ellie knew she should have seized the moment to leave the room, to get upstairs and put the chair under the door handle. But she still held the letter she'd written and she desperately wanted to get rid of it. What had possessed her to spill out all her thoughts like that in the first place?

She stepped quietly towards the kitchen range and Bert shifted in his chair.

"What you up to?" he muttered.

"Making you a cup of tea, Dad."

She lifted the round hotplate and poked the fire, glancing quickly at her father. He appeared to be dozing. But as she reached across to thrust the sheets of paper into the glowing embers, his hand shot out and grasped her wrist.

"What's this then?" he snatched the letter from her and several of the sheets drifted to the floor. "Dear Harry — what yer writin' ter 'im for? It's a waste of time — never was any good and now he's got himself shacked up with a bleedin' Kraut."

Bert's grip on her wrist was painful and Ellie tried to pull away. She reached out for the letter. "I was only telling him about Gran being ill," she said.

"Then why were yer puttin' it in the fire?"

"I made too many mistakes. I've written it all out again in my best writing," she told him, hoping desperately he'd believe her. Besides, he was too fuddled with drink to be able to read what she'd written — wasn't he?

He pulled her closer, tightening his grip, and with the other hand held one of the pages up to the light. A short mirthless laugh escaped him. "So that's the way the wind blows is it? I might've known. You was always moonin' round 'im like a little puppy dog." He shook her roughly. "Yer a little tart — just like that sister of yours."

Ellie whimpered as he threw the letter down and grasped her shoulder. His eyes raked her figure and she shivered, suddenly aware that she was dressed only in the thin satin slip.

"Yes, you deserve everything that 'appens to yer," Bert said, throwing her down on the floor and straddling her body. This time she didn't try to fight him off. She just turned her head to the side, slow tears squeezing past her closed eyelids. With each thrust into her bruised body, he muttered, "Bitch, tart. Bet yer wish it was 'im doin' this, don't yer?"

When it was over he didn't let her go. "Well, now I know what you really are, there'll be no more of this 'No, please Daddy'. You've bin after 'im all along, aven't yer? Darlin' 'Arry, the blue-eyed boy." He stood up and fastened his trousers, then bent and picked up the sheets of writing paper that were scattered across the floor. He waved them in Ellie's face and she flinched. "Wouldn't do fer yer mother to hear about this, would it?"

And Ellie knew he wasn't just referring to the letter.

CHAPTER
ELEVEN

"Hurry up, Helen — there's the sandwiches to do yet."

"Half a sec, Trevor. I can't do everything at once," Ellie replied, coming through from the kitchen and wiping her hands on the front of her blue nylon overall.

"Sorry, love. Didn't mean to snap. But Norah's not turned up yet and there's three lorries parked outside waiting for us to open."

Trevor put the tray of sizzling sausages and bacon on the hotplate to keep warm. He'd already fried a huge stack of bread and was now cutting tomatoes in half to go in the pan. The lorry drivers who plied the busy main road between Colchester and London were well-known for their love of the traditional English fried breakfast.

Ellie glanced at the tables to make sure each had its complement of cutlery, salt and pepper, tomato ketchup, brown sauce and mustard. The sugar-shakers were newly filled and there was a brightly coloured metal ashtray in the centre of each red-checked tablecloth. In the grey dawn of a chilly March morning the long room looked warm and welcoming. She went to the front door, pulled back the bolts and put up the snib on the Yale lock.

Almost before she was back behind the counter, the café seemed full of men, young and old, tall and short, fat and thin. They brought with them a blast of cold air and a feeling that life still went on in the outside world. Since starting work for Trevor, Ellie had hardly left the sanctuary of the busy transport café, except to take Rex for a walk across the fields that stretched flatly into the distance behind the long low building. She'd been nervous of the big Alsatian at first, but in the months since she'd started work at Trev's she'd come to love the fierce-looking dog. He was more likely to lick her to death than to bite. Luckily, though, their more stroppy customers didn't realize that, she thought with a smile.

As she dashed about, slapping plates of greasy fried food in front of the customers, she responded to their cheeky banter with a smile. Although her recent experiences had left her wary of men, she knew that most of them meant no harm by their teasing jokes. But there were one or two she instinctively mistrusted, something in the way they looked at her, and she always made sure Rex was near by when she went outside.

She was glad of the loose blue overall, which had belonged to Trevor's buxom ex-wife and did nothing at all for Ellie's slimmer figure. Her hair was scraped back from her face and secured with an elastic band and she never wore make-up. The shame and degradation she'd felt on that dreadful night, the conviction that she had somehow been to blame, had made her determined not to call attention to herself.

Over the months she'd started to regain her confidence but it was hard to put up with the occasional wandering hands of the customers. She was getting a bit fed up with it — not to mention the long hours on her feet. She didn't mind being behind the counter, dispensing tea into the thick china mugs and cutting sandwiches for the men to take with them on the next leg of their journey — even the endless washing-up in the kitchen out the back. But each day it was becoming harder to handle these rough men with their sly grins and hot eyes.

Maybe she was being silly, judging them all in the light of her experiences. They couldn't all be bad. Trevor, for instance, had been kindness itself and had never put a foot wrong. She glanced at him as she filled the mugs with the thick black brew that passed for tea. His face was redder than ever and a thin film of sweat gleamed on his bald forehead. He slapped another slice of bacon on to the plate he was holding and took it across to the table by the door.

When he came back he leaned against the edge of the counter and sighed. "Rush seems to be over — for the minute. Let's have a cuppa, shall we?"

Ellie poured out two cups of the strong brew, putting a generous heap of sugar into Trevor's. As she handed it to him, he smiled at her. "You're a good little worker, Helen. Don't know what I'd have done if you hadn't come along when you did. Lady Luck must've been smiling on me that day."

"I'm the lucky one, Trevor. What would've happened to me if you hadn't taken me in?"

He looked at her sternly. "You'd probably have gone back to your family — like I keep telling you to. They

127

must be worried sick about you. Not that I want to lose you, mind. But I still think you should let them know you're OK."

"They don't care about me." By now, Ellie had almost convinced herself it was true. "Besides I told you — I sent a card at Christmas." She put her mug down and picked up a tray. "I'd better start clearing these tables."

"Hey, Scotty, let's have another cup of tea," one of the men called out.

"Here, less of your cheek — the girl's name is Helen," Trevor said sharply.

"I don't mind, Trev," Ellie said quickly. She still found it hard to respond to "Helen", let alone the nickname the lorry drivers had given her. But it was too late now to tell anyone her name wasn't Helen Scott. Besides, Ellen Tyler no longer existed.

Ellie could scarcely remember the events which had led to her banging on the door of Trevor's Transport Café or how she had ended up trudging along the busy A12. She could only recall her desperation to get away from the flat in Kendall Street — to leave everything that reminded her of her childhood — even if it meant leaving the East End she knew and loved.

She had stumbled up to her room, leaving Bert glaring after her, his face contorted with hatred. What had she ever done to make him look at her like that? What had made him call her "bitch" instead of "Angel"? She didn't understand but she knew she couldn't stand it any longer.

Once in the sanctuary of her room, it would have been so easy to fall on the bed, pull the eiderdown over her head and give way to tears of despair. But with grim determination she began to stuff things into her old school gym bag — none of the posh clothes bought with Tommy Green's money, though. Just a change of underclothes, a couple of her old school blouses, a jumper and skirt. After a brief hesitation she reached up to the top of the wardrobe for the box containing her paints, the brushes, pencils, charcoal and the remains of a sketch pad. She packed them carefully into the leather school satchel, now shapeless and battered from constant use. Silly really, but she couldn't bring herself to leave them behind. Also in the satchel was her post office savings book — the money that had been destined to help her through college — and her purse containing the few shillings she'd earned running errands for Sid.

The crumpled photo of Harry was there too. When she'd finished packing, she'd screwed it up and thrown it into the corner of the room. She wanted no reminders of the past. But at the last moment she'd run back and snatched it up, smoothing it out and tucking it into the savings book.

With no clear idea of where she was going, she ran round the corner into Roman Road, past the deserted market stalls, shrouded in fog, through narrow streets and desolate islands of rubble or towering concrete. The grimy brick façade of the hospital loomed up out of the mist and she paused. How could she have forgotten about Gran?

They probably wouldn't let her in. But she'd try to see her grandmother before she left London for good. She pushed through the main door and wandered along a corridor. Her footsteps echoed and she looked round nervously. But no one was there. She didn't need to ask the way. Her mum had worked here for years and she had often called to meet her from work. She guessed which ward her grandmother was in and hoped to sneak in and see her without anyone knowing.

She climbed a flight of stairs and, hearing footsteps, she dodged back out of sight, peering round the corner. Her mother and Auntie Vi were talking to a tall man in a white coat. Ellie couldn't hear what he was saying but when Auntie Vi burst into noisy tears and her mother began to sob too, she knew what had happened.

Gran couldn't be dead. But Ellie knew it was true. There was no point in staying. With tears streaming down her face, she ran out of the hospital and along the sleeping streets, coughing as the fog caught in her throat.

Almost without realizing it, she found herself at Bethnal Green station. She sat down on one of the wooden benches in the booking hall. The ticket windows were closed, the platform deserted. She took a shuddering breath and dried her eyes. Although she'd been determined to run away, she'd gone to the hospital in one last desperate bid to avoid taking such a drastic step. Surely Gran would have helped her? But now it was too late.

A train pulled in, filling the station with smoke and steam. It stayed there for a few minutes, the engine

130

hissing softly. There was still no one about, and almost without thinking Ellie went on to the platform, opened the door nearest her and got into one of the carriages. She didn't care where the train was going — she just had to get away.

She looked out of the window as the train picked up speed, realizing that the fog was clearing and it was starting to get light. She'd been up all night. Leaning back with a sigh, she closed her eyes and within a few minutes, the rhythm of the train had lulled her into a deep sleep.

The train stopped a couple of times, but still she didn't stir. The piercing shriek of the whistle and the whooshing sound of another train passing jerked her out of her troubled dreams. She sat up and rubbed her eyes, gasping as she saw the green fields and trees rushing past. Where on earth was she?

The train slowed, rounded a bend and pulled into the station. Ellie peered out, looking for the station sign. Chelmsford — how did she get here? She got off the train and stood for a minute looking around her. The platform was crowded, men in suits carrying briefcases, girls in smart two-piece costumes, workmen in dungarees. They all had somewhere to go, Ellie thought, a sob catching in her throat.

She went into the ladies' cloakroom, feeling grubby and unkempt. As she splashed her face with cold water and combed her hair, she tried to work out what to do. She didn't know anyone here but there was no one in London who'd help her either. She couldn't go back. She'd just have to find a place of her own. She had enough money to tide her over till she could get a job — she'd have to draw some out of the post office and then set about finding lodgings.

Outside the station she looked up and down the busy road, trying to decide which way to go. The railway station seemed to be some distance from the town centre.

After walking for what seemed to be a long time she realized she'd made the wrong decision. The houses had petered out, giving way to a group of small factories and workshops. She should have gone the other way.

She sat down at the edge of the road, shivering as the cold of the damp and misty autumn day seeped through her clothes. Her feet were hurting and she took off her shoes, massaging her toes. Last night's blisters had burst and her stockings were stuck to her feet. She'd have to draw some money out of the post office to buy new stockings and some plasters. That was if she could find a post office.

As she turned to retrace her steps, her brain fogged with exhaustion, she almost missed the sign: *Best Breakfast this side of London — stop at Trev's Transport Café.*

It was probably too late for breakfast but at least she could get a cup of tea.

The potholed gravel in front of the long, low building was empty as Ellie stumbled towards the café. Trev's breakfast can't be that great if none of the lorries stop here, she thought. But at that moment she didn't really care. It wasn't until she reached the door that she saw the closed sign. She bit her lip in dismay — surely these places stayed open all day and most of the night?

She peered through the windows. But there was no sign of life. What should she do now — carry on walking or wait for the café to open?

The decision was made for her when her legs started to tremble and she knew that if she didn't sit down, she'd pass out. The events of the previous night had at last caught up with her.

She sat on an empty lemonade crate and leaned her head against the wooden fence which enclosed a small yard to the side of the building. She was sheltered from the keen East Anglian wind here. At least it wasn't raining and her feet didn't hurt so much.

She'd almost dozed off when she felt a warm tongue on her cheek. She leapt up in alarm, backing away from the huge Alsatian.

"Well, what do we have here?" A big man with a shiny red face and thinning black hair was looking down at her. "Down, Rex." He pulled the dog away from her. "He won't hurt you. He's a big softie really." He bent to stroke the animal, giving a deep chuckle which shook his meaty frame.

Ellie reached out and tentatively ruffled the dog's fur, smiling when he licked her hand. The man reminded her a bit of Sid — maybe that was why she decided to trust him.

When he asked what she was doing so far from town, she said, "I was hoping to get a cup of tea. But the café's closed."

"Well, I'll open up — just for you," the man said, laughing at her expression. "I'm Trev — Trevor Ridley at your service." He gave a mock bow, took a key from his trouser pocket and unlocked the gate at the side of the café.

"Come on through," he said. "I'm not due to open for an hour or so yet. But you look dead beat. You can tell me what you're doing out here on your own while I put the kettle on."

She hadn't told him the whole story of course — just a little white lie about her Gran having died and that she was on her way to stay with her sister. He'd given her a stern lecture on the dangers of hitch-hiking and, when she'd mentioned needing a job, had offered to take her on temporarily until she found something better. Norah only worked part-time and he was desperate for another pair of hands.

Six months later, she was still here. She picked up a tray and went to clear the tables. The door banged open, bringing in a blast of cold March wind. The men sitting near the door grumbled as usual, but their moans turned to laughter as a thin little woman in a plastic mac and brightly printed headscarf stamped in, swearing. "Bloody bike — got a puncture, didn't I? Had to walk to work, didn't I?"

Norah was often late and her excuses were colourful and varied. Ellie wondered why Trevor kept her on when she was so unreliable. But he'd told her that Norah's husband had been his best mate when they were in the forces during the war. They'd both come

134

through it all right and Bob had gone back to his old job in the silk mill on the other side of Chelmsford, the place where he and Norah had both worked since leaving school. Not long afterwards he'd been killed in an accident with one of the machines, leaving Norah very badly off. Trevor had given her the job out of sympathy and now he hadn't the heart to fire her. Besides, he said, when she was here she worked like a Trojan and the customers liked her.

Ellie liked her too, although her tongue could be a bit sharp at times. But there was a rough kindness beneath the brusque manner.

Now, Norah breezed through the café, pulling off her headscarf as she went to hang up her coat. When she came back, tying her flowered wrap-around overall and patting her hair into place, she grabbed a tray and darted between the tables, loading the dirty plates and mugs dangerously high.

"You get on with the sandwiches, love," she said. "I'll get this lot cleared. I expect you're all behind with me being late." She dashed around as she spoke, returning with the loaded tray and pushing the swing door open with her hip.

"Sorry, Trev. I'll make it up to you." The words were flung over her shoulder and by the time Trevor turned to answer, she was gone again.

"She may be little, but she's a real bundle of dynamite, that Norah," one of the men said, coming up to the counter with his mug held out for a refill. Ellie laughed and poured the tea, then started buttering bread for the sandwiches. She was glad the other woman had turned up. The work was easier when it was shared. Maybe it wasn't so bad here after all.

She was absorbed in her work when Norah came back with her empty tray. But she looked up quickly at the older woman's words.

"By the way, Trev. I saw your missus when I was in town yesterday. She asked me if you'd come to your senses yet."

Trevor gave Norah a lift home in his old van when the café closed that afternoon. But for Ellie, work wasn't finished for the day. She wiped the counter down, put out clean mugs, changed the tablecloths and laid the tables for the afternoon and evening rush. They weren't usually quite so busy during the second session.

It was mostly fried food, sometimes steak-and-kidney or shepherd's pie. But these days Trevor didn't have time for all the preparation, although he was a good cook and Trev's Café used to be famous for its home cooking.

As Ellie worked, she wondered what Norah had meant by her remark about his wife. She looked up at the photo on the mantelpiece. Gloria Ridley was a pretty blonde with a well-developed figure who looked younger than her years. She had her arm round a young girl of about thirteen and both of them were laughing into the camera. The girl, Julie, had dark hair and brown eyes like her father.

Ellie picked the photo up, wondering what had made Gloria leave a nice man like Trevor — he was kind, hard-working and, as Norah had told her, he idolized

Julie. She was still holding the photo when Trevor came in, Rex gambolling at his heels. He took it from her and sat down at the table in the middle of the room, sighing heavily and gazing at the picture. The dog put his head on Trevor's knee and he fondled it absently.

"You know, Helen — that day I first saw you — I thought it was Julie come back to see me. You still remind me of her a bit — not just your hair. You've got spirit — you don't let people walk all over you."

If only he knew, Ellie thought. It had taken a great deal of determination to stand up for herself — to stick her chin out and pretend she didn't care when the customers tried it on. But Trevor was right. No one was going to tread on her ever again. She turned away and started to dish up their meal. It wouldn't be long before they had to open again and they should make the most of the brief break.

When she put Trevor's plate in front of him, he was still staring at the photograph.

"You must miss them very much," Ellie said, sitting down opposite them. She hadn't liked to mention his family before but she couldn't help being curious, especially after what Norah had said earlier about him coming to his senses.

"It's my fault she went," Trevor said. "I thought she'd come back after a couple of weeks — just teaching me a lesson, she said. But it's been more than a year." He sighed and pushed his plate away.

"What did you do? Was it something very bad?" Ellie wondered if he'd had an affair. But poor Trev — what chance did he have, working all the hours there were?

137

Trevor laughed. "If you can call being a boring lump with no ambition something bad," he said. "She was right though. I'm happy here — I like having my own business, I like cooking and I like knowing my customers, having a bit of a laugh with them all."

"What's wrong with that?" Ellie couldn't see that Gloria had anything to complain about — unless she didn't like having to work as hard as her husband. She had seen in the short time she'd been here that it needed more than one person to keep the business going.

"Gloria had plans — big ideas. And why not? When we first got married I was a chef in a big hotel — I was trained by a top French chef — cordon bleu, me." Trevor stuck his chest out and grinned. "Gloria was pleased I wanted my own business and we saved for years. But this was the only place we could afford. Gloria wanted somewhere posh — worthy of my talents, she said."

Ellie nodded sympathetically. "Is that what she meant by coming to your senses — she wants you to sell up and move on?"

"That's right, love. But the posh stuff isn't really me, love." Trevor sighed and ran his hands through his thinning hair. "Gloria took Julie and went to live in town — said she'd come back when I saw sense."

"Do you miss them?" Ellie asked.

"I did at first — Julie more than anything. I let the business slide for a while. Then Norah gave me a good talking-to." He gave a little laugh and Ellie smiled.

"She's good at that," she said.

138

"You can say that again. Anyway, I pulled meself together and now at least I'm doing well enough to make sure Julie's OK." He pulled his plate towards him and started to eat. But Ellie noticed that he left most of it.

She scraped the remains into Rex's bowl and washed up while Trevor rolled himself a cigarette. It was nearly time to open up again and she went to switch on the illuminated sign at the entrance to the car park.

It was late when the last customer left and they locked up. Ellie cleared the tables and relaid them for the morning before going through to the kitchen and starting to run hot water into the large stainless-steel sink.

"Leave that," Trevor said. "You've done enough for one day. Norah can do it in the morning."

"How will she get here without her bike? It's quite a way from the village."

"I'll pick her up in the van first thing — and she'd better be ready."

Ellie laughed at Trevor's mock angry expression.

"Seriously, Helen. I had a chat with her earlier and it seems she's not been too well lately — she keeps getting these pains in her legs. But she didn't want to let me down, she said." He gave a short laugh. "Silly mare. Anyway, I've arranged to pick her up and take her home — at least until she's feeling better. And she's promised to see the doctor about her problem."

"You're a good boss, Trev," Ellie told him.

He shrugged, looking embarrassed. "Like I said, Norah's a friend, not just an employee." He stood up. "You'd better be getting off to bed. It's been a long day."

Ellie went along the passage to her room. The pictures pinned to the wall above her bed — a black-and-white enlargement of Pat Boone and a coloured poster of Dickie Valentine, all dark curly hair and white teeth — reminded her that this was still Julie's room. A china doll in a pale-blue crinoline sat on top of the chest of drawers, next to a framed photo of Trevor and Gloria. A bookcase against the far wall held *School Friend* and *Bunty* annuals and a selection of pony stories. Perhaps Gloria had told her they wouldn't be away for long. Ellie wondered what would happen to her if they came back. Where would she go?

Next morning Trevor was in his usual place at the stove, expertly flipping sausages and bacon so that they browned evenly. He looked up as she came through to the café and put down his spatula. "I'm just off to get Norah — won't be long. Keep an eye on these for me. If any lorries turn up, you can let them in and take their orders. Won't hurt them to wait."

Left alone in the café, only the quiet gurgling of the tea urn and the spattering of the frying food breaking the silence, Ellie's concerns about the future resurfaced. She knew she couldn't stay here for ever. Already there'd been sly remarks and knowing looks about Trev's "new girl". Perhaps she should be looking for another job, or at least somewhere else to live.

Beyond the steamy window, the pink-streaked sky heralded another bright spring day and, already, a couple of lorries had turned into the car park.

Ellie unlocked the door and switched on the outside lights indicating that Trev's was open for business. She stood by the open door, breathing in the country smells until another lorry pulled into the car park, bringing with it a whiff of diesel, and listening to the roar of traffic, reminding her of London; but the noise and smells were all she missed, she told herself.

By the time Trevor returned with Norah, the café was full and Ellie was rushed off her feet. There was no time to dwell on her problems while trying to sort out who had ordered two eggs with their sausages and bacon, and who wanted fried bread but no tomatoes, or bacon but no eggs. Even in a brief lull there were tables to be cleared and re-set, sandwiches to make, tea to be poured. Norah, in deference to her poor legs, was spared the running around, ensconced in the kitchen, up to her elbows in sudsy hot water.

Ellie and Trevor worked side by side until the morning rush was over and he locked the door behind the last customer. This two-hour break before they opened again for the evening was usually just as busy with preparations and clearing up. But today Norah had worked hard behind the scenes. The kitchen surfaces were sparkling, the floor had been mopped and the smell of something other than fried food warmed the air. The table in the centre had been laid with a white cloth and sparkling cutlery. As Ellie and Trevor sat down, Norah brought a steaming meat pie, its crust light and crisp and golden, to the table.

"What's all this in aid of then?" Trevor asked, holding his plate out for Norah's generous dollop of mashed potato.

Norah flushed. "It's just my way of saying thank you for being so understanding about my problems. You know how much I need this job — not just for the money." She flushed, then with a return of her old tartness, she said, "Go on then — eat up. Don't let it go cold."

"Good pie, Norah. Can't beat home cooking," he said with his mouth full.

Norah went red again, and with a sudden flash of insight Ellie realized that the older woman was in love with Trevor. And why not? With her hair in its tight bun, her wrap-around overall and her "poor legs", Ellie had thought her old, comparing her with Gran. But she'd been at school with the glamorous Gloria and must be about the same age — barely into her forties.

And, knowing the glamorous Gloria with her red mouth and blonde locks, Norah must feel she couldn't compete. Poor Norah, Ellie thought. She would never let Trevor know how she felt, while Trevor, being a man, wouldn't see the treasure right under his nose.

As she put the remains of the pie into the fridge, Ellie smiled. Norah wasn't silly. She must know how a man like Trevor could be wooed — hence the home-made steak-and-kidney pie.

CHAPTER
TWELVE

A few days later, when they were locking up after the morning and lunchtime session, Norah asked Trevor to take her in to Chelmsford instead of going straight home.

"How long will you be? I've got to open up again at five," he said.

"I only want you to drop me off at the hospital. The doctor's given me a letter about my veins. I don't expect you to wait around for me. I can go home on the bus," she said.

Next day she told them she wouldn't have to wait long for her operation.

"Well, until you get it done, I'm not having you standing," Trevor said. He found a tall stool in the shed out the back and cleaned it up for her. Now she could "take the weight off" as she put it, while washing up or doing the sandwiches. Not that Norah had a lot of weight to take off. Her problems had been caused by years of standing at the machines when she worked in the silk mill.

She still gratefully accepted the lifts to and from work, although she kept saying she ought to start riding her bicycle now that summer was almost here. But Ellie had a feeling that Norah was making the most of these few minutes each day alone with Trevor. Now that it seemed Gloria was off the scene permanently, perhaps she thought she stood a chance with him. Good luck to her.

As a thank you, Norah brought in a batch of her home-made scones and a Dundee cake. Trevor put them under the glass dome on the counter, next to the basket filled with cellophane-wrapped slices of cherry fruitcake and little packets of biscuits. Norah's cakes sold out and Trevor asked her when she was going to make some more. They'd make a good team, if only he could see it, Ellie thought.

Ellie realized how much they depended on Norah when she went into hospital for her operation. They only kept her in a few days but she wasn't allowed back to work for two weeks. And even then she had to rest.

As she tidied the kitchen and made sure everything was ready for reopening, Ellie smiled. Trevor had confessed to missing the little woman while she'd been away.

He'd just taken Norah home and the café seemed quiet after the bustle of the morning. Ellie switched on the radio and hummed along to "Singing the Blues". Trev's Café didn't have a juke-box, or a pinball machine like many roadside cafés did. He said it attracted the wrong sort of people like the motorbike gangs who roared up and down at weekends on their way to Clacton.

She finished laying the tables and went back to the kitchen, first turning the wireless up so that she could still hear it while she went to tidy her bedroom. She'd never really got used to how quiet it was when the café was closed.

There was just time to change the sheets and make her bed. She went into Trevor's room. It looked as though a hurricane had whirled through it. He never put anything away. After taking the dirty linen downstairs and loading the surprisingly modern twin-tub washing machine, she made up Trevor's bed, then on impulse tidied his clothes away. As she dusted the dressing-table and replaced the ornaments and photographs, she sang along to the wireless which was tuned to Radio Luxembourg. They were playing Bill Haley now and, as she gave a final tweak of the bedspread, she danced a few steps and twirled round.

She stopped short, her hand to her breast as she realized that someone was standing in the doorway. Before she could speak, the woman launched into a tirade.

"What the hell are you doing in my bedroom? And where's that rat hiding himself?" She strode across the room and wrenched open the wardrobe door. "Trevor, come out — now," she shrieked.

If she hadn't been so terrified, Ellie would have laughed. But the woman — it must be Gloria — was still shouting, as if she imagined Trevor was hiding somewhere.

"I might have known as soon as my back was turned you'd find some floozy to keep your bed warm. Well, I won't have it — you hear me, Trevor?"

She eventually ran out of steam and turned to Ellie, who still hadn't moved. "Well, what are you doing here? Get out — now."

"But Mrs Ridley, I can explain. I just work here," she stammered.

"Work." The word was spat contemptuously. "I bet that's not all you do. I hear things you know. Just because this café's out in the sticks doesn't mean he can get away with anything. I know what he's been up to — you've been living here for months. Don't deny it."

"Yes, I do live here — but it's not like you think. Trevor's been very kind to me." It was the wrong thing to say.

"Is that what you call it?" With a harsh laugh Gloria was off again. When she'd calmed down again, she looked round. "Well, where is he?"

"He's gone out somewhere," Ellie said. She wasn't going to tell Trevor's wife that he'd taken Norah home.

"Well, I want you out of here — before he gets back. You'd better start packing." She stood over Ellie, her blue eyes cold, as she stuffed things into her bag haphazardly. There wasn't much. She got her old satchel with the art things from the bottom of the wardrobe where it had remained undisturbed since her arrival six months earlier.

"To think I was willing to come back," she heard Gloria mutter, as she almost pushed her through the door. She could feel the woman watching as she stumbled across the potholed car park, her head still reeling from Gloria's tirade. Why was she so determined to believe the worst of her? Why hadn't she let her explain?

Everything had happened so fast. And now, here she was, trudging along the same stretch of road that she had toiled along all those months ago — worse off than she'd been then. The long grass of the verge was wet against her bare legs and she shivered. Despite the earlier sunshine it was going to be a cold night. The light was beginning to fade as heavy clouds built up and Ellie choked back a despairing sob. Where could she go?

As she reached the junction leading to Little Howe, it crossed her mind that Norah might take her in. But how could she face her friend, knowing how she felt about Trevor? She might even think Gloria's accusations were true.

Ellie sighed and leaned against the bus stop. No, she'd go into town and find a hotel or bed-and-breakfast. She spared a thought for Norah's feelings when she heard that Gloria had decided to return to her husband. But when the threatened rain started to fall in earnest, her only concern was how soon the bus would come along. The black clouds had brought an early dusk and Ellie shivered, peering through the gloom, mesmerized by the hazy lights of the cars and lorries swishing through the rain. But no bus came.

Wrapped in misery Ellie didn't notice the van until it stopped beside her, showering her with muddy water. She shrank away as Trevor opened the door. "What the hell are you doing out here?"

Ellie didn't answer.

"Don't be silly, get in. You're soaked."

"Gloria's back."

He muttered a curse and ran his hand through his sparse hair. "And I suppose she threw you out? The silly cow."

Ellie nodded. "I'm not coming back — not after what she said."

"OK, then, Helen, have it your way. But for Pete's sake get in out of the rain. I'll take you to Norah's. She'll look after you. I'll come and fetch you when I've sorted Gloria out."

Ellie got into the van beside him, shivering now inside her damp coat. As Trevor pulled away, she turned her face towards the side window, ignoring his attempts to start a conversation.

At Norah's cottage, Trevor gave a hurried explanation before jumping back in the van and driving off. Norah drew Ellie inside, helped her off with her wet things and wrapped her in her own candlewick dressing-gown. She sat the girl down in front of the wood stove, which now had its little glass doors wide open to reveal a satisfying blaze. "A hot drink is what you need, my girl," she said.

As she clattered crockery in the tiny kitchen Ellie heard her muttering, her exclamations interspersed with the occasional swear word. But by the time Norah returned carrying a laden tray, she was asleep.

Norah put the tray on a side table and looked down at the sleeping girl. Fond as she was of Trevor, she felt a spurt of anger that he hadn't foreseen the trouble it could cause — letting a young girl like that stay at the café. But he was such a happy-go-lucky sort of bloke, as well as being straight as a die. It would never occur to him that people might read more into his relationship with a girl young enough to be his daughter.

Mind you, she could understand Gloria's outrage on returning home to find Helen there — especially in what had been her bedroom. She might have left him but that didn't mean she'd relinquished all claim on her husband. Jealousy was an unpredictable emotion — as Norah herself knew all too well.

The arrival of the girl had triggered off feelings she'd hardly been aware of. She shouldn't have been jealous. Helen was such a scrawny little thing with her hair scraped back and those huge eyes in her thin white face. But over the months she'd filled out, her eyes had lost their haunted look and she had gained in confidence.

Norah had seen the way the male customers looked at her, had also seen Trevor's eyes light up when she came into the room. And she'd been jealous — not of the girl's beauty — she'd had her own share of looks when she was young. And she didn't care how many men fancied Helen — just as long as Trevor didn't. That was when she'd realized her feelings for him were more than friendship — not that he'd ever notice her, she thought, not while Gloria kept coming back to mess things up.

Helen, or Ellie as she now liked to be called, stirred and mumbled, then settled deeper into the armchair, her feet stretched out to the warm blaze. Norah set the cup down near her, but she hadn't the heart to wake her. She looked so young and defenceless.

Norah knew there was nothing in Gloria's accusations — she'd be able to tell if anything like that was going on. Trevor was just fond of the girl in the same way as he was fond of his daughter, Julie.

But men did silly things when they were lonely. Maybe it was just as well things had turned out this way. She should have asked Ellie to stay with her before now. She touched the girl's arm. "Drink it while it's hot, love — and have a biscuit too."

Ellie sat up, rubbing her eyes. "I don't want to be a nuisance," she said.

"Don't worry about it. You're staying here," Norah said firmly. "I'll cook us some supper in a minute. Now — tell me exactly what happened. Trevor just said Gloria found you in his bedroom and threw you out."

"She said some awful things — but I was only changing the sheets. I didn't, I couldn't . . ." Ellie burst into tears.

Norah let her cry for a few moments. Better to let it all out. She perched on the arm of the chair and put her arm round the girl. "I believe you, love. Some people have nasty minds. But I know Trevor — he'd never do anything out of place." She patted Ellie's arm. "Anyway, no need to worry any more — you're not going back there."

She wasn't surprised when Ellie joined her in the kitchen and, without a word, started to help lay the table. She smiled and let her get on with it.

Over scrambled eggs and toast she asked the question she'd been dying to ask ever since Trevor had deposited Ellie on her doorstep. "Is Gloria back for good?"

"She gave me that impression, but I didn't see any luggage."

"Maybe she just came for some of her things. Never mind, we'll soon find out," Norah said. But Trevor didn't come back that evening and she tried not to think that Gloria might decide to stay this time — or that Trevor had welcomed her back.

But she needn't have worried. When he arrived to pick them both up for work the next day, Trevor told them he'd thrown Gloria out, angry at the way she'd treated Ellie.

He tried to persuade Ellie to return to the café, promising there'd be no more trouble from his wife. But Norah insisted that Ellie must stay at the cottage. "Then there'll be no more misunderstandings," she said.

Although she didn't want to outstay her welcome, Ellie agreed. She also told them she ought to find another job. She dreaded another confrontation with Gloria, as well as the thought of being the subject of gossip in the village. From what Trevor's wife had said, everyone was talking about the young girl who'd "shacked up" with the café owner.

Norah said it was nonsense — Gloria was just being her usual bitchy self — but Ellie was ready to move on anyway. When the local paper came out each week she scoured the situations vacant page as well as the advertisements for lodgings and rooms to let in nearby Chelmsford. But they all seemed very expensive.

"No luck?" Norah asked, as once more Ellie folded the paper with a sigh.

"Most of the ones I've seen offer training on the job. But you don't get paid much while you're training and I need to be able to pay my way, and there'd be things like bus fares," Ellie replied. She still had her savings and had added to them considerably, having no opportunity to spend much while she'd been at Trevor's. But she would need some more clothes and she still hadn't given up hope of going to evening classes, perhaps even to college one day.

"You needn't worry about lodgings. My spare room is yours for as long as you want it," Norah said, picking up the paper. "There must be something. What were your best subjects at school?"

With a little laugh, Ellie said, "Art and history — not much use really, are they?"

"S'pose not. Still, I can tell you've had a good education. You must have had ambitions — something you dreamed of doing. Perhaps it's not too late."

Ellie hesitated. It was a long time since she'd allowed herself to think about it. She couldn't bear it if Norah ridiculed her. "It was always too late. Deep down I always knew they'd never let me go to college. I wanted to study art. But they made me leave school and get a job."

"Well, I'm darn sure you can get a better job than dogsbody in a café."

"Maybe — but who's going to give me a chance?" She helped herself to another scone and started to relax in the homely atmosphere of Norah's cosy sitting room. It was almost like being back at Gran's.

Norah broke the silence, reaching out to touch Ellie's arm. "Why don't you go home, love? Whatever the problem was, I'm sure it's all blown over by now. They'll be so pleased to have you back, they won't be angry with you."

Ellie's eyes filled with tears. "You don't understand . . ."

Norah sat back in her chair. "I was right then. You did run away? And Helen Scott's not your real name?"

Ellie nodded.

"But you have got family? Trevor said you were supposed to be going to your sister after your grandmother died." Norah touched her arm again. "Why don't you get in touch with her? Surely she'll be pleased you're safe."

"She's only my half-sister — and she doesn't really care," Ellie said.

"But Helen, she's family." Norah sighed. "It's only when you've got no one left that you realize how important that really is."

"Gran was the only one who cared," Ellie said. She wouldn't think of Mum — or Harry. Her mother should have stood up to Bert. And if Harry really loved her, he wouldn't have married that German girl.

"I'm sure your sister cares too. At least get in touch with her — tell her you're safe."

"I sent a card at Christmas. They know I'm all right," Ellie said. "Anyway I can't go to Sheila. I can't stand her husband. Just being in the same room with him . . ." She gave a little shudder and bit her lip.

Norah nodded. "Some men make you feel like that, don't they?" she said with a smile.

"I don't know what she sees in him," Ellie said. She remembered his sleazy smile, the way he'd looked her up and down. She'd tried so hard to forget that part of her life. Why had Norah brought it up? She began to shake and tears spilled over.

Norah put her arms round her and let her sob. At last she gave a shaky sigh and sniffed away her tears.

"That's better, love. Now — tell me, what brought all that on?" Norah said. "Do you miss your family — is that it? Why can't you go home, love?"

"You don't understand." Ellie bit back another sob. She couldn't confide in her friend. Better to try to forget them all — Harry as well. She leaned forward in her chair. "I'm sorry. I know you're only trying to help and I do appreciate all you've done for me."

"That's what friends are for," Norah told her.

"I don't know what I'd have done without you — Trevor too, but it's time I started standing on my own feet. I don't want to be a waitress all my life. I want to make something of myself so if I do ever go back home I can show them my education wasn't a waste of time."

"Education's never a waste," said Norah.

Ellie smiled and changed the subject. "Trevor told me you used to work in a silk mill. What was your job, Norah?" she asked.

"I was a throwster," Norah said proudly.

"What's that?"

"I worked the machine that twisted the silk threads, before they were woven into material. It's a very skilled job."

"They used to make silk in Bethnal Green — not far from where I used to live. There was an old row of weavers' cottages, with big windows upstairs. But they were pulled down a couple of years ago. And there aren't any mills left in London," Ellie said. "I didn't realize there were any left in this country at all." She remembered the beautiful fabrics she'd seen in the Victoria and Albert Museum and her efforts to reproduce the designs for her art portfolio.

"There's not many — most of them have converted to making these new materials, nylon and such, especially up north. I sometimes wonder how Turner's keeps going," Norah said. She sighed and began to reminisce about her old job and Ellie listened fascinated. During the war, the mill at Withies Green had woven thousands of yards of silk for parachutes and Norah had been proud doing such important work. "We'd stopped throwing our own silk by then — I went on to the weaving," she said.

"Why did you leave?" Ellie asked.

"I couldn't face going back after Bob's accident," she said. "He came back there to work after the war — got his arm caught in a machine and lost a lot of blood. He should have been all right. But he was weak after being so long in the prison camp. He couldn't fight the infection, you see." Norah's voice trailed away and Ellie squeezed her arm sympathetically.

155

"I'd like a job like that — something I can take pride in," she said.

"So, what are we going to do with you, then?"

"I really don't know." Ellie said, "But, listening to your tales of working in the mill, I'd like to do something like that. Do they still make silk there?"

"I think I'd have heard if Turner's had gone out of business," Norah said. "But, Ellie — for all the skills you need, it's just factory work really. Are you sure that's what you want?"

Ellie gave a bitter little laugh. "I'm not really in a position to be choosy, am I?"

"I suppose not. But really it's nimble fingers you want — not brains." Norah held out her red, work-worn hands. "I'd be no good now." She gave a little laugh.

Ellie, her imagination full of images of rainbow-hued silks spilling out of the machines, nodded enthusiastically when Norah promised to write to her old boss to see if there were any vacancies.

CHAPTER
THIRTEEN

Ellie ignored the jolting of the bus and read the letter again. Although she was nervous, she was determined to impress Mr Turner with her willingness to work and her genuine interest in the business of silk manufacture.

When she'd been invited for an interview, she'd gone to the library in Chelmsford to read up about it, discovering that Essex had once been a thriving centre for the silk industry. Fascinated, she read avidly until she felt she was almost an expert although she'd never seen a spinning-machine or a loom in her life.

Turner's Mill was midway between Chelmsford and Braintree and when the conductor called out "next stop — Withies Green", Ellie made her way to the front of the bus. She consulted the piece of paper on which Norah had written the directions. Yes, this was the right stop. There was the church and tucked away behind it was the mill, a tall building with large windows set under the eaves, surrounded by several smaller sheds and outbuildings. Some of them looked a bit run down, but it was a pretty scene and, for the first time in months, Ellie felt the urge to get out her paints.

She crossed a bridge over a stream and approached the huddle of buildings, hearing the clatter of machinery. A man crossed the yard in front of her, his arms full of pieces of different-coloured material — samples, she guessed. Maybe he was a sales representative. She ran after him.

"Excuse me — I'm looking for Mr Turner. I have an appointment," she said.

"Well — you've found him," the young man said, smiling down at her from his considerable height. "However, if I had made an appointment with such a lovely young lady, I'm sure I'd have remembered."

Ellie's cheeks reddened under his scrutiny as she explained that she'd come about a job.

"Oh, sorry — wrong Mr Turner." He laughed. "You want my father — through that door there," he said, pointing.

Ellie hurried away, conscious that he was watching her. Although his manner seemed pleasant, she hadn't liked the way he looked her up and down. She hoped Mr Turner senior wasn't too much like his son.

She knocked on the door of the long, low building beside the stream and entered hesitantly. A tall, stooped man with grey hair looked at her over his glasses.

"Ah, you must be Miss Scott — or may I call you Helen?" he asked with old-fashioned courtesy. "Do sit down."

Ellie sat in the chair opposite the wide oak desk which almost filled the tiny room. She folded her hands over her handbag, clenching her fingers nervously.

Mr Turner smiled over his glasses and proceeded to question her about her education and background. She answered as truthfully as she could without being

158

specific and held her breath as he picked up the letter she had written, reading it through again.

"Well, young lady, I was very impressed with your handwriting and spelling. But I have to say that, despite your seeming interest in our products, this isn't really the place for a girl with a grammar-school education."

Why had he wasted her time asking her for an interview then? Ellie stifled her protest and stood up, ready to leave. Mr Turner raised a hand, gesturing her to sit again.

"Wait — I haven't finished yet. I do have a job for you."

She leaned forward eagerly but Mr Turner sighed as he confessed that the mill wasn't doing very well. As Norah had told her, they no longer threw their own silk but bought it ready twisted ready for weaving. And the market for silk had dropped off — ousted by cheaper fabrics from abroad, as well as the synthetics that were being produced more cheaply by mills in the north.

"I don't understand," Ellie said.

"We won't close down — not if I can help it. I just hope my son will be ready to take over when I decide I've had enough." Mr Turner took off his glasses, rubbing his eyes. "He'll go over to man-made fabrics though — if he wants to keep in production."

"Norah — Mrs Jenkins — told me the mill had been in your family for over a hundred years," Ellie said.

"Yes. We have a long history — Digances, who owned it before, were a family connection, so you could say the family tradition goes back more than three hundred years." He smiled at her. "We used to do everything here — throwing, dyeing, weaving all sorts of fabrics — damasks, crêpe, brocades. Now it's just plain material — the sort of thing used for ladies' petticoats and such."

She wondered when he'd get round to explaining what the job was. But he seemed to be rambling now. "Thought Turner's would go on for ever — foolish old man that I am. Would've been different if Philip was here to take over. Michael's not interested." Ellie remembered Norah saying that one of his sons had been killed in the war.

Mr Turner stopped speaking abruptly and looked up, focusing on Ellie. "Don't mind me, young lady." He straightened the papers on his desk. "Oh dear, I haven't told you what your duties will be. You must think me very unbusinesslike." He gave a little laugh. "It's all these papers, you see. I need everything sorted out and put in order. I haven't been too well lately and I've rather let things slide. The last girl I had left rather suddenly and my son's been too busy to see to it."

Ellie's heart sank. She didn't know the first thing about office work. And Mr Turner seemed so vague. But Norah had said he was a good boss — and she had taken a liking to the old man. The loss of his elder son had clearly affected him deeply. Ellie felt a stab of anger towards the young man she'd encountered in the yard. Surely he could take more of an interest — if only for the sake of his father?

"Well — will you take the job?" Mr Turner asked.

"Thank you — yes, I'd love to," Ellie said. She'd worry about what to do when the time came. It

160

couldn't be that difficult to sort out a few papers and file them away.

Ellie's first day in her new job went well, although she was disappointed that Mr Turner himself wasn't there to show her the ropes. When she entered the cramped little office her heart sank as young Mr Turner — she couldn't call him Michael — rose from behind the desk.

She didn't like the way he smiled at her — or the insinuation in his voice when he said, "I think we're going to enjoy working together."

She hoped he'd show her what he wanted done and leave her to get on with it. But first, he took her on a tour of the mill. The office was a partitioned-off area at the end of a long, low building which had once been the throwing shed but was now filled with a jumble of old, worn-out machinery.

Michael smirked as he opened the door and imparted this information and Ellie guessed he thought she knew nothing about silk production. The smirk disappeared when she asked, "Where do you get your thrown silk from now? Is it imported from abroad?"

"It comes from France and Italy usually. But we buy ours from an import firm based in Bristol," he said.

"And what happened to the throwsters when they lost their jobs. Did you find them work in the weaving and dyeing sheds?"

"Some of them — most left to go and work in Chelmsford." As they crossed the yard he said, "I didn't realize you'd worked in the silk industry before."

She smiled and didn't enlighten him. He opened the door to another building and stood back to let her see. "I don't suppose I have to tell you what goes on here?" he said.

A row of vats from which arose a pungent smell told Ellie this must be the dyeing shed. She could see that Michael was put out by her knowledge and she felt a little burst of pleasure that the hours spent in the library hadn't been wasted. She had a feeling that Mr Turner Junior loved feeling superior and lording it over the people in his employ. What would he be like if he ever did take over from his father?

In the weaving-shed the noise was deafening and Ellie flinched. Norah had warned her about this and she was glad she wouldn't be working here. She didn't think she could stand it for long. But the girls standing at the rows of machines didn't seem bothered. As their fingers flew nimbly back and forth they were laughing and talking, although it seemed impossible that they could hear each other.

Michael shouted in her ear, explaining that she would be required to collect the time sheets from the workers at the end of each shift and make sure they were filled in properly. Ellie nodded, stepping closer to the machine to examine the fabric that was spilling off the rollers at the end, a blue figured silk.

Ellie smiled at the girl working the machine and she smiled back. But, after a quick glance at Michael, she ducked her head and concentrated on her work. Ellie saw her surreptitiously nudge the girl next to her and in seconds the laughter and chatter had died and heads were bent industriously over the machines.

Michael Turner took hold of Ellie's elbow and drew her outside. "Nothing like the sight of the boss's son to keep them on their toes," he said. Catching Ellie's expression, he laughed. "Just joking. They're not a bad crowd. Still, I'd better have a word with the overseer."

Ellie had been at Turners for a couple of weeks and had picked up the office work very quickly. Now all the files were in order and she had time to deal with the litter of orders and correspondence overflowing the baskets and trays on the desk. She had even started learning to type — using old scrap paper and picking out the letters hesitantly, like a hen pecking at corn. She wished she could do it properly and made up her mind to go to evening classes.

From her perusal of the ledgers and order-books she had deduced that things weren't as bad as old Mr Turner had hinted. But the old man was in poor health and just didn't seem to care any more. And Michael only seemed interested in strutting around, looking important and watching out for slackers.

Her first impression of him hadn't changed and she dreaded him coming into the office, leaning on the edge of the desk and smirking as she tried to work.

He was there again today and she was glad when a sudden silence indicated that the machines in the weaving shed had stopped and work was finished for the day. Ellie put the cover on the typewriter and grabbed her jacket off the back of the chair.

"No need to rush off, Helen," Michael drawled, getting up and blocking the door. "I'll give you a lift home."

"I'd rather catch the bus," Ellie snapped, pushing past him. She rushed out into the yard as the crowd of girls from the weaving-shed dispersed, hoping frantically that Jackie Wilson hadn't gone yet.

Her new friend, a bubbly vivacious girl a little older than herself, caught the same bus home. Whenever Ellie went into the weaving-sheds it was her laughter that could be heard above the noise of the machines and she seemed very popular with the other workers, old and young alike. They'd become friendly when Ellie collected the time sheets. One or two of the girls seemed to resent anyone from the office encroaching on their territory. But Jackie smiled and introduced herself. While they chatted, her fingers flew busily, checking the tension on the warp and watching for any broken threads.

Ellie watched fascinated, wishing she could pluck up the nerve to ask if she could have a go. But she was afraid of offending the girl. Neither of them noticed that Michael had entered the shed until his sharp voice interrupted them.

"You're paid to attend the machines — not to stand around gossiping," he said. He turned to Ellie, "Miss Scott — your place is in the office."

Flustered, Ellie indicated the bundle of time sheets. But Jackie didn't seem put out. She smiled at the boss's son. "Oh well, you know what they say, Mr Michael — all work and no play." She laughed. "It would be a poor show if we had to be miserable all the time — like some I could mention."

Michael only glared at her and stalked away after snapping at Ellie. "Don't be long — I need those sheets in the office."

Jackie grinned. "There's one that knows how to play all right. Pity he doesn't set us an example and do some work himself for a change." She handed her time sheet to Ellie and turned back to her machine. "See you at the bus stop," she said.

The funny thing was, Jackie's cheek never seemed to get her into trouble. Ellie envied her confidence and wished she too had the courage to speak up for herself.

Jackie and a few of the other girls were still at the bus stop and Ellie breathed a sigh of relief when the bus came along before Michael had time to turn his car round in the yard and come after her.

"Young master been making a nuisance of himself, has he?" Jackie laughed as they flopped into a seat. She gestured out of the window, where the silver-blue Triumph could be seen streaking away down the main road in a cloud of exhaust.

Ellie felt herself reddening. Maybe she was reading too much into young Mr Turner's remarks. But, for someone who seemed to do very little work, he spent a lot of time in the office.

"I wish he'd leave me alone," she muttered.

Jackie laughed. "Some might say you could do worse — the boss's son, and a good-looking feller at that."

Ellie shook her head. "I wouldn't care if he was a millionaire," she said.

"I'm glad you've got your head screwed on right," Jackie said, abandoning her teasing tone. "I wasn't sure at first — thought you might actually like him. But I ought to warn you — he's the same with all the new girls. Tries it on, butters them up — then when he's had what he wants, he goes on to the next silly cow who's taken in by those baby blues." She looked at Ellie thoughtfully. "You ought to be careful though. He's been known to make life very difficult for those that refuse him."

"Don't worry — I've met his type before," Ellie said, smiling. She wondered what the other girl would say if she knew Ellie had been propositioned by a famous film star — Philip Devereux, no less. She bit her lip. That part of her life was over. No one must ever know how she'd almost been drawn into a life of shame and degradation — even if it had been none of her doing.

She looked out of the bus window, only half-listening to Jackie's gossip, lost in memories of her former life — memories she'd tried hard to suppress over the past year. Gradually she was beginning to realize that she shouldn't feel such shame and guilt — the only person to blame was the man she'd once called "Dad". Now, she felt nothing but hatred for the man who'd blighted her childhood and made her grow up all too soon.

CHAPTER
FOURTEEN

Although she was no nearer achieving her ambition of going to college, Ellie had started shorthand and typing classes and was becoming more and more absorbed in the business of weaving silk. She loved her job as well as living with Norah in the little cottage. She had become used to the quiet of the country — not that it was that quiet with cockerels crowing, tractors and combine harvesters scraping the hedges on either side of the narrow lanes and cows pleading to be milked. Here she felt safe and, in her work at Turner's mill, she felt valued and appreciated.

Mr Turner was full of praise for her improvements in the office. If it weren't for his son, Ellie would have been content. He just wouldn't leave her alone. It was all right when his father was around, but over the last few months the old man's health had deteriorated. He'd begun leaving more of the management of the business to Michael.

Ellie wondered whether he realized how little work his son actually did. She was now practically running the office on her own. Turner's had been ticking over nicely — even if it wasn't the thriving business it had been before and during the war. But, as she told Norah, things were going downhill under Michael's mismanagement.

And now there was something else to worry about. Norah would be sad when she heard the news. Although she'd left Turner's years ago, she still felt involved in the business and always spoke of her old boss with respect and affection. But Ellie would have to tell her — if only because it meant she might be out of a job herself soon.

They'd finished their evening meal and, as it was a warm spring evening, they decided to sit in the garden with their cups of tea. Ellie brought her sketchpad and box of watercolours out with her. Now that her life was more settled her interest in painting, which had lain dormant for so long, had been reawakened. It could have something to do with her beautiful surroundings, she thought as she breathed in the country scents, so different from what she'd been used to all her life.

She sighed. Despite her outward content, she still missed her family, her mother most of all. She tried not to think about Harry. She would always love him, but remembering him brought only pain. She just hoped that he was happy with his German bride and their child. He must be out of the army now. Had he returned to London to work in the market with Sid? She'd never know — there was no way she would ever go back to the East End.

She sighed and turned her attention to what Norah was saying. The older woman was always eager to hear what was going on at Turner's.

"So, young Michael hasn't knuckled down to the job then?" Norah finished her tea and set the cup down on the grass at her feet. "His dad must be so disappointed."

"I think that's why he's made the decision to sell up," Ellie said.

Norah looked up sharply. "Sell up — what do you mean?"

"He's had an offer from a textile manufacturer from up north — Manchester, I think. He hung on, waiting till Michael had learned the business. But I think he's now realized that he'll never be ready to take over." Ellie gazed across the garden, her face sad. "He was really broken up when he told me — angry too at seeing all those years of tradition being lost."

"That young man never was interested in work," Norah said tartly. "I could understand it when he thought his brother would take over. But, he's the only son now Philip's dead — the mill would have gone to him eventually."

Ellie bent to pick up the teacups but Norah detained her. "Let's stay out here a little longer — it's a lovely evening."

Norah had cut the grass earlier and the sweet smell lingered on the still air. The borders were awash with spring colours which glowed in the deepening dusk and overhead a couple of early swallows coasted on the warm breeze in search of a late supper. Ellie was reluctant to spoil the perfect moment but there was something else on her mind.

"I know I haven't much experience of business," she began hesitantly. "But I'm sure the mill was doing all right, although Mr Turner told me that things went downhill after they stopped producing parachute silk. He said they've been losing money ever since. But, according to the books, they should still be making a profit."

"You did tell me things were in a bit of a muddle when you first started there," Norah said. "After he lost his son, the old man went to pieces — lost interest in the business altogether for a while. As you've said, Michael isn't much help — only interested in chasing girls and swanning around in fast cars."

"I suppose that's it — as you say, things were in a muddle. Maybe I've got it wrong." Ellie changed the subject, asking teasingly how things were going with Trevor. Norah spent a lot more time at the café these days. Her home-made cakes were now a regular item on the menu and it seemed that Gloria was off the scene for good.

Ellie smiled, pleased that her friend was happy, but she had other things on her mind. She'd sorted out all the old paperwork and the office was now well organized. Everything was ready for the final stock-take before the new owner, Alex Cameron, took over. But she was worried about what she thought were discrepancies. If only she could discuss it with Mr Turner, but he was hardly ever there these days. She'd mentioned it to Michael and he'd laughed, saying she was mistaken. It wasn't her mistake though — she was sure of that.

★　★　★

Although no one was supposed to know until it had been officially announced, news of the take-over leaked out, causing consternation among the weavers. At lunch time next day Jackie accosted Ellie. "It's all round the factory. Why didn't you tell me? I thought we were supposed to be friends."

"I was told in confidence," Ellie said defensively, biting her lip as she remembered that she had told Norah.

"Well, I think we should have been warned if we're about to lose our jobs," Jackie told her huffily.

"I'm sorry — you're right. It was just as much of a blow to me, you know." Ellie touched her friend's arm, aware that the other girls were listening. "But I don't know why you're worried. I'm sure the new owner will keep you all on. It's not as if the mill's closing down altogether."

"That's not what I heard," Jackie said, hunching her shoulders and moving away as the bus drew up.

The next day the staff assembled in the weaving-shed, where Mr Turner informed them of the take-over and introduced the new owner. Ellie had already met Alex Cameron. He had spoken to her about her role in the firm just before the meeting and she'd been reassured by his firm handshake and the direct look from his grey eyes.

"Will Turner has told me how much he relies on you," he said. "I'm sure I'll be able to depend on you, too, Miss Scott — or may I call you Helen?"

"My friends call me Ellie," she told him.

She liked Alex Cameron and felt that the business couldn't be in better hands. Her only concern was that he'd told her Michael Turner would stay on as manager.

Alex stood on a box and looked over the twenty or so heads gathered in front of the machines, smiling down at them as they shuffled their feet apprehensively.

"I know the news over the take-over has come as a shock. However, before I go any further, I would like to reassure you all that your jobs are not in jeopardy. And, for the time being at least, we will continue to produce silk fabrics." There was murmuring and shuffling of feet and he held up a hand for silence.

"You may have heard rumours that changes are planned — and it's true. Change is inevitable — not just here, but in the wider economy of the country. We must move with the times, and that means updating our practices and our machinery. But, to implement those changes and to make Turner's a thriving business once more I shall need workers." He paused and pointed a finger, encompassing them all. "You."

There were collective sighs of relief and Ellie realized that there'd been a very real fear of job losses.

Alex then told them that, as he would have to make frequent trips back to Manchester to deal with his other business interests, he had decided to keep Michael on as his manager. "So, although Turner's will no longer be a family firm, the interest and traditions developed over the years by the Turners and their forebears will, I hope, still continue."

Alex smiled and stepped down from the box, moving among the machines, shaking hands and greeting by name all his new employees.

172

Ellie caught Jackie's eye and walked towards her. "You're not still angry with me, are you? I felt really bad — not saying anything."

"It's OK. I'm sorry I got a bit huffy — but when rumours start flying round, you don't know what to believe. And I like my job here."

"So do I. What do you think of our new boss, then?"

Jackie's eyes sparkled. "He's quite a dish. If I wasn't spoken for already, I wouldn't mind . . ." She giggled. "Is he married?"

"Don't think so — not that I'm interested. Besides, he strikes me as being more interested in business than in personal relationships."

Jackie laughed, nodding towards Michael, who was talking quietly to his father. His face was flushed and Ellie wondered what they were discussing.

"Pity he's not going instead of his father," Jackie said. "The creep."

Ellie shuddered. "You don't have to tell me. Anyway I'm sure Mr Cameron won't let him get away with as much as his father did."

"Yes, he looks like he's not easily fooled," Jackie said. "Who knows, Michael may mess things up so badly that Cameron will give him the sack."

Ellie hoped her friend was right. Her job would be so much easier if Michael was out of the way.

Alex Cameron came through to the office from the old throwing-shed, a swatch of samples in his hand. He was frowning as he flicked through them.

Ellie looked up from her column of figures and smiled at him. "Any luck?" she asked.

"I haven't quite cracked it yet — but I'll keep trying," he said.

"I'm sure it'll come right eventually," she said encouragingly. From the moment they'd met six months ago, Ellie had been impressed with Alex Cameron's dynamism. He radiated energy — from the fierce grey eyes to the large capable hands which moved expressively as he outlined his ideas. She also felt comfortable with him. He was one of the few men she knew who didn't look her up and down with a certain gleam in his eye. And he also spoke to her as an equal, never assuming that she wouldn't understand what he was talking about.

"I've invested a lot of money in this venture," he said. "I can't afford to fail."

"But you're still making cloth in the Manchester mill — and we're doing all right here. A new order came in this morning," Ellie said.

"I'm not bothered about the silk. If things go to plan we'll be putting in new machines and making the new fabric before too long."

The dilapidated throwing shed had been cleared of all the old and broken machines that had been stored there for years. The roof had been mended and the interior painted white to reflect the light. Alex had cleaned up and renovated some of the old machines for use in his experiments, including the old hand-loom.

There was also a new machine, lovingly tended by Donald Blair, an old friend of Alex's, who had recently

174

joined the firm to help with the experiments. Donald was so confident of their eventual success that he'd moved his wife and family down from Manchester.

Alex, seeing Ellie's genuine interest, smiled at her. "I know you think making silk is the only thing that matters — I admire your dedication to the business, especially as Mr Turner told me you're still fairly new to it. But we have to move forward. We've been struggling against the import of cheap ready-made silk and cotton from India for years — and now there's all these synthetic fabrics coming on the market. We're making a type of nylon ourselves up in Manchester."

"I know — horrid slippery stuff that's supposed to not need ironing," Ellie said with a cheeky grin.

"That's the whole point of these experiments," Alex said, perching on the edge of the desk and displaying the samples. "Imagine if you could make a material that looks and feels like silk but has the properties of nylon — durability, non-iron and so on. That's what I'm trying to do — make a combination thread — part man-made, part natural fibre. It's been done before, of course — but not with silk."

Ellie fingered the material, smiling at his enthusiasm. The sample squares were easily pulled out of shape and she knew that if they were made up into a garment it would soon become baggy and unwearable. Earlier samples had turned out coarse and scratchy or had not held the dye well. There were also problems controlling the build-up of static as the thread passed through the winding machine.

"If we can't solve that we can't proceed. It's one of the biggest problems with synthetic fibres," Alex said.

"If anyone can do it, you can. You're obsessed." Ellie laughed and he laughed with her.

"Maybe," he said. "But that's how most new things come about — the inventors wouldn't give up even though everybody else thought they were mad." He stood up and stretched. "I came to ask if you'd get me a cup of coffee — I need something to keep me going."

"OK. I'll bring some for Donald too, shall I?" Ellie got up and went towards the door. In old Mr Turner's day the workers had brought their own sandwiches and flasks. Now Alex had turned one of the disused buildings into a rest room, containing a small kitchen area with an electric kettle and fridge.

Ellie welcomed the chance of a break and a walk across the yard in the fresh air. While she was waiting for the kettle to boil Jackie came in with one of the other girls. They were laughing as they flopped into chairs and got out their cigarettes. That was another of Alex's innovations — the chance for the workers to have a cigarette in comfort. There was a strict rule against lighting up in the storerooms and weaving-sheds, with instant dismissal for anyone caught breaking it. In the past it had been the custom to sneak out and have a quick puff in the shelter of the porch. Naturally enough, in bad weather it was tempting to hide behind one of the machines or bales of material. Now, there was no excuse and consequently less risk of fire in the mill.

"I was gasping for that," Jackie said as she took a long drag.

Her friend held the packet out to Ellie but she shook her head. The kettle came to the boil and she filled two mugs and brought them over to the table.

"What about you?" Jackie asked.

"I'm making some for Alex and Donald — I'll take mine over to the office as well," Ellie said, refilling the kettle at the sink. She turned to her friend. "That's a pretty blouse."

Jackie had undone her overall, revealing pale-blue silk with an embroidered collar. "Made it myself," she said proudly.

"It is silk, isn't it?"

"Of course — only the best for me," Jackie laughed. "I made it from an offcut — well two, actually. It was hard to get two matching pieces big enough though."

Ellie remembered that the weavers were allowed to take offcuts — the ragged pieces of fabric left as the roll came off the machine. Sometimes material would get damaged or smeared with machine oil. The scraps were put in a box by the door and everyone was allowed to help themselves.

"Why don't you do the same?" Jackie asked her.

"I'm no good at sewing," Ellie said. But Jackie had given her an idea.

When she got back to the office, Alex had disappeared again. She went through to the laboratory, once the old throwing-shed. The two men had their heads together, intent on the machine which tested the breaking strain of the thread, as well as the amount it had stretched under tension.

"Maybe this one will work, Donald," Alex said.

His colleague nodded thoughtfully. "We've got to adjust the acrylic fibre to match the breaking strain of the natural thread. Once we've calculated that, we'll be home and dry." He indicated the pointer which measured the tension on the thread.

Neither of them noticed as Ellie put the coffee down beside them and she smiled as she went back to her desk.

Perusing her sheet of figures once more, her smile turned to a frown. There was definitely something wrong. Now she had a good idea why Turner's hadn't been making the profits it should. She could no longer put off talking to Alex about it. But would she be able to hold his attention long enough to make him see how serious it was? And, wrapped up in his experiments, would he really care?

CHAPTER
FIFTEEN

Ellie didn't get the chance to talk to Alex before he dashed off on one of his frequent trips to Manchester, saying that Michael would sort out any problems. But she was sure now that Michael was the problem.

This time Alex was gone for six weeks and Ellie didn't know what to do. Whenever Michael came into the office she bit her lip and clenched her fist. She was sure that if she was measured on the thread-testing machine she'd find she'd reached her own breaking strain. She laughed at herself, dismissing the fanciful thoughts. All the same, she willed her boss to return soon. He'd have to listen now.

She'd had her suspicions before, and they'd been confirmed when a customer phoned asking why his order was late. Michael told her there'd been a delay in the delivery of the thrown silk from their new supplier in Manchester.

But Ellie was sure they'd received it. She remembered the invoice arriving and Alex signing the cheque in payment just before he went away. Surely she hadn't made a mistake and paid for goods not received. And hadn't Jackie told her how quickly they'd managed to get the order out? Or was that for another customer?

She smiled at Michael, appearing to accept his explanation. But when he left the office, she went through the invoices carefully, then phoned the supplier to check the delivery date.

On the bus going home that evening she asked Jackie how soon the bolts of silk would be ready for packing. Somehow she wasn't surprised when her friend told her they'd gone off the previous week. But what had happened to them if the customer hadn't received them?

Puzzling over it in bed that night she remembered the strange van that had been parked near the loading bay a few days previously. Michael and someone she'd never seen before had disappeared in the direction of one of the disused buildings down near the stream. When she asked Michael who it was he'd told her it was an old friend who'd dropped in to see him. She didn't believe him but his bold stare deterred her from asking more questions.

Now, she was sure that Michael was working some sort of fiddle — maybe selling their fabric privately and pocketing the money himself. She couldn't think of any other explanation. Remembering the muddle the books had been in when she first came and how an apparently thriving firm seemed to be losing money, Ellie was sure it had been going on for some time. How could Michael cheat his own father, especially when he must have known it would mean the loss of the family business? Maybe he just didn't care, Ellie thought indignantly. Well, he wasn't going to get away with it. She must find a way of stopping him.

It wouldn't be easy now that he was in and out of the office so much. For a while, he'd left her alone and she'd thought that at last he had got the message that she wasn't interested in him. Lately though, he'd taken to sitting on the edge of her desk again, watching her work. Had he realized that she was suspicious?

If only Alex would get back.

The cottage was so quiet that Ellie could hear the rain on the roof and the wind in the trees. Norah was at the café, where she seemed to spend even more time lately. Usually on a Saturday Ellie went in to Chelmsford on the bus to shop or go to the pictures but she didn't fancy it in this weather.

She wandered aimlessly from room to room, peering out at the sodden garden through the streaming windows. It was a good time to try out her idea.

She'd never painted on silk before but before long she was totally absorbed, and her concerns about Michael faded into the background. She became fascinated by the way the colours sank into the material, giving a soft muted feel to the design. She used her watercolour tubes and a wet on wet technique which seemed to work well with the design she was doing. But if she wanted a hard edge, how would she stop the colours running into each other? The other problem was that the colours wouldn't be fast.

Ellie bit her lip. There must be a way: special paints perhaps. She'd ask at the art shop next time she was in Chelmsford.

She sat back and looked at the finished design. Now she was ready to transfer it to a larger piece of fabric. How lucky she'd been to get that long narrow piece off the end of the roll. It had an oil smear in one corner, but she could cut that off and still have enough left for a scarf. Her sewing skills weren't good enough for the fine stitches she'd need on this delicate material and she decided to tease out the threads at the edge to make a fringe.

But how to fix the material while she worked? She didn't want to use drawing pins as she had with the practice piece. Perhaps Norah wouldn't mind her borrowing her embroidery frame. If the scarf proved a success, she'd give it to her as a thank you present.

With the silk firmly in place, Ellie soon transformed the white material into a bright swirl of mauves, pinks and blues. It reminded her of the wallpaper design she'd painted — so long ago now it seemed — and her eyes closed against the remembered pain of her father's contemptuous expression as he screwed the paper up and threw it aside. She thrust the thought away. No one would ever do that to her again. She knew she had talent — and one day everyone would know it, including Bert Tyler.

Norah was delighted with the scarf and only too happy for Ellie to use her embroidery frame. "You could make those and sell them," she told her.

Ellie laughed. "It's just a hobby," she said. "Besides, I'd have to charge a lot if I had to buy the material — I was lucky to get this piece for nothing."

182

She was pleased that Norah seemed impressed with her artistic talents and it gave her an idea. It was getting near Christmas and she would make scarves for the girls she'd become friendly with at the mill. She didn't want to dip into her hard-won savings to buy presents.

. She asked Jackie to get some more scraps for her, unwilling to enter the weaving-shed unless she had a genuine errand in case she encountered Michael lurking behind the bales.

She couldn't avoid going across the yard for ever though. The time sheets had to be collected and she wanted to talk to Fred, the overseer, about the latest order. It was Michael's job to monitor the work in progress but Ellie didn't trust him. Last time the bales had gone missing she'd had a hard job persuading the customer not to cancel his order.

Everything seemed to be all right this time and Ellie wondered if she might have been mistaken. Or perhaps Michael was aware of her suspicions and was lying low. She said goodbye to Fred and collected the time sheets.

When she opened the shed door she was dismayed to see that the fine drizzle had turned to driving sheets of rain. She stepped back inside, hoping it would soon ease off.

As she leaned against one of the bales, Michael appeared in the doorway, shaking the drops off an umbrella. He spotted her and smiled.

"I'm just going to have a word with Fred, then I'm going back to the office. If you wait, you can share my umbrella," he said.

Ellie would like to have refused but the rain seemed set to last. She wondered why Michael needed to talk to Fred. Were they working the fiddles together? She didn't believe so. Fred had been with Turner's since he was a boy and was now nearing retirement. Besides, she liked the old man and couldn't bear to think ill of him.

She jumped when Michael touched her shoulder. He opened the umbrella and grasped her arm, pulling her closer as he threw open the shed door. She flinched away instinctively and he hissed through his teeth.

"What's the matter with you, girl? All I've ever done is ask you to go out with me — to have a bit of fun. But you keep fobbing me off with excuses."

"I've already told you — I'm not interested," Ellie said, trying to keep her voice steady. She couldn't tell him she just didn't like the way he looked at her.

"Got your eye on the new boss, have you?" he sneered. "Not good enough for you now, am I?"

"You never have been," she retorted, regretting her words instantly as a flash of anger darted across his face and his grip on her arm tightened.

He threw the umbrella down and pushed her towards the pile of bales. As she fell against them he lunged at her, his lips curled in what was almost a snarl. "I'll teach you who's boss."

"Oh no you won't," she muttered through clenched teeth as her knee came up and caught him between the legs. He reeled away, his face contorted in pain and anger, and Ellie grasped the opportunity to dive for the door.

She raced across the yard and burst into the office, leaning against the door and trying to catch her breath. She was shaking, fighting the urge to burst into tears. Gradually her breathing eased and she became conscious of the rainwater dripping from her clothes to pool at her feet. She ran her hand through her tangled hair and looked up to see Alex Cameron perched on the edge of her desk, a sheaf of papers in his hand.

She gaped at him foolishly. When had he returned? "I just went over for the time sheets," she said lamely.

He looked at her without smiling and she realized she must have dropped them in her flight across the yard. "Never mind the time sheets." He thrust the papers in his hand at her. "I'd like you to explain the meaning of this."

Ellie reached out a hand for the papers which were covered with scribbled figures in her own handwriting. She was sure she'd put them away, worried that Michael might see them and realize their significance. As she collected her thoughts she wished she'd had time to work out what she was going to tell Alex. Why had he come back so unexpectedly?

"Well, girl — explain," he said brusquely.

Ellie bit her lip. He'd never spoken to her like that before. Surely he didn't think she was the dishonest one? Stammering, she tried to explain the discrepancies between the amount of thrown silk purchased for weaving and the finished cloth sent out to their customers. Someone must be selling off the surplus for their own profit. The amount was too great to be accounted for by spoiled material and natural wastage.

She couldn't bring herself to mention Michael, unsure whether Alex would believe her.

Throughout her halting explanation, Alex did not move from his perch on the corner of the desk, his grey eyes, hard as flint now, fixed on hers.

Ellie's voice trailed away and she felt herself reddening as Alex continued to stare at her in silence. She felt embarrassed — guilty almost — as if it were her fault that such things had been allowed to go on.

"Why didn't you tell me of your suspicions before now?" he asked.

"I wanted to — but you were always so busy. I planned to speak to you as soon as you got back from Manchester."

"Never mind. I'll deal with it now," he said sharply, getting up and striding out of the office.

Ellie sagged against the desk in relief. It wasn't her worry any more. She hoped fervently that there would be no second chance for Michael Turner and that he would get the sack as he deserved. But she spared a thought for old Mr Turner's distress when he found out what his son had been up to.

Alex realized he still had Ellie's sheaf of notes and calculations in his hand when he sat down at the bench which ran along the far end of the laboratory. He'd managed to complete his business in Manchester earlier than expected and couldn't wait to get back to his experiments. That was where his real interest lay and he resented time spent away from Essex.

Donald spoke from his end of the bench, where he was testing a new batch of fibres. "Glad to see you back, Alex. Come and take a look at this."

"Not now, Don. I've got other things on my mind at the moment."

Donald swivelled round at the impatient note in his friend's voice. "Things didn't go well up there then?" he asked mildly.

"Oh, no. It's something else that's come up. I just need to go over some figures."

"Business before pleasure, eh?" Don said with a laugh, turning back to the thread-testing machine.

Alex didn't reply, his head bent over the notes in Ellie's neat handwriting. He'd have to do something about this. When he'd taken over Turner's, he'd been fully aware that the business was going downhill. It hadn't troubled him unduly. So long as the Manchester textile mill kept making money, he could afford to indulge his own interest. All he needed from Turner's were the premises and the machinery — somewhere to conduct his experiments.

It was part of his agreement with old Turner that he kept the existing staff on as long as possible. They were good and loyal workers and he hoped to keep things ticking over until he was ready to start producing the new material. He hated the idea of putting any of them out of work. It would be hard for them to find new jobs in the industry, especially out here in the sticks, although there were a couple of silk mills still in production in Essex — one just up the road in Braintree.

But this new development was something else, he thought, as he pored over Ellie's figures. He might not care about making money. But he did care about being cheated. He sat back and rubbed his chin, deep in thought. It must be someone who knew the business thoroughly — someone who also knew what a muddle the books had been in when he took over.

Could it be Ellie? He knew very little about her background, except that she wasn't local like the rest of the workers. But he'd seen how hard she worked and been impressed with her genuine interest in the silk business, as well as in his experiments. He hoped his growing attraction to her wasn't clouding his judgement.

Until recently his work and his experiments had been his whole life. But it wasn't just the desire to know how the latest batch of thread-testing had gone that had brought him back from Manchester in such a hurry. His disappointment when he found Ellie wasn't in the office was like a physical blow.

And now this. Was Ellie cheating him? He didn't want to believe it but the figures in her neat handwriting, spoke for themselves. She must have an accomplice. Who was it, he wondered as he paced the room, pausing by the window. The heavy rain had brought an early dusk and the lights from the weaving shed reflected off the deepening puddles. A movement caught his eye and a figure came out of the shadows and slunk across the yard, disappearing in the direction of the disused mill building down by the stream. What was young Turner up to? Alex, aware of his manager's reputation with the mill girls, wondered if he'd arranged to meet one of them there.

Or was there something else behind his furtive movements? Much as he disliked Michael Turner, Alex couldn't believe he'd cheat his own father. Still, it might pay to keep an eye on him in future.

Christmas had come and gone and the dark days of January made travelling to work a nightmare. But standing at the bus stop, blowing on her hands and stamping her feet to keep warm, Ellie laughed and joked with Jackie and the other mill girls, grateful for their friendship. She was grateful too that there were no longer offers of lifts in the mill manager's car. Since their painful encounter some weeks ago, Michael had kept his distance.

Nothing more had been said about the firm's losses since Alex had confronted Ellie with her scribbled calculations. For days she waited for the sparks to fly — as she was sure they would when Alex exposed Michael's dishonesty. But nothing happened and as time passed she began to wonder whether Alex had taken it seriously. When she hesitantly raised the subject he had brusquely fobbed her off.

She still monitored the orders, incoming and outgoing, and as far as she could see the losses had stopped. Perhaps Alex had spoken to Michael, threatening him with dismissal if it happened again. She shivered, not entirely from the cold, as she realized that Michael had probably guessed he'd been rumbled and that she was the one responsible. Hadn't she tried to discuss it with him — before she realized he was the culprit? She shivered again, pulling her scarf more closely about her neck as she prayed for the bus to arrive.

CHAPTER
SIXTEEN

Ellie smiled as she stood up to clear the plates away, firmly pressing Norah back into her seat. "You stay there and entertain our guest," she said, grinning at Trevor over her friend's head.

Since spending Christmas Day with them, Trevor had got into the habit of coming to the cottage for Sunday dinner and Norah wore herself out preparing roast lamb or pork with all the trimmings, finishing off with one of her delicious puddings.

Trevor licked his lips and his eyes gleamed in appreciation as Ellie set the light golden apple sponge down on the table, together with a jug of thick creamy custard. Yes, the way to a man's heart — at least this man — was through his stomach, Ellie thought, recalling one of her mother's sayings with a little pang.

By the time they'd finished eating, the short winter afternoon was already drawing to a close.

Trevor looked at his watch. "Time we were off, if we want to catch the first house," he said, helping Norah on with her coat. They were going to the pictures in Chelmsford to see *The Flame and the Arrow*. Norah, a great fan of Burt Lancaster, had missed it the first time round. The little cinema, known locally as the "fleapit", always showed older films on Sundays.

"Are you sure you don't want to come with us?" Norah asked for the third time.

"Now why would I want to be cramped in the back of Trev's van when I can sit here in front of a warm fire?" Ellie laughed at the obvious relief on the older woman's face. The couple might spend the best part of the week in each other's company but Sunday afternoons and evenings were special. She went to the window and watched as Trevor solicitously helped Norah into the van, settling her comfortably before closing the door. It seemed that at last Trevor was ready to forget Gloria and begin to appreciate the treasure right under his nose.

Ellie fondly hoped that this outing would be the turning point in her friends' relationship. When she'd finished tidying the kitchen, she was ready to get her equipment out and start work on her next project. Much as she enjoyed the company of Norah and Trevor, she now relished these precious hours of solitude when she could lose herself in her painting.

The scarves she had made and given as Christmas gifts to the mill girls had been so popular that she'd been inundated with requests for more. The girls wanted them as presents for their own friends and families. They had each given her their share of the offcuts and scraps from the mill to work on. But if she got any more orders, there wouldn't be enough in the scrap bin at work. She would have to start buying material and charging for her services. As it was, she only accepted a token payment from her friends to help with the cost of the dyes.

After her first tentative experiments with watercolours, Ellie had made another trip to the library to read up about the different techniques for silk painting. The art shop only had ordinary fabric paints which weren't suitable for silk. So to obtain the special dyes she needed, and the gutta — a wax resist to stop the colours running into each other — she had to make a special trip to Colchester. As well as Norah's embroidery frame, which her friend had been delighted to lend her, she now had a number of square frames so that she could work on several designs at once.

She got out her materials and turned to the page in her sketchbook where she had drafted out her next project. She was making a square headscarf for Fred's wife, whose birthday was due soon. The overseer had been stumped for a present until he asked Jackie where she'd got her scarf.

His approach to Ellie had been rather hesitant and he'd smiled shyly when she agreed. He was a reserved little man who did his work quietly and efficiently, always ready to help when something went wrong and never blaming the girls when their machines broke down or the warp snapped. He and Ellie had always been polite to each other. But she'd been a little worried that he might think she was usurping his authority when she came into the weaving shed to check the progress of a job, or to see how many books of silk were left before recordering. Now she realized he was just shy and she was delighted when he made his request.

Ellie always tried to match the scarf to the person it was intended for and the stained-glass window design she'd chosen was based on Fred telling her that his wife regularly attended the village church. With practice she'd become more proficient in using the gutta to draw the lines between the blocks of colour and now she was confident that the finished design would live up to her imagination.

She'd already stretched the piece of silk on the frame and drawn the design. Now, she carefully painted raised lines in the white latex solution, following the pencilled design. While she waited for it to dry, she put on rubber gloves and started to mix the dyes — ruby red, purple, jade green and sapphire blue. She hoped the jewel-like colours wouldn't be too bright for Fred's wife — if she was as quiet and mousy as her husband she'd probably be too timid to wear it. Perhaps she should have asked Fred what colours his wife liked.

Ellie shrugged. If he seemed unsure she could always keep it for herself and make another one for his wife.

She switched on the wireless for company. But soon she was so absorbed in her work that she scarcely noticed the strains of the Palm Court Orchestra, shortly followed by the Adams Singers singing "something simple". Usually she avoided the programmes which reminded her so painfully of evenings at home with Harry and her mother — times which had been happy as long as Bert was out of the way. Now, in her new-found contentment with her job and having found an outlet for her creativity, the old songs had lost their power to make her sad. Occasionally, it was true, a small lump would lodge somewhere in the middle of her chest. But it was swiftly dismissed as she tried to do what Gran had always advised: "Count yer blessings, girl".

Ellie looked up in surprise as the door opened and Norah came in, her cheeks rosy with cold — or was it something else? Behind her, Trevor was unbuttoning his coat and laughing. How had the time passed so quickly? She had almost finished the scarf and all that remained was to let it dry before removing the rubbery solution to reveal crisp white lines between the colours. It wasn't like a real church window, of course and Ellie wondered whether there might be a way to paint black lines to enhance the stained-glass effect. Or maybe she could do them in gold or silver. All sorts of ideas sprang into her mind. But for the moment this would have to do. She was sure it was one of the best she'd done so far.

She put her things away and put the kettle on. "You look as if you've enjoyed yourselves," she said. "Was it a good film?"

"It was OK." Norah blushed and caught Trevor's eye.

He grinned at Ellie. "To tell the truth, we didn't see a lot of it."

"Trevor!" Norah squealed, punching his arm. But she smiled up at him affectionately and Ellie smiled. Norah deserved a second chance after losing her first husband so tragically.

It wasn't until she was in bed later that night that Ellie wondered what would happen to her if Norah and Trevor decided to get married. She didn't know whether her friend owned the cottage or rented it. But if she moved into the café with Trevor it wouldn't matter either way. Ellie herself would still be looking for somewhere to live.

A few days later Ellie had finished the scarf for Fred's wife. Wrapping it in tissue paper, she put the parcel in her bag and left the house, having to run for the bus as she saw it turn into the lane and stop outside Little Howe church.

Although she was worried about the possibility of having to move out of the cottage, Norah looked so happy these days that Ellie couldn't bring herself to broach the subject. Besides, there was plenty of time. Trevor was still married to Gloria and, as she knew, divorce could take a long time — years even. And she couldn't imagine Norah moving in with Trevor unless she had a ring on her finger.

She got off the bus at Withies Green and crossed the mill yard to the weaving shed. She wanted to give Fred the scarf and see his reaction before she started work.

The overseer was helping one of the men to set up the warp on his machine and Ellie waited patiently until he looked up and saw her. She followed him into his little cubby-hole at the back of the shed, biting her lip as he opened the tissue-wrapped package. She had put so much work into this one and she desperately wanted him to like it.

196

As he held up the gaudy scrap of flimsy material she held her breath, relaxing in a smile as he grinned at her. "Just the job, Helen. The missus will love this."

"Really — are you sure it's not too bright?"

"She loves colourful things, does my Doris. Reckons she needs something to brighten up her life — and I'm not much use in that direction." He gave a mournful smile and Ellie smiled back, realizing that Fred was actually making a joke.

"I'm glad you like it, Fred." Ellie turned, her hand on the door. "I must get across to the office. Mr Cameron will think I'm not coming to work today."

"Wait, I haven't paid you yet," Fred said. "How much do I owe you?"

Ellie hesitated. She usually only charged her friends a few pence. But she'd put in an extra lot of work this time. "Would two shillings be all right?"

"More than all right," Fred said, pressing a half-crown into her hand. "You ought to get a lot more than that."

"Well, I didn't pay for the material — otherwise it would be more," Ellie said, with a laugh.

"Miss Scott, come into the office at once." The voice behind her made her jump. "And Fred, you're wanted in the dyeing shed." It was Alex.

"Sorry, Mr Cameron. I didn't realize it was so late," Ellie stammered, wondering what was wrong. It wasn't like him to be so abrupt.

She followed him across the yard, stumbling another apology for being late.

"Never mind that," he snapped.

He held the door open for her and she swallowed nervously as she saw Michael Turner lounging in the chair behind her desk, smiling sardonically.

Alex gestured to her chair at the other side of the desk. She sat down, hands clasped in her lap. As her employer began to speak she realized why Michael was looking so relaxed — and Alex so grim.

"I understand you've been making silk scarves and selling them to the mill employees," Alex said. He reached across the desk and picked up a scrap of material. It was a scarf she'd made for one of the girls in the dyeing shed.

Ellie glanced at Michael but he was gazing at the floor with seeming disinterest. "Yes — but I've been doing it in my own time — not when I should be working," she said.

"Was that one of your creations I saw in Fred's office?" Ellie thought she detected a sneer at the word "creations", but she could have been wrong. By now she was twisting her fingers nervously together.

She nodded wordlessly.

"Didn't I just hear you telling Fred that you hadn't paid for the material. What did you mean exactly?"

"I use waste material — offcuts that are left over when the material comes off the loom."

"I see." Alex sat on the edge of the desk, swinging his leg and tapping his chin as if deep in thought.

He stood up abruptly. "Can you tell me how many of these scarves you've made?" he asked, going to the window and looking out at the yard.

Ellie half-closed her eyes, trying to calculate. It was hard to remember — she'd been making one or two a week since well before Christmas. "About two dozen — maybe more. I can't remember." She felt a little spurt of anger. Why was he questioning her? "May I ask why you want to know?" She was pleased that she managed to keep her voice steady.

"All in good time." Alex remained at the window.

Ellie was really apprehensive now. She glanced again at Michael and caught a glimpse of his calculating smile, before his gaze slid away and he contemplated his shoes again. She caught her breath as the realization dawned on her. Alex had tackled Michael about the missing fabric and he was trying to blame her. She gasped in protest, but Alex waved her to silence.

He stepped away from the window and faced her. "It has come to my notice that bolts of woven silk are going astray. Turner seems to think you might be" — he paused as if looking for the right word — "appropriating the fabric for your own use. And it certainly seems as if you've got quite a little cottage industry going here." He dangled the scarf in front of her.

Ellie's chin jutted and her eyes flashed dangerously. How dare he? She clenched her fists at her sides and took a deep breath. Losing her temper wouldn't help. "I told you — I've only used the stuff I'm allowed to take. I haven't stolen anything." Her cheeks were flushed and she was breathing heavily. She glared furiously at Michael, who was now imperturbably examining his fingernails.

"It must have taken rather a lot of offcuts to make such a quantity of scarves," Alex said.

"Yes, but I only took what I was allowed. The other girls said it was all right . . ." Ellie was floundering now. Surely Alex didn't really suspect her.

"So now you're trying to blame your workmates," Michael's voice interrupted smoothly.

Alex silenced him with a raised hand. "I said I would handle this, Turner. Perhaps it would be better if you waited outside." He turned back to Ellie and she was sure he missed the malicious look Michael directed at him.

Michael rose slowly from the chair where he'd been lounging and sauntered towards the door. He stopped, leaning on the doorframe. "She's not going to confess you know, Cameron. But the evidence is there." He gestured towards the scarf, which still dangled from Alex's hand. "I can tell you, there wouldn't have been all this time-wasting talk in my father's day. The slightest suspicion of theft would be enough to send them packing with no references."

"This is my business now, Turner — and I'll handle things in my own way. I could blame you — since you're the manager. It seems that you have allowed blatant thievery to go unchecked in my absence."

Michael closed the door without answering. With a sigh, Alex threw himself into the chair that the other man had just vacated. As he ran the scarf through his fingers, Ellie dared to peep at him beneath her lowered lashes. His brow was furrowed, as if he was trying to frame the words of dismissal, she thought. He believed she was a thief — and she couldn't blame him really. She had taken more than her fair share of the offcuts, although her colleagues had agreed to her having them. And she was making money — albeit only a small sum — from selling her scarves. It looked bad for her, she had to admit. But surely Alex couldn't believe she'd stolen a whole bale of silk — let alone a dozen. And she knew from her own investigations that at least that many were unaccounted for.

A hysterical giggle, hastily disguised as a cough, bubbled in her throat as in her imagination she saw herself manhandling a huge bale on to the bus at the end of the working day. Even a single bolt would be too heavy for her to carry by herself.

I wish he'd get it over with, she thought, standing up. She straightened her shoulders, determined to take it bravely. She wouldn't let him see how much his lack of trust hurt her.

To her surprise he smiled. "What an obnoxious young man," he said, jerking his head in the direction of the door. "And what, I wonder, have you done to make him dislike you so?"

Ellie couldn't find the words to reply. She was still trying to take in his abrupt change of mood.

Alex leaned towards her. "Never mind. I want to apologize, Ellie — for putting you through such an ordeal. I could hardly believe it when I confronted him with your figures and he immediately tried to shift the blame to you."

"You don't believe him, then? You're not accusing me?" Ellie didn't know whether to be relieved or angry.

He had certainly given her — and Michael — the impression that she was about to be dismissed.

"Of course not. You're perfectly entitled to take the offcuts — and use them in any way you like. And if the other girls are willing to let you have their share, that's their business." He smiled at her. "It's very enterprising of you — and if this is a sample of your work" — he held up the scarf — "I'm most impressed."

"So why did you practically accuse me of stealing?" Ellie wasn't ready to be flattered into letting the matter drop.

"It was Michael Turner who did the accusing," Alex said, leaning towards her. "I'm sorry, Ellie — I can't apologize enough. I checked all your figures and I've been keeping a close eye on young Turner, waiting to catch him out. When he accused you, I knew he was only trying to shift the blame. He couldn't know, of course, that thanks to you and your vigilance, I was well aware that the thefts had been going on for some time — long before you came to work here."

"So you let him think you believed him . . ."

"In the hope that he would convict himself — yes."

"Why did you let him go, then?"

"Don't worry — Donald is keeping an eye on him. I've got a feeling he'll try to get rid of the evidence. We discovered a bale hidden in the old mill — down by the stream. His car's parked round the back there and he's probably loading it right now."

"Will you get the police?" Ellie asked.

"There's nothing I'd like better than to see that young man in gaol where he belongs. But, for the sake of his father, I'll just see him off the premises with a strong warning as to what will happen if I ever clap eyes on him again."

"Poor Mr Turner," Ellie murmured, remembering how kind the old man had been when she first came to work here.

Alex stood up. "I'd better go and see what's going on. I just felt I owed you an explanation." He paused at the door. "I really am sorry for putting you through this."

"I understand," Ellie said.

His grey eyes sparkled, lighting his face in a smile. "Am I forgiven, then?"

Ellie nodded. She liked and respected Alex Cameron, although for a few moments that feeling had wavered as she came under his cold scrutiny. Now that she understood the reason for his play-acting, it wasn't hard to forgive him. In fact she admired the way he had handled the situation, as well as the consideration he'd shown for Michael's father. She had thought any human feelings he had were overridden by his passion for his work and his dedication to his experiments. It gave her a little warm glow of pleasure to think that she might have been wrong.

CHAPTER
SEVENTEEN

Harry was wet and cold and thoroughly miserable. This wasn't how he'd planned to spend his life — standing under a dripping awning gazing out at equally wet, cold and miserable people. But at least it was a job of sorts.

As a lad he'd loved working the market with Sid, but joining the army had broadened his horizons. For the hundredth time he wished he hadn't given in to the impulse to cut short his army career. If he'd stayed on he'd have finished up with a proper trade. He'd learned a lot about engines and vehicle maintenance, but it wasn't enough to get him taken on as a mechanic and now he was too old to do a proper apprenticeship.

Now, here he was, weighing out potatoes and trying to summon up enthusiasm for the bananas and oranges which had once been luxuries but which now seemed to be available all year round. Not that many of the people round here could afford them and if they could, they weren't hanging around on such a grey day.

There weren't even any kids around whom he could ask to keep an eye on things while he went for a warming cuppa at Bob's Café.

He looked across at Maisie Jones, who was already packing up her second-hand clothes stall.

"You might as well do the same, love," she called. "Can't see many more customers turnin' out in this lot."

"I'll hang on a bit — just till the factory shifts turn out. Gotta try and keep things going for Sid," Harry said.

"How is the old sod then?"

"Doin' OK — though it'll be a while before he's out of hospital."

"Might pop in and see 'im later — if 'e 'asn't got anyone else goin' in."

"Only me," Harry said. "I go every day — just to put his mind at rest about the stall."

"Will you carry on here when 'e's back on 'is feet?" Maisie asked.

"Don't know — depends on Sid, I suppose." Harry didn't really want to, he had been thinking of joining up again. It would be different if he only had himself to think about but he couldn't leave Mary now she was so poorly. Since Ellie had run away, she had really gone downhill. He sighed and peered up through the awning at the louring sky which really matched his mood today. He wondered sourly if Bert would be there when he got home and if he would be sober. Fat chance, he thought.

He'd thought he'd be happy, back on his home ground, surrounded by his family and old friends. But Bert's drunken behaviour had worsened and it was all he could do to stop himself lashing out when he saw how his foster mother was treated. He didn't know how much longer he could put up with it and he felt the familiar churning in his stomach at the thought of what he was going home to.

He managed to summon a grin as Maisie, the contents of her stall already packed away into the handcart she used, came and thumped him on the shoulder.

"Cheer up, mate. It might never 'appen."

"It already has," Harry groaned.

"No word from the council yet, then?"

Harry shook his head. He'd put their names down for a flat as soon as he got back to London, hoping that he could persuade Mary to leave Bert, but there was a long waiting-list for people without children. Besides, deep down he knew that wasn't the problem.

Everywhere he went there were reminders of Ellie. People still asked if there was any word and each enquiry sent a fresh dagger through his heart. Why had she done it? he asked himself, as he had so many times. She was naïve and inexperienced but surely that one kiss hadn't been enough to drive her away.

He sighed and turned away to serve a customer. When the woman had gone, the rain-swept street was almost deserted and he decided to call it a day. Maisie stayed to help, packing boxes with the fruit and vegetables still fresh enough to be sold the next day. The wilted and speckled items went into another box to be left under the stall. They'd be gone by morning. There were still people eking out an existence in the narrow streets and alleys of Bethnal Green for whom the chance of free food was a godsend.

When the van was packed he offered to pull Maisie's handcart through the streets to its nightly berth under the railway arches. He'd come back for the van later.

Maisie grinned at him from under her shaggy mop of grey hair. "I ain't past it yet, son," she said. "Besides, I ain't goin' 'ome yet. I'm gonna pop into Bob's fer a bite to eat. Come and have a cuppa with me."

"Why not?" Harry said. What did he have to go home for?

They squelched their way through the puddles and debris of the market to the comforting warmth of the café on the corner. Bob greeted them with his usual grin, plonking two thick mugs of strong tea down on the counter.

Maisie led the way to a table in the corner and leaned back in her chair with a sigh. "It's good to take the weight off me dogs," she said. "This weather really gives me the screws."

Harry hardly noticed Maisie's chatter as he took a sip of his tea and looked out of the steamy window at the darkened street, now bustling with home-going workers. It all looked so normal. Nothing seemed to have changed since he went away — and yet, everything had.

He sighed, drinking his tea without tasting it, pondering the changes in his family since he'd been away. Sheila and Tommy were married now with two children, living in their big posh house out Chingford way. They had two little girls and Mary doted on Vickie and baby Debbie. But she'd never really forgiven her daughter for taking up with a married man and being the cause of his divorce — a fact blazed across the Sunday papers, to Mary's intense shame.

Harry was worried about his foster mother. She'd always been quiet, stoically enduring her hard life. Being married to a no-good bastard like Bert Tyler didn't help. But she'd got worse since he'd been away — and he knew why.

Ellie. His stomach churned painfully as he allowed her name into his thoughts, into his heart. Where was she? Why had she never got in touch with them? How could she do this to her mother — to him? He was furious with her and if she were here he'd shake some sense into her, although he knew he was as much to blame as anyone. But despite his anger, he understood and with all his heart he hoped she was well and happy. But it was agony not knowing.

He'd left Sheerness and the army with no regrets, glad to be going home. Back in London he could search for her. He had never given up hope that she'd turn up one day, reluctant to believe, as so many had hinted, that something dreadful had happened to her. He had to hang on to the belief that, confused by her feelings, she'd run away from him. And one day, she'd come back.

Maisie leaned back in her chair, her hands clasped for warmth round the thick china mug. Harry looked up to see her gaze fixed on him, sympathetic, kind, as if she knew what he was going through.

"Life's a bitch, ain't it?"

"Too right — still we just have to get on with it, don't we?"

"Something worrying you? It helps to talk, mate."

He was tempted to pour it all out, but he couldn't tell anyone, least of all Maisie, the biggest gossip in the market, how he felt about Ellie.

"It's Mary," he said. "She doesn't complain but she looks ill and she seems so tired all the time."

"Not surprising, considering what she's gone through the last couple of years," Maisie said. "Bad enough losing her mum, and all that business with your Sheila. But it must have nearly killed her when your Ellie disappeared."

Harry stared into his mug, unable to speak. Ellie again.

"You'd think she'd write — let her mum know she's safe," Maisie stopped abruptly, her hand over her mouth. "You don't think anything's happened to her, do you?"

Harry reassured her, although the thought was never far from his mind. "She sent a card not long after she left. Said she had a job and was staying with nice people. Twice she's written — but we've heard nothing for ages. And she didn't put an address."

"So you've no idea where she is, then?"

"No, the last one was postmarked Colchester — but that doesn't mean she's there. She could have got someone to post it for her."

"Have you tried to find her, then?"

"Wouldn't know where to start," Harry said, draining his mug and standing up. He didn't want to discuss it. Of course he'd tried to find her, written to the

209

Salvation Army, the *News of the World*. But nothing. What more could he do?

Ellie *was* happy — or so she managed to convince herself, as long as she didn't allow thoughts of her family and former life to intrude.

It was easier these days, with Michael Turner out of the way and her friendship and respect for Alex Cameron growing daily. Her work at Turner's Mill was interesting and, best of all, her new hobby was satisfying her artistic instincts.

The cottage at Little Howe was her home now and she missed the noise and bustle of London less with each day that passed. If sometimes she woke in the night, ears straining for the rattle of trains over the bridge at the end of Kendall Street, the mournful hooting of tugs from the river — well then, it was just a dream, she told herself.

Her days were filled with activity, whether at the mill or at home working on her designs. After the confrontation with Alex over Michael's dishonesty, she found herself looking forward to the time she spent with him, discussing his experiments. Gradually she confided her own ideas and ambitions.

Her confidence had grown so much that one day she summoned the courage to ask Alex whether she could buy a bolt of silk from the mill. The scraps and offcuts were no longer enough for her. She had bigger things in mind. When he agreed good-naturedly she seized the moment and asked if she could try some of the dyes they used in the mill. The craft shop in Colchester only stocked small quantities.

He smiled indulgently. "Are you sure you don't want to take over the whole mill for your enterprise," he said with a laugh.

"I wouldn't mind just a little bit of it," she said, surprising herself. The idea had just that second popped into her head.

His eyebrows rose and for a fleeting second she thought his eyes hardened to that flinty greyness she'd seen before when he was angry. Perhaps she'd gone too far. But he laughed and said "Perhaps we could discuss it over dinner."

She laughed too, then realized he was serious. Her stomach fluttered a little at the thought of going out with the boss. But it would be a chance to discuss what she wanted to do — purely business of course — and he might be able to help. She wondered fleetingly what her workmates would think. But it was none of their business. Swallowing her misgivings, she smiled and agreed when Alex arranged to pick her up from the cottage later that evening.

"I'll deliver the silk and the dyes at the same time," he said. And Ellie relaxed. Alex was a businessman and she was not only a colleague, but a customer now.

When she told Norah she was going out with Alex that evening, the little woman couldn't hide her pleasure. "You deserve an outing — but what will you wear, love?"

Ellie hadn't given it a thought. Despite her flair for design and her interest in fabric and colour, she rarely thought about clothes for herself. She had her serviceable dark-blue costume and a selection of smart blouses that she wore for work, a couple of summer dresses and cardigans. And that was it.

"I'll just wear my blue cotton dress with my costume jacket. That'll look OK," she said. After all, it wasn't a proper date.

Norah wasn't so sure. "He might take you somewhere posh. You don't want to let him down." She disappeared, leaving Ellie to survey her meagre wardrobe. In seconds she was back, a long midnight-blue dress over her arm. "I haven't worn this since Bob died," she said, holding it up against Ellie. "Good job you're slim round the hips." She indicated her flat chest with a laugh. "I had a bit more up top in those days too, so it should fit. Try it on, love."

After a token protest Ellie slipped the dress over her head, smoothing it down over her hips. She was a lot taller than Norah and the soft folds of the chiffon layers reached only halfway between her knee and her ankle.

"That looks lovely, Ellie," Norah said, stepping back and surveying the girl with satisfaction. "It could have been made for you. Even the length's right — they don't go in for full-length dresses so much nowadays."

Ellie went through to Norah's room to look at herself in the wardrobe mirror. She felt a bit overdressed but, she had to admit, the colour suited her and with her hair washed and curled and a little bit of powder and lipstick, she'd do.

Norah was standing behind her and Ellie smiled at her reflection. But the image wavered and, in its place she could see her mother's proud face, telling her how grown-up she looked all decked out in her finery for the opening of Tommy's Paradise Club. That was the last time she'd seen Mum, apart from that one brief glimpse at the hospital just after Gran had died.

She gave a little gasp and tears spilled through her fingers as she covered her face with her hands. She sank on to the edge of Norah's bed, leaning against the little woman, whose arms comforted her as she sobbed.

Norah was still patting her back, murmuring meaningless words, as the last of her tears were shed. She was still shaking but she sat up straight and tried to smile. "Don't know what got into me — it was the dress. It reminded me . . ."

"You don't have to tell me, love. I know from the little you've let slip that you had a hard time at home. But that's all behind you now." She patted Ellie's back, then stood up. "Wash your face and let me do your hair for you. Mr Cameron will be here soon."

"But I can't wear this dress" — Ellie almost started to sob again — "and I can't go out with him."

"Don't be silly, girl. You can't spend the rest of your life shut away here with just an old woman for company. You're young, with the rest of your life in front of you — and it's time you started living it."

Ellie almost managed to smile. "You're not old," she said.

"Go on with you." Norah gave her a little push.

As she sat at the dressing-table letting Norah brush and coax her hair into smooth waves, Ellie wondered if she was doing the right thing. Maybe Norah was right and she should start living a little. She had tried to block out the past but it kept intruding — just little things would set her off. But wasn't it time she began to accept that what had happened in the past was over? Bert could no longer hurt her. Neither he nor Tommy Green had any power over her. She could live her life as she pleased, work to fulfil the dreams she thought had been thwarted by her father's selfishness. And if Alex Cameron could help her achieve her ambitions, what was wrong with that?

Ellie stood up and took her latest creation — a soft silk shawl painted in shades of blue — and threw it round her shoulders. A knock came at the door and she ran downstairs, pasting a smile on her lips.

When she opened the door she was glad she'd dressed up. Alex looked so smart in his dark dinner jacket, a snow-white shirt gleaming in the dark of the porch. At least she wouldn't feel out of place.

The hotel restaurant was just as Ellie had imagined, tastefully decorated with low lighting and soft-footed waiters. At first she felt a bit nervous, but Alex was good company and she began to enjoy herself.

When he'd picked her up at the cottage, looking her up and down with frank admiration, she'd been a little wary, wondering whether she'd have to spend the evening fending off unwanted advances. But she saw him every day at work. Surely he'd have made a move before now, if he was that sort of man.

As the meal progressed she relaxed, reminding herself that he'd only taken her out so that they could talk about her ideas for expanding her "cottage industry" as he called it. As they waited for dessert she swallowed and took a deep breath. "We were going to talk about my business," she said.

"I have something to discuss too," he said, smiling. "But you go first. What can I do to help?"

"I don't have enough room at Norah's. I was wondering if I could use one of the old outbuildings. I'd pay rent of course."

"You're serious about this, then?"

"I thought you realized that."

"Have you thought it through, though? For instance, what will you do if you get so many orders you can't cope with them all?" he asked.

At least he hadn't laughed. "I don't know," she admitted, toying with her glass.

He leaned back and tapped his chin. "I have an idea. Why don't you use screen printing instead of painting the scarves by hand. That way, you could produce them in bulk. I could sell them for you — I've plenty of contacts in the rag trade."

"It wouldn't be the same," she said. "I want my designs to be unique — one-offs, exclusive."

He didn't seem to understand. "You won't make much money doing it your way," he said.

"It's not about making money," she said.

His eyes hardened. "Being in business is all about making money," he said, pouring another glass of wine. As he lifted his glass the hard expression melted and he smiled. "Anyway, forget about business. That's not why I asked you out."

Her heart began to thump. Had she been wrong about him? She was so agitated that at first she didn't take in what he was saying.

". . . buying a house, not far from the mill on the outskirts of the village. I've been too busy to think about moving till now. But if I'm going to settle in this part of the world, I can't stay in those cramped rooms. I need somewhere for my books, to hang my paintings."

She smiled nervously. What did this have to do with her?

He reached across and took her hand. "Ellie, would you share it with me?" The pressure of his hand increased and he looked into her eyes. "I'm asking you to marry me."

She stared at him, fighting the urge to giggle. It must be the wine. Surely he was joking. She'd never thought of him that way — not really — and it had never occurred to her that he might be in love with her.

He was looking at her intently, his grey eyes serious, but with a hint of laughter in them. Her hand still lay in his and, as she tried to pull away, his other hand covered it. He leaned towards her. "Say something, Ellie, please."

She eventually managed to extricate herself and looked down at her plate, picking up her fork and pushing the food around. "I don't know what to say," she said, her voice a low whisper.

"Well at least you haven't said an outright no," Alex replied with a little laugh. "I'm sorry, Ellie. I shouldn't have sprung it on you like that. But you must know how I feel about you."

"But you're my boss."

"More than just that, I hope."

"Well, I did think we were becoming friends. You've been so kind, helping me with my 'cottage industry' as you call it." Ellie managed a little smile.

"But I wouldn't have done it for just anyone — it's because I care about you."

He hadn't mentioned the word love, Ellie thought. But she didn't love him, did she? So why was she even thinking about his proposal? Why hadn't she just said "no" straight away?

Alex seemed to sense her confusion. "You need time to think about it, don't you? I'll take you home now — we can talk again tomorrow."

While he paid the bill, Ellie went into the ladies' cloakroom. She looked into the mirror above the wash basin. Earlier, she had been flushed and hot. Now her skin was pale and there were shadows beneath her eyes, which looked enormous in her thin face. Her cloud of thick dark-brown hair reflected copper highlights from the harsh overhead light, making her seem even paler by contrast. For the first time for months she looked like the frightened waif she'd been when she ran away from home.

In the security of Norah and Trevor's friendship, her sense of self worth had grown as she mastered her demanding job and rediscovered her artistic talent. Now, with those few seemingly careless words, Alex had undone all that. For with the mention of marriage had come the fear. She was fond of Alex but she didn't love him — not in the way he deserved to be loved. The very thought of the intimacy that marriage demanded made her stomach churn with apprehension. Still, the temptation was there. Alex could offer her security, a home, maybe a family of her own one day. And maybe in time, she'd be able to overcome those feelings brought about by memories of what had been done to her as a child.

She splashed her face with cold water. It was no good. How could she even be thinking of accepting him? He was too nice a man to be used like that. Besides, he knew nothing about her — and she would have to tell him about her past. Although she had never told anybody why she had run away from home, she'd never lied about it. And Alex, of all people, deserved total honesty — that was, if she intended to accept his proposal.

On the drive home he didn't refer to their earlier conversation, helping her out of the car and guiding her up the dark path in his usual courteous way. But as she went to open the front door, he pulled her round to face him.

"I meant it, Ellie. I love you and I want to marry you. But I won't press you for an answer. All I ask is that you think about it." He cupped her face in his hands and dropped a light kiss on her lips. "We'll talk tomorrow," he said, and walked quickly away down the path.

Alex sat in the car for some minutes before switching on the ignition and reversing out of the narrow lane. The evening hadn't turned out a bit as he had planned. It was his own fault. He really should have given Ellie an indication of his feelings before just blurting out his proposal like that.

But he couldn't help it and he had dared to hope that she felt more for him than just friendship. Maybe it wasn't love — not yet. But already she turned to him for help, relied on his advice, appeared to enjoy his company. There was no one else in her life — of that he was certain. And, in time, he was sure he could make her love him — that is, if he hadn't blown his chances already by his hasty action this evening.

His hands gripped the steering wheel and he put his foot down hard on the accelerator as he turned on to the main road. The need to concentrate as he sped through the dark night almost succeeded in driving the tormented thoughts from his brain. But when he reached his lonely bachelor flat, he paced the two tiny rooms above the back-street tobacconist's, unable to settle to sleep. Although he knew he would have to be up early the next morning to help Donald with the next batch of testing, he could not get Ellie's face out of his mind.

He had noticed the brief glint of laughter in her brown eyes at the mention of marriage, quickly followed by a gasp of dismay. Had she really thought he would joke about such a thing? And when she realized he was serious, was it really such a dreadful prospect as to leave her so pale and distraught?

He groaned aloud. This was no good. He must get his thoughts under control. At work tomorrow he would have to face her, behave as if nothing were amiss. He had said he would give her time — and he meant it.

But God, it would be hard to talk about orders and invoices, when all he wanted was to take her in his arms and feel her soft lips on his, her body moulding itself to his.

Alex drove to the mill through misty drizzle, his eyes gritty from lack of sleep, longing to see Ellie, yet almost dreading the moment when she would walk into the office. Would she wish him "good morning" and sit at her desk with that brisk, efficient demeanour she usually exhibited during working hours? Or would she greet him with a dazzling smile and the confession that she had thought about his proposal and that the answer was "yes"?

Despite his sleepless night, he arrived early as he always did. Only Donald was there before him and before long they were both immersed in the work that until recently had occupied his every waking thought. But they were nearing the breakthrough, he was sure, and there would be more time in the future for his personal life. He would be able to court Ellie as she should be courted, to buy her flowers, take her out. If he was patient he knew he would win her in the end.

As he wound the new sample of thread on to the break-testing machine he tried to concentrate on the calibrations, but all he could think of was Ellie. He realized he knew very little about her, beyond her enthusiasm and capacity for hard work, as well as her undoubted artistic talent. He knew she had worked in the café before moving in with Norah and coming to work at Turner's. But she never spoke of her life before that. Although she was usually bright and vivacious, he had sometimes caught her in an unguarded moment, her eyes clouded and inward looking, and he guessed that she had not always had a happy life. Well, he would change all that. If he had anything to do with it, she would never want for anything again.

CHAPTER
EIGHTEEN

Ellie opened the office door, shook the raindrops off her umbrella and hung it with her coat behind the door. She had hesitated with her hand on the doorknob, expecting to see Alex perched on the corner of her desk, swinging his leg and smiling that quizzical smile. But the room was empty.

After a sleepless night wrestling with her conscience, she had come to a decision. But it was a relief to be able to put off telling Alex a little longer. Norah, of course, had been delighted. Marrying the boss had been every young girl's dream in her day. But Ellie still wasn't sure whether she was doing the right thing. True, she was fond of Alex and they shared common interests in the textile business. As his wife, she would continue to work at his side and, she was sure that together they would be a successful team. But was that enough?

Unwittingly Ellie thought of her mother. Mary had married her first husband for love, but after his death, struggling to bring up a family alone, she had been tempted into a loveless match which had proved disastrous. Mary must have asked herself the same questions she was asking now, trying to persuade herself that affection and commitment were enough.

Ellie took the cover off her typewriter and gave herself a mental shake. It wasn't the same at all. Alex was good, kind, hard-working and Ellie knew he would try to make her happy.

And she would make him happy — *she would*, she told herself. A little shiver ran across her shoulders and she thought someone had opened the door. She turned, but there was no one there. As she settled to work, she promised herself she wouldn't put off telling Alex what she had decided. And there was something else she couldn't put off either. She must confess her past. If this marriage was to work, there must be no secrets between them. Alex deserved total honesty.

Norah smiled across the table at Trevor. He was looking very pleased with himself — as well he might, she thought. A new business and a new wife — both in one day. Well, not quite. They wouldn't be able to get married until his divorce was final. But that shouldn't take long, now that she'd persuaded Trevor to allow her name to be cited in the petition. He had tried to protect her from Gloria's vindictiveness, never staying the night at the cottage and refusing to let her remain at the café after it was closed. After all, Gloria had left him and he didn't see why he should be the guilty party in the divorce.

But it had dragged on too long. Norah wanted it all settled — neither of them was getting any younger after all. And if it meant she had to bear the brunt of any scandal, she could put up with that. Trevor had needed quite a lot of persuading though, the dear old-fashioned man that he was.

She touched his hand as he spread the papers across the table, the deeds and inventory of their new business.

He smiled up at her. "Happy, love?"

Norah nodded. She hadn't been this happy for years, not since Bob had come home from the war, a shadow of his former self. That should have been a new beginning, but she had always had a queer feeling that it wasn't meant to be. Now, after the years of loneliness she was being given a second chance.

"You're sure you're gonna like Southwold? I mean, you've always lived in and around Chelmsford. It won't be too much of a change will it?" Trevor's brown eyes gazed into hers anxiously.

"I love it — I've always wanted to live by the seaside." Norah sighed with pleasure. She'd never dreamed it would really happen. Trev's café was sold, she'd given notice to her landlord and by Christmas they'd be in their new home. She wasn't going to wait until Trevor was free to marry before moving in with him. As far as their new neighbours were concerned they were already man and wife.

The little cottage on the seafront near the pier was ideal for turning into a tearoom. And there was a spare room so that Julie could come and stay in the holidays if she wanted to. The planning permission for the tearooms was all settled and they would make a start on the work in the new year. By the time the summer

224

visitors arrived in the picturesque little Suffolk town, they would be ready to open.

And it would be no greasy-spoon café either — not like Trev's Transport. They would serve good wholesome home-made food, Trevor's pies and pasties and Norah's cakes and scones. There'd be no opening at the crack of dawn either, or staying open all hours. They'd still have to work hard of course. But with Trevor at her side, Norah wouldn't mind that.

The only worry was Helen — Ellie as she now liked to be called. "Do you think she'll be upset?" she asked.

"Why should she? She must have realized something was up."

"I've been afraid to say anything until it was all settled. I don't know how I'm going to break it to her that she'll have to find somewhere else to live."

Trevor put his arm round Norah. "She'll be all right, love. Didn't you say the boss had proposed to her?"

"But suppose she turns him down."

"She's not that daft," Trevor said with a laugh. "Besides, if she does, she can always come and live with us in Southwold."

Norah gave a little laugh. "She won't want to do that. I can't see her working in a café again now that she's doing so well at Turner's. She'll be able afford a flat in Chelmsford." She sighed as she heard the click of the front gate and Ellie's heels clicking on the stone path.

Ellie hadn't expected to see Norah back yet and had been so preoccupied with her own thoughts that she hadn't noticed Trevor's van parked on the grass outside.

She'd been surprised when Norah told her Trevor was closing the café for the day and taking her to Southwold. They'd been there several times on Sundays throughout the summer, taking Ellie with them once or twice. It wasn't like Trevor to take a day off in the week though, especially a wet autumn day like today.

Now, her own news went right out of her head as she stopped just inside the door, looking from Norah to Trevor and waiting for one of them to speak. They both looked like naughty schoolkids caught out in some prank — part guilty, part excited.

Ellie looked at Norah. "Go on, tell me," she said.

"Trev's bought a café in Southwold. We'll be moving up there in a month or two."

Ellie squealed with pleasure and gave Norah an unrestrained hug, then turned to Trevor and hugged him too. He blushed a little and ran his hand through what remained of his hair. "Don't know what she sees in a boring old codger like me," he said with an embarrassed grin.

"I do," Ellie said warmly. "She's a very lucky woman — and you're a lucky man. And I hope you'll both be happy in your new life."

Norah was looking worried. "But what about you, love. I feel awful — as if we're turning you out on the street."

"You mustn't feel that way," Ellie said sincerely. "Besides, I've got some news of my own. I'm getting married too."

"You said yes," Norah squealed.

After that the evening got rather noisy. Norah got out the bottle of gin she kept for special occasions and they drank toast after toast. Norah and Trevor were so happy that Ellie was relieved they didn't seem to notice she wasn't celebrating quite as enthusiastically as her friends.

Later, as she lay in bed listening to Trevor's old van coughing its way down the lane, she wished she hadn't blurted it out like that. She hadn't even told Alex her decision. As she drifted into sleep she realized that marriage to Alex would solve the problem of where she would live. But was that a reason to accept his proposal?

Alex was in the laboratory when Ellie arrived at work next day. But he came into the office seconds after she'd hung her coat up.

"I heard you arrive. I don't want to rush you, Ellie, but I need to know. Have you thought any more about . . .?"

"Oh, Alex, please . . ."

"I'm sorry." He shook his head. "There isn't anyone else, is there?"

"No, Alex. I would have said." Ellie felt herself flushing and gave a mental shake of her head. Stupid to hold on to dreams of Harry. It had been so long now, and besides, he probably had a couple of children by now.

Alex sighed and turned away. "Better get on with some work then." He went back into the laboratory and

Ellie sat down at her desk, trying hard to concentrate on the column of figures in front of her. She had intended to give Alex his answer today. She was fond of him and they worked well together. But now her mind was in turmoil again.

She typed frantically for a few minutes, then muttered under her breath. Another mistake. She ripped the sheet of paper out of the machine and screwed it up just as Alex opened the door. He was holding a fabric sample, his expression grim.

"What's wrong?" she asked, her own concerns temporarily forgotten.

"Another failure, that's what," he said, handing her the material.

"This one looks OK. I don't understand," she said.

"Yes, I really thought we'd done it this time. But do you know how long it took, just to weave this small sample? It kept unravelling; we couldn't seem to maintain the twist on the yarn."

Alex explained that they'd tried several different synthetic fibres, twisted with the raw silk in different weights but there was always something not quite right, whichever proportions they used.

"We've tried just about everything," he said, pacing the floor.

Ellie fingered the material, deep in thought. "I know this probably sounds silly," she said hesitantly. "Have you tried — no, I'm sure you would already have thought —"

"What, what? Tell me. I'll try anything once," Alex interrupted.

"Well, let's see if I've got this right. You make the synthetic yarn on Donald's machine, adjusting the spinnerets to make different weights — deniers — right?"

Alex nodded. "Go on."

"Then when you've got a length of yarn, you take a length of the raw silk and throw them together." Ellie paused. She wanted to put this in the right way, so that it made sense. "Have you tried mixing them up before you put them through Donald's machine?" She was watching Alex's face, sure that he'd burst out laughing.

But he didn't laugh. He didn't tell her she was a genius either.

"No, no. Forget it. It's a silly idea," she said, wishing she'd kept her mouth shut.

But Alex's thoughtful frown turned to a wide grin. He leapt up and threw open the door to the lab. "Donald, Don, listen. I think the fair Ellie's cracked it for us." He turned round and blew her a kiss, his face red with excitement. Then he closed the door with a bang.

Ellie couldn't help being pleased that she might have been of some help. This was what she liked about Alex, his enthusiasm. She hoped the experiment turned out well. He deserved to be successful.

The two men were hunched over the spinning machine, which broke down the chemicals and heated them to the right consistency before passing them through the spinnerets. They didn't look up when Ellie put her head round the door to say she was going home. Alex continued to scribble notes in the little book that he carried everywhere, while Donald carefully dismantled the machine. As he worked he spoke in a low fast voice, explaining what he was doing and Alex nodded agreement.

Neither of them seemed aware of her presence and Ellie couldn't help thinking that, despite his seeming eagerness, marriage now seemed to be the last thing on his mind.

"I'm off — goodnight," she said again in a louder voice.

"'Night," they both said, without turning round.

When she got home there was no sign of Norah but a note propped up by the teapot in the middle of the kitchen table said that she was staying at Trevor's for the night. Ellie smiled but the smile was tinged with sadness. How she'd miss her friends when they left for their new life.

She turned the wireless on for company and took her coat off. She didn't feel like cooking supper just for herself. She looked round the cosy kitchen, suddenly realizing that it wasn't cosy any more. Norah had already started sorting things out and packing for the move and, without the little ornaments and knick-knacks which usually crowded the windowsill and shelves, the room looked bare and unwelcoming.

As she paced the room, she realized that, despite her interesting job and her growing pleasure in being able to use her artistic talents, she was really quite lonely. Yes, she had friends. She didn't know how she would have got through these last years without Trevor and Norah's love and support. And there were Jackie and the other girls at the mill, Fred and Donald — and Alex. What was she going to do about Alex?

She sighed and got the bowl of eggs out of the pantry. As she beat them into a froth, there was a knock at the door. Alex stood there, a broad smile on his face. He swept her into his arms and swung her round. "You did it, Ellie — we did it."

"What?" She struggled to free herself. "Alex, what's got into you?"

"The new thread — it worked."

"It wasn't a stupid idea, then?" She took his arm and led him into the cottage. "I was just cooking myself some supper. Come in and tell me all about it."

He followed her into the little parlour and sat down in Norah's old armchair.

"I'll just go and finish off in the kitchen. You will join me? It's only scrambled eggs." Ellie guessed that Alex hadn't bothered to eat.

She left him gazing into the fire and hurriedly prepared the meal. Instead of laying the kitchen table she brought the food into the parlour on a tray. Alex had closed his eyes but he sat up quickly as she put the tray down on a low table between them.

"Sorry, I'm shattered. We've been working flat out on this," he said.

"You must eat though." Ellie passed him a plate and a knife and fork. He began to devour the food and she looked on, amused. Between bites, he told her about the experiments. "Donald was still there when I left, working out the calculations for recalibrating the machine. And he's got an idea of how we can break down the raw silk and mix it with the liquid chemical before extruding it through the nozzles on the spinneret." Alex stopped speaking and grinned at her. "It's all down to you, Ellie."

She flushed with pleasure. "You would have got there in the end — I know you would."

"Well, there's a lot of testing to do yet," Alex said. He put down his knife and fork and leaned across to put the plate on the tray. "That was delicious — a good cook too."

The flush on Ellie's face deepened and she looked away. He stood up. "Perhaps I'd better go. It's been a long day. I just wanted to thank you."

She didn't try to stop him although she had enjoyed his company and dreaded the rest of the evening alone in the cottage.

At the door he took her hand and drew her towards him. "We make a good team, Ellie. Have you thought any more . . . ?"

On impulse she leaned towards him. "Yes, Alex. I will marry you."

CHAPTER
NINETEEN

Ellie and Alex were married in the village church at Little Howe a month after his proposal. He hadn't wanted to wait — the house was ready and Ellie herself would have had to leave Norah's cottage by the end of January when she and Trevor moved to Southwold. By the time Ellie and Alex returned from their Italian honeymoon, they would be firmly settled in their new life, with only Rex, the old Alsatian dog, to remind them of Trev's Transport Café.

Everyone from Turner's was invited to the reception in the village hall. Trevor gave Ellie away, with Jackie as bridesmaid and Don as best man. Norah looked on as proudly as any mother as Ellie floated down the aisle on Trevor's arm, turning to smile gratefully at the woman who had indeed been a mother to her over the past few years.

Ellie managed to swallow a sob as she thought of her own mother. Clinging to Alex's arm, she managed to convince herself, for the moment at least, that she'd done the right thing. Her new life beckoned — the door was firmly closed on the old.

She still hadn't told Alex everything, her resolution draining away at the horror of revealing the real reason why she'd run away from home, cutting herself off from her family. Alex had nodded understandingly when she told him of her sister's involvement with the dubious nightclub owner and her fears that she would be drawn into that shadowy world. But when it came to putting into words the reality of Bert's assaults on her body, she just couldn't find the words, the remembered shame and fear choking in her throat. And she hadn't mentioned Harry at all. Her feelings for him were still mixed up in her mind with the awful things her father had said to her on that dreadful night.

So she had let Alex think she'd run away to escape being forced to work in her brother-in-law's nightclub and he had reassured her that the past was irrelevant. He loved her and their future together was the only thing that mattered now.

And, as Ellie had sat by his side at the reception in the village hall, responding to the teasing and laughter of their friends with a flushed and smiling face, looking round at the people she now thought of as her family, the future had indeed seemed rosy.

How quickly things had changed — and how devastating the realization, when it was too late, of the terrible mistake she had made.

Now, two years later, she was rapidly reaching her breaking-strain; like one of the threads being tested on the machine at the mill, she was stretched as far as she could go. She wasn't sure whether she could go on much longer. She *should* be happy, she told herself, as she gazed round the elegant room, blinking as the sun struck prisms off the cut-crystal vase on its low table by the window and bounced across the polished wooden floor. She had a loving husband, a beautiful home, everything a girl could wish for. She even had her own little car bought with her own money, a pale-blue Morris Minor, tucked away in the garage. The evidence of her success in breaking away from the past was all around her. Nothing remained in her life to remind her of those earlier struggles. But she was beginning to realize it all meant nothing.

Alex's house — she still couldn't think of it as her own — had originally been a farmhouse, a long, low rambling building, added to over the years to create a delightful jumble of rooms and passageways, odd little corners and stairways. It was the sort of house Ellie had often dreamed of. But Alex had chosen the furnishings before their marriage and she had never really felt at home, although he had told her to feel free to make any changes she wanted. But she couldn't summon up sufficient interest to do so.

Ellie sighed and moved restlessly. It wasn't the house that was the problem. It was Alex. She didn't blame him — no other man would have been so patient for so long. But his patience was showing signs of running out.

She thought back to their honeymoon in Italy when she'd been so sure that everything would work out for the best. She enjoyed Alex's company as he showed her the sights of Rome and Florence, delighting in seeing at first hand the paintings and sculptures so familiar from books and prints. Later, as they sat drinking wine or coffee at outdoor cafés, Ellie wished the days would never end.

It was the nights she had dreaded — and still did. She had hoped things would improve in time but, despite his unfailing patience and understanding, their relationship had gone from bad to worse, so that now she was at the end of her tether. And she knew Alex felt the same.

Ellie shook her head and bit her lip to stop the sob escaping. She had tried — God knows she had tried. During the day she would tell herself that this time it would be different. Alex loved her — and she was fond of him, wanted to please him. He had given her so much. Surely it wasn't too much to expect that she should give herself to him in return?

That first night together, she hadn't even given it a thought, looking forward to the time when they would be alone. Unlike many girls of her age, she wasn't apprehensive of what was to come. After all, she wasn't some gently-brought-up young maiden ignorant of the facts of life. And she had enjoyed Alex's kisses and caresses before their marriage — provided he didn't try to go too far. When she had pulled away he had laughed and said, "I can wait, darling. I understand if you want to save yourself for our wedding night. Our love will be all the sweeter for the waiting."

She had kissed him fervently, believing it to be true. Marriage — lovemaking — with Alex would wash away the bitterness and hurt of the past.

In their honeymoon hotel room she had gone into his arms willingly, opening her lips to his passionate kisses,

236

pressing herself against his hard masculine body, her own flushed and rosy through the thin silk as he ran his hands down her back and over her buttocks. When he slipped the flimsy nightdress down over her shoulders, letting it slide to the floor, she was ready for him.

But, as he laid her on the bed and lowered himself beside her, taking her in his arms, it was as if an icy wind had entered the room. She began to shiver and she had to clench her teeth to stop them chattering. Perhaps mistaking her reaction for a shudder of desire, Alex had rolled over on to her, unable to hold back his own fierce need.

Ellie had lain beneath him, unseeing eyes fixed on the corner of the room. When it was over, he had stroked her damp hair away from her face, kissing her neck tenderly. "I didn't hurt you, did I, my darling?" he murmured.

"No. It's all right, Alex. I'm all right," she whispered back. Turning away from him, she bit hard on her knuckles as slow tears slid down her cheek.

When she woke next morning to the cacophony of revving engines and impatient horns outside their Rome hotel, for a brief moment she was back in her attic room above the shop in Kendall Street. She stretched and rolled over, flinching away as her naked body encountered the warmth of another.

Then it all flooded back. She was in bed with her husband — and she knew at that moment that she should never have married him.

If only she had someone to talk to, she thought now. But Jackie had married her Dave and now lived the other side of Ipswich, busy with her baby son and another child on the way. And she couldn't talk to Norah about her problems.

The last time she had visited the Ridleys Norah had given a knowing smile. "Landed on your feet there, girl," she said. "You're a lucky one."

Ellie had smiled and nodded agreement. What else could she do? How could she confide in her friend that the merest touch of Alex's hand, the soft breath of his lips against her cheek, turned her to marble?

How she wished things were different. She had tried to explain to him how she felt but it was hard to put into words and, for the first few months at least, he had persisted in thinking that somehow the fault was his.

Just lately though, he'd become impatient and when the inevitable tensing of her body communicated itself to him, instead of trying to coax her as he usually did, he would fling himself away, sitting on the edge of the bed, his head in his hands.

Last night he'd grabbed her shoulders, his eyes blazing. "Christ, Ellie — you drive a man to . . . I'm not trying to rape you, for God's sake. But you're my wife, I want, I need . . ." He pushed her away with a stifled groan.

She could only whisper that she was sorry, the tears running unchecked down her cheeks. But he seemed unmoved and had got up, leaving her to sleep alone.

This morning he'd seemed his usual self, dropping a kiss on top of her head before helping himself to toast and coffee and immersing himself in the morning paper.

After he'd left for the mill, Ellie tidied up the kitchen, reluctant to do too much — she had to leave something for Mrs Mills to do. She would like to have done the housework herself — at least it would help fill the long days. But Alex had insisted that they keep the housekeeper on. If only he'd let her work. Naïvely, she had assumed that she would carry on as Alex's secretary, as well as continuing to build up her silk-scarf business. Why shouldn't things go on as before — at least until she started a family?

It had come as a shock to find someone else sitting at her desk when she entered the office after returning from their honeymoon.

"You'll have more time for your painting," Alex told her when she protested. "Besides, the business is doing well. You don't need to work."

It was true. The problems with the new "silkene" thread had been ironed out and the old looms adapted to weave the fabric. The disused buildings had been renovated and the thread was once more spun on the premises — as it had been when Turners produced all their goods, from silk-moth cocoon to finished material. The firm was prospering and Alex made it clear that he was in a position to support his wife in luxury.

Ellie, needing something to distract her from the disaster she now knew her marriage to be, fought for her independence. Alex, wanting her to be happy, had the old stables converted into a studio. But she couldn't help feeling it was like a consolation prize and besides, she could no longer summon up any enthusiasm for her art. Maybe if she had a child to love it would take away this dreadful ache, which never seemed to go away.

Ellie sighed, knowing what was at the root of her depression. This morning she had woken once again to the knowledge that she wasn't pregnant. She blamed herself, wondering whether something inside had been damaged when her father assaulted her. The doctor had said there was nothing wrong, but then, she hadn't confided her deepest fear even to him.

She opened the back door and picked her way across the lawn, her feet squelching on the soggy turf. Even the surly monosyllables which passed for conversation with George, the gardener, would be preferable to the silence indoors.

He scarcely looked up in response to her determinedly cheerful "good morning" and, after a few remarks about the weather and the state of the garden, Ellie gave up and walked through the gate at the side of the house towards her studio. No expense had been spared in fitting it out and she had all the frames, dye baths and other equipment she could possibly need — now that she no longer had the inclination to use them.

She entered the light airy room for the first time for weeks, telling herself she must snap out of it, find something to fill the empty hours. It was no good mooning around hoping that everything would come right one day. In the past she'd always taken positive action to solve her problems. But what could she do this time? Other than running away again, the solution seemed to be beyond her.

240

As she stood in the doorway, she seemed to hear her grandmother's voice: *"Don't give up, girl. You're strong, like your mum. Look at all she's had to put up with over the years — she never ran away, just made the best of things, like you must."*

"Make the best of things!" It was hard, but she would do it. Fired with new determination, Ellie walked over to one of the frames which stood under the window. On it was a half-finished painting. She hadn't touched it since before Christmas, and a film of dust now dulled the brightness of the colours. She brushed her hand over it, almost absent-mindedly. Art had always been her solace. Why shouldn't it work its magic now?

Perhaps it was because there was no incentive. She didn't need to earn a living and she had no one to prove anything to. However successful she was, her family would never know — the name Helen Cameron would mean nothing to them. For the first time for weeks a spontaneous bubble of laughter rose in her throat. Helen Cameron was still Ellie Tyler at heart — and who did she think she was, anyway?

Another little voice made itself heard. She could still paint — there were galleries in Chelmsford and Colchester. Surely Alex couldn't object. It wasn't as if she'd be "working". Perhaps she could make Alex understand that she didn't want to paint pretty pictures as a hobby. Like him, she needed to be *doing* something that engaged her brain as well as her aesthetic senses?

Like most men of his generation, Alex seemed to think that caring for home and husband — and in time their children — was enough for a woman. It wasn't as if they needed the money, he'd said.

It was all right for him, Ellie thought. Not content with the success of "silkene" he and Donald were looking for ways to improve the yarn and were working on a new type of fabric which meant long hours spent at the mill. Ellie wouldn't have minded if only, when he came home, he would share his enthusiasm with her, talk about his experiments as he had in the days when she'd been his secretary and assistant. But he fobbed her off, intimating that she wouldn't understand.

Now, she brushed her hand across the half-finished panel again, disturbing the cloud of dust, She picked up a soft brush and, hardly thinking, carefully cleaned the silk. She inspected the tins of dye which had lain undisturbed on their shelf for so many weeks.

Before long she was immersed in her work, scarcely noticing as the sun crept lower in the sky and the afternoon drew to a close. It was only when it was too dark to work that she threw down her brush and looked at her almost finished work with a glow of satisfaction. Tomorrow she would make an early start and get it finished. She couldn't wait to start on the next one; her head was buzzing with shapes and colours. And she didn't care what Alex said. Would he know, or even care, what she got up to in the long, lonely hours that he was away?

Ellie tried not to feel too disappointed as she left the shop and pushed her way through the crowds which thronged Colchester's narrow High Street. It was only

242

what she'd expected — although she'd set out full of confidence.

She'd tried four shops already and no one seemed to be interested. No — that wasn't strictly true. Two of the buyers she'd spoken to had been very impressed with her samples. But one had indicated that, because they were individual designs, there would only be a limited number available and therefore would be too expensive for his shop. And the other had been very enthusiastic until she told him that she could not produce them in the quantities he wanted.

"Why don't you get the design printed on to the material and run off as many as you can sell? I'd buy them in bulk — at the right price," he said. "You've got to produce them in quantity if you want to make a profit."

She agreed — up to a point — but the whole idea was that no two of her scarves were alike. She could tailor the design to what the customer wanted — like an art commission in fact. After all, silk painting was still only a hobby.

But was it? Since the day she'd picked up her brushes again she had begun to feel like her old self. Even the problems with Alex had faded now that she had something else to think about. Her old ambitions were stirring once more. Painting scarves wasn't just something to fill the empty hours. If she could sell just a few it would prove to Alex and everyone else who'd laughed at her ambitions how wrong they'd been.

Ellie turned into a narrow lane just off the High Street. She might as well try one more shop before giving up. *Sylvia — Accessories*, was painted in flowing script over the blue-painted shop front. It was just the sort of shop Ellie had imagined selling her scarves, its window draped in purple velvet with a matching hat, handbag and gloves tastefully arranged in the centre, a chiffon scarf thrown artistically across the bag. But it wasn't a patch on any of hers, Ellie thought. She hoped the shop owner would agree.

Thirty minutes later she was drinking Earl Grey out of delicate bone china, trying to give the impression that she had business meetings like this every day of the week. Her samples were spread across the table in the back room and Mrs Marshall, the shop's proprietor — "Call me Sylvia, dear" — was enthusing about the colours and designs as she ran a pale-blue-and-mint-green scarf through her long slim fingers.

"I was trained as a milliner and it was always my dream to have my own little shop," she told Ellie. "But so few ladies wear hats nowadays — except to weddings. So I've started branching out into other accessories — even a bit of costume jewellery. I want to expand my stock even more and your scarves are just the thing. So individual, dear."

When she left the shop, promising to deliver a dozen scarves by the following week, Ellie could hardly stop herself leaping in the air and shouting for joy. The silly grin was still on her face when she started up her car.

Sylvia had asked her if *Helene* scarves would be exclusive to her shop. Ellie didn't want to be restricted to one outlet. "Exclusive to Colchester," she said, thinking quickly.

Sylvia had smiled happily. "I'll mention that in my advert in next week's local paper," she said.

It had been Norah's idea to give Ellie's "creations" as she called them a name. "You must have your own label," she'd said, suggesting she use her name. Now each scarf was signed *Helene* in the corner — with an "e" because it looked more classy, as Norah said.

As she drove through the country lanes, her mind busy with new designs, she itched to get home and take up her paintbrushes. Her success in Colchester was the start of a new phase in her life. Next week she'd try Ipswich, maybe London — not her old home ground but exclusive West End shops. She couldn't wait to get home and tell Alex her news, hoping he'd be pleased for her. But something told her not to say anything just yet.

When she opened the front door she was greeted with silence. Mrs Mills had gone home, leaving a casserole simmering on the Aga and a note on the table saying that Alex had phoned to say he would be late.

Disappointed, Ellie sat down to her own meal. She was just finishing when the phone rang.

"Sorry, darling. Crisis at the Manchester plant. I've got to rush up there. Hope to be back tomorrow if I can sort things out."

"Do you have to go tonight?"

"If I drive up now, I'll miss the worst of the traffic and be ready to start first thing." He gave a short laugh. "Don't say you'll miss me."

"Of course I will," she replied.

"I phoned earlier. Where were you?"

"Colchester." Ellie was about to tell him her news but he laughed again.

"Spending my hard-earned money, eh?" He laughed. "Must go. See you tomorrow but if I can't get back, I'll ring. You will be in, won't you?"

She put the phone down and went back to the dining room. She couldn't quite put her finger on it but Alex hadn't sounded his usual self. It wasn't unusual for him to go away on business and, in a way, she was relieved. Perhaps now wasn't the right time to tell him she was going into business for herself.

CHAPTER
TWENTY

Harry was working even longer hours in the market. Sid was still unwell and he had taken over the more arduous work of running the stall. Leaving Sid to serve the customers, he did all the setting up, the dismantling of the stall and packing away at the end of the day. Recently, he'd started doing the books as well.

If only Sid would admit that he'd never be able to work full-time again, they could find someone else to take over the pitch. Then Harry could look for a "proper job" doing something he enjoyed. He still hoped to work with cars one day. But Sid was determinedly cheerful in the face of his recurring stomach problems and swore he'd be "back on his feet" before long. Until then, Harry continued to keep things ticking over for his mate.

Today he was worried about Mary too and had popped home to make sure she was all right. He crossed the landing to her room. She was lying on top of the bed, fully dressed, her hands clasped across her stomach. Even in the dim light filtering through the partly closed curtains, he could see she was in pain.

"You must see a doctor, Mum." The old name that he seldom used now slipped out. She *was* his mum in all but blood ties. He laid his hand on her arm, smiling down at her.

"I'm OK, son. Just needed a rest, that's all, but I should get up. I'm due on the ward this evening."

"Oh no, you're not. I'll phone from the box on the corner — tell them you're sick. You're in no condition to be running around with bedpans."

Mary didn't argue and, as Harry went down the echoing stairs and through the empty shop, he thought she must be really ill to take time off work. Why shouldn't she, when Bert was earning good money at the Club? He always seemed to have money to splash around — although Harry knew he was prone to being "a bit short" when the rent was due, or when Mary desperately needed something like a new winter coat. Although she only worked part-time now, Mary had told him she needed the little bit of security it gave her, and he could understand that.

After phoning the hospital he hurried across the road to the market, pushing his way through the crowds thronging the stalls. The cacophony of horns blaring, lively chatter and the stallholders' raucous patter was music to his ears.

Sid was inundated with customers and he greeted Harry with relief. "It's been bedlam 'ere, mate," he gasped. "Am I glad to see yer — I need a breather."

Harry finished weighing out the potatoes and tipped them into the woman's waiting bag, topped it with a hearty cabbage and a pound of cooking apples. He totted the money up in his head and gave her change, then turned without pause to the next in line.

248

Half an hour later there was a pause and Harry turned to Sid, who was sitting on an upturned orange box. "You OK, mate?"

"Bin overdoin' it. The doc told me, no lifting 'eavy weights." He gave a short laugh. "Ow does 'e expect a fruit and veg man to avoid 'eavy liftin'? Them spud sacks are no joke."

"You should've waited for me to come back. Sorry I was so long," Harry apologized.

"Mary all right, is she?" Sid asked, his kindly face creased in concern.

"I'm worried. She ought to see the doctor — but you know Mary — stubborn as hell."

"Well, tell 'er not to leave it too long — like I did. They said at the 'ospital, if I'd gone sooner they could've done more for me." He put his hand on Harry's arm. "You don't think she's got my trouble, do yer?"

Despite several operations, Sid continued to lose weight and often seemed to be in pain and Harry knew his old friend was more ill than he let on. He would never tell anyone exactly what the doctors had said, but Harry had his suspicions.

He hastened to reassure him, knowing how fond Sid was of Mary. "I'm sure it's nothing too serious." He coloured a little. "It's just — women's trouble. You know."

Sid nodded in understanding. "Still, she oughter get 'erself sorted out. Don't do to leave these things — you tell 'er from me."

Harry turned to serve another customer, glad for once that the crowd was thinning out. Maybe he'd be able to get off early for a change. He turned back to Sid and suggested he go home. "You look knackered, mate. I can finish up here," he said.

When he got back to the flat, it was dark and chilly and he realized he'd forgotten to bank up the range before leaving. He riddled the dead ashes and carefully relit the fire, waiting until he was sure it had caught, before going into the next room to check on Mary. She was still lying on top of the bed as he'd left her and he tucked a blanket round her. Best let her sleep, he thought.

As he went downstairs to fill the coal bucket, the side door opened and Bert came in. He grinned at Harry. "Still runnin' around after that lazy mare?" he asked.

Harry brushed past without replying.

When he got back upstairs, Bert was sprawled at the kitchen table. "No grub ready, I see."

Harry stared him down, remembering how as a small boy he'd been intimidated by this nasty little man. But no more. Even for Mary's sake he wouldn't keep quiet.

"Always thinking of yourself," he said. "What about Mary? She's in bed — sick. You haven't even asked how she is." He turned away and threw coal on to the fire, his knuckles white on the handle of the shovel.

Bert backed down, as he'd known he would. "I thought she was at work," he mumbled.

"She's too ill to go to work. You'll have to get yourself something to eat. I'm going to see if she's OK."

250

Mary still appeared to be sleeping but she opened her eyes. "Back so soon? I'll get you some tea."

"No you won't. I'll get some fish'n'chips later. How do you feel now?"

Mary struggled upright. "A bit better. It's OK if I don't move around too much."

"Well, you stay there, I'll fetch you a cuppa."

Bert was having a wash at the kitchen sink — too lazy to go downstairs and use the bathroom — and he moved grudgingly aside to allow Harry to fill the kettle. He slicked his hair down with Brylcreem and put his jacket on. "I'm off," he announced.

Harry banged the kettle down on the cooker. That selfish bastard hadn't even looked in on his wife. Concentrating on getting the teapot out of the cupboard, laying a tray with cup and saucer, a plate with a couple of biscuits to tempt Mary's appetite, he knew at that moment he was quite capable of going after Bert and giving him a good hiding.

When his breathing was back to normal he took the tray into the bedroom, almost dropping it when he saw Mary sitting on the edge of the bed, doubled over in pain, her face grey and beaded with sweat.

He had a long wait before the doctor appeared, his steps echoing in the long empty corridor. "Are you the next of kin?" he asked.

"Not exactly. I'm her foster son — I'm not sure where her husband is at the moment. He went out just before she collapsed."

251

"Well, I ought to have a word with him. We're going to have to operate. Tell him to come in as soon as he can — I'm on duty all night."

"I'll try and get hold of him," Harry said, then blurted out, "Can I see her? She's going to be all right, isn't she?"

"Oh, I'm sure she is. But I think we ought to let her rest now. Come back at visiting time tomorrow." The doctor was already turning away. "And don't forget to let her husband know."

"Sod Bert," Harry muttered as he went down the stairs and crossed the entrance lobby. "He doesn't care anyway." Scarcely reassured by what the doctor had said, Harry wasn't sure what to do next. He couldn't just go home and wait.

He spotted a telephone near the door. Sheila — he ought to let her know her mother was ill. Not that she could do anything at this time of night and with two little kiddies to look after. But he'd feel better talking to someone.

He fumbled in his pocket for some coppers, struggling to remember the number. Sheila didn't sound unduly worried when he told her what had happened.

"Lots of women have the same trouble," she said airily. "She'll be fine once she's had the operation." She rang off after promising to come to the hospital the next day.

Reluctant to go back to the empty flat, Harry walked through the deserted streets. It was much later than he'd realized — he must have been at the hospital hours. He cut across the tarmac play-area in front of

252

the flats where Mary's mother had lived for such a short time, and where her Auntie Vi still lived. He ought to let her know too, he thought. But no lights showed in the twelve-storey block which dwarfed the remaining terraced houses around it. Harry smiled, remembering Ellie's description of the lit-up flats as fairytale castles. In the dark, they could be anything your imagination wanted them to be. The smile changed to a twisted grimace as he wondered yet again where Ellie could be, wishing there was some way he could let her know how ill her mother was.

Beneath the sadness of missing her, as he still did even after all this time, Harry felt a surge of anger. However unhappy she'd been, she shouldn't have hurt her mother like that. The anger helped mask his worry that something must have happened to her. He could understand her cutting herself off from him, but to lose touch with her mother so completely . . .

He sighed and turned the corner, passing the deserted market and quickening his steps as he neared home. He must get some sleep, otherwise he'd never get up in the morning, and Sid was depending on him to do the Covent Garden run.

The flat appeared to be deserted. Bert was at the club of course. He stumbled upstairs, but before entering his own room he opened the door to the room that had been Ellie's. Reminders of her were everywhere — her paintings pinned to the walls, her school blazer still hanging behind the door. He sighed — he must make one more effort to find her — and not just for Mary's sake either.

CHAPTER
TWENTY-ONE

Ellie lined up the sheets of silk, taut in their wooden frames, and switched on the overhead spotlights, adjusting each one to shine directly on to the painting. She stepped back to let Alex see.

"These are excellent, but what else could I expect from my talented wife?" He dropped a kiss on her head. "I don't want you overdoing things, though."

She ignored his condescending tone. Since she'd told him she was pregnant, he treated her as if she might break. At least the tension between them had lessened and she didn't want to jeopardize the fragile thread that held them together.

She smiled. "Painting relaxes me," she said. "I was a bit worried about these though — it's the first time I've tried anything really modern or abstract."

"We must get some proper frames made," Alex said, pointing. "I like that one — it'll look good on the dining room wall over the fireplace."

Ellie bit back a reply. She'd been working on the new designs for several weeks and, although Alex seemed pleased that she'd regained her usual zest for life, he still treated her art as if it were a hobby. She knew she should have told him about her commissions for Sylvia

254

before now but the opportunity hadn't arisen. Besides, he wasn't really interested. All he could think about was the baby and whether she was taking care of herself.

Would it do any good to try again — to make him see that she needed more than just being a wife and mother? She took a deep breath. "Alex, I've had an idea," she said as if she had only just thought of it. "Why don't we use some of these designs on the new fabric?"

He frowned. "I don't think so. The plain material is doing well. Besides, Don and I have some ideas of our own."

"But Alex —"

"No, Ellie, you won't have time for all that once the baby comes."

Ellie bit back her reply but later, as they sat down to their meal, she decided to try again. Before she could frame the words, Alex raised his glass and smiled at her across the table. "Here's to my beautiful, clever wife," he said.

Smiling, she took a small sip of wine. Perhaps this wasn't the right moment. It was good to see Alex looking so happy. To him, the coming baby had set the seal on their marriage. It would be stupid to spoil things.

But he had to know about her business venture some time. Her hand-painted scarves were now being sold in exclusive shops in Ipswich and Norwich as well as Sylvia's in Colchester and she'd recently been in touch with one of the new boutiques in London. How could she keep it secret now that demand for her work was increasing? She'd even started reproducing her designs in bulk ready for the expected influx of orders. At one time she'd have asked Alex for help but, wary of his reaction, she had found a screen printer in Chelmsford who had agreed to run off small numbers to start with.

Deep in thought, she didn't notice he was staring at her, one eyebrow raised. "Is everything all right, darling? You looked a little worried."

"Everything's fine." She touched his hand, hesitated. "Alex, I've something to tell you."

Before she could continue he squeezed her fingers. "It's not the baby, is it?"

"No — I told you, everything's fine." She took a deep breath, wondering why she felt so nervous. She hadn't done anything wrong.

"You know how much the girls at the mill liked my scarves. Well, I made some more. And when I went into this lovely little shop in Colchester, the woman there admired the one I was wearing. She asked me where I bought it."

"Don't tell me she wanted you to make one for her," Alex said with an indulgent smile.

"No, she wanted me to make half a dozen — for her shop."

"Very flattering, darling. I hope you refused."

"Of course I was flattered but I didn't see any harm in agreeing to make a few scarves for Sylvia — exclusive to her shop. I've been wanting to do something like this for ages."

"But why? You're my wife, you have this house, our baby soon. Isn't that enough for you?"

"The baby's not due for months and Mrs Mills does everything in the house." She paused. "I get bored, Alex. I'm not used to a life of leisure."

"I don't understand you, Ellie. Most girls would give anything for the kind of life you have. Look at those mill girls, and your friend Norah — ask them if they'd like a life of leisure."

"I didn't think you'd understand," Ellie said, pushing her chair back. She rushed out of the room.

Upstairs she sat at her dressing-table, brushing her hair with furious strokes, fighting to hold back the tears. She wished she'd kept quiet now but she already had enough secrets from Alex. Besides, she understood in a way. He was concerned about her — and the baby.

She looked up as he came into the room and carried on brushing, looking at him in the mirror.

After a few moments he said, "I didn't mean to upset you, darling, but you must see things from my point of view. I'm the factory owner. I can't have you producing things in competition with me. Besides, what's the point of telling this woman you can supply her when you won't be able to keep it up? She'll want more when those are sold and, once the baby comes, you won't have time for all this nonsense."

"How dare you say it's nonsense," she said. "Besides, she's already sold them and I've promised her a new batch next week."

"You can't do it, Ellie. I forbid you."

"But Alex, I've promised her. I can't let her down."

He sighed. "Well, I suppose it won't hurt. But that's it — no more."

257

As Ellie opened her mouth to protest, he grabbed her wrist. "I mean it. You must think of the baby. I can't let you wear yourself out like this."

Ellie nodded. Let Alex think he'd got his own way. She felt a twinge of guilt — she really had meant to tell him everything.

The next day she phoned Norah, listening with a smile as her friend rattled on about how good life was in their little seaside town. "And what about you, love? Keeping well, are you? I bet you and Alex are excited. Have you thought about names yet?"

"Not really." She paused and took a deep breath. "Actually, we had a row last night. I told him about making the scarves for Sylvia's shop."

"And he didn't like it, I suppose?"

"He called my business nonsense, said I'd forget all about it when the baby comes."

"Maybe you will, love. Babies take up a lot of time. Besides, it was just a hobby wasn't it — something to keep you occupied while Alex was spending so much time at the mill?"

"It's not just a hobby. Why doesn't anyone understand?"

"I do, Ellie. But what about Alex?"

Ellie bit her lip. "I didn't tell him everything. He thinks I just made a few for Sylvia."

"Oh, Ellie. You must tell him everything."

"I can't, Norah. He'll insist I stop. Besides, I'm committed now. I've got an order from a shop in London — a boutique in Carnaby Street."

258

Norah shrieked. "Carnaby Street! I've been reading about those shops and all those weird fashions. Well, I've got to admire your guts, Ellie. But is it worth risking your marriage?"

"I suppose not. But I can't let the shop down now. I'll just have to tell them I can't keep up production." She paused. "I expect you've guessed things aren't right with me and Alex. I've tried to put a brave face on things . . ." Her voice choked on a sob.

"Don't cry, love. I'm sure things will get better once you have the baby."

They spoke for a few more minutes and when she rang off she felt better. She picked up the phone again. There was one more thing she had to do. But she was too late. The editor of the magazine told her regretfully that the issue with the article about her had already gone to press.

How she wished she'd refused to be interviewed when the reporter had got in touch with her. She'd agreed almost without stopping to think. That'll show them, she'd told herself, remembering Auntie Vi's snide comments and her father's taunts. The fact that they were most unlikely ever to see the expensive glossy publication didn't matter. But Alex was sure to hear about it. Should she own up before the article came out?

But she didn't get the chance. When her complimentary copy dropped through the letterbox, Ellie snatched it up, flicking through the pages eagerly. The two-page spread showed her in her studio and there were pictures of her designs including the original one of delicate butterflies and flowers that she'd done for Sylvia.

Later, she bought an extra copy of the magazine to send to Norah, knowing how proud her old friend would be. "It doesn't sound like me at all," she wrote in the accompanying letter. "They've made me out to be a sort of leader of fashion — but I've only copied what everyone else is doing. To be honest I'd rather be painting the more traditional stuff."

A couple of days later she had a reply. "Alex must be so proud of you," Norah wrote.

Ellie bit her lip and glanced up to see Alex watching her. "From Norah?" he asked. "How are they? We must invite them over while the café's closed for the season."

She managed to smile back at him. "I don't think I could cope with visitors the way I am now," she said, putting a hand over her growing bulge. "Maybe after he's born."

"It's up to you, darling," Alex said, getting up from the table and kissing her goodbye.

As he left for the mill he said, as he had every morning since she'd told him about the baby, "Don't go overdoing it now. Remember the doctor said you must rest."

She nodded dutifully, telling herself it was good that he cared, although it still irritated her when he chided her for overdoing things. She'd tried to make him see that it was natural to feel a little tired at the end of the day. And she was a healthy young woman — the doctor had told her there was no reason why she shouldn't carry on normally as long as she felt able to. Sometimes

260

she felt that it wasn't her Alex was concerned about, but the baby.

He probably felt she was putting her work before the welfare of their child, but she didn't see why she couldn't combine a career with motherhood. Her own mother had done it — out of necessity it was true. But Mary had gained a satisfaction and fulfilment from nursing in addition to her very important contribution to the family finances. Ellie didn't need to work — not for money anyway. But she had always felt that her life was incomplete without her art. And earlier this year, when she'd been feeling so depressed, it was her art that had saved her.

Alex didn't mind her doing it in her spare time, but she didn't want to be a hobby artist. There was far more satisfaction in seeing her creativity giving pleasure to others. If it came to it, Ellie wouldn't give in easily. She would fight for what she wanted.

Harry served the queue of customers, automatically exchanging his usual backchat with the regulars, but his heart wasn't in it. Mary was out of hospital but he was worried about her. Even a couple of months after her operation, she was still weak.

She'd been warned to do only light housework, but Harry often came home to find Mary leaning on the edge of the sink, her face pale and drawn, as she struggled to peel potatoes for their evening meal. He did his best to help but there weren't enough hours in the day. If Bert lent a hand, things would be easier. Fat chance, he thought.

As if he didn't have enough to worry about, there was his concern for Sid. He seldom complained, although it was obvious he was in pain and he refused to go to the doctor.

"I don't want to die in 'ospital, 'Arry. I wanna be in me own bed," he said, clutching his stomach, his forehead beaded with sweat, even though the day was freezing.

"You won't die, Sid. They can do wonders nowadays," Harry told him with more conviction than he really felt. He didn't want to believe his old friend was dying but he had a feeling it wouldn't be long.

Sid knew it too, although he continued to make light of his symptoms. He heaved himself up from the chair which Harry had provided to replace the wooden box he'd always used as a seat. "I'm a bit tired, son. You can carry on 'ere, can't yer?"

"Yeah, go home, mate. I'll bring the takings round later," Harry told him. "Won't be able to stay long though."

"Mary still poorly, is she?" Sid asked.

"Not too bad — but she will overdo it. I can't get her to rest."

"That lazy bugger of a husband should pull his weight. I bet 'e don't do sod all."

Harry didn't answer. The mere thought of Bert made him see red. Fortunately, he spent more time hobnobbing with Tommy and his cronies than he did at home and Harry managed to keep out of his way. It was at times like this that he wished he'd stayed in the army. But what would have happened to Mary if he hadn't been there? Sheila hardly ever came round these days and Ellie had disappeared, apparently without trace.

When Sid had left, Harry found himself thinking about Ellie, as he did so often these days. When Mary was taken ill he'd been determined to find her and had used some of his precious savings to hire a private detective. He'd made enquiries in Colchester, where the cards Ellie had sent had been posted, but had drawn a blank.

"The thing is, Mr Scott, she may not want to be found," the detective said, shrugging. "She could have got someone else to post the cards for her."

Harry didn't want to believe that Ellie had cut herself off deliberately. She'd been hurt and unhappy when she ran away, scarcely more than a child. Even if she regretted her hasty action she probably thought her family wouldn't forgive her. If only he could find her, he would make her see how much she was loved and missed. He pictured the joy on Mary's face when she was reunited with her long-lost daughter — a tonic that would surely set her on the road to recovery. If only for his foster mother's sake, he'd have to try once more to find her. He tried not to think what it would mean to him to have her home again. But just to know she was safe and happy, surely that would be enough . . .

He called in at Sid's flat and made him a hot drink, leaving it on a side table with his tablets. "Make sure you take them — and if you still feel bad in the morning, don't worry about the stall. I'll manage," he said as he went out of the door and down the stairs. The newsagent's shop under the flat was closed, Mr

Cook having locked up and gone home to his wife and family hours ago. Harry reflected that if Sid were taken ill during the night there'd be no one to hear. He should have the phone put in, he thought, resolving to see to it himself.

It had rained earlier in the day and with nightfall the air had grown colder. The wet pavements underfoot were slippery but he strode along, anxious to get home.

Seating himself opposite Mary, Harry thought the cosy domestic scene was reminiscent of the days before he'd joined the army — times when, like today, Bert had been working late — or more likely was down the pub. He smiled across at Mary, who had her feet on the little wooden stool he'd made for Ellie so long ago.

She had picked up a magazine and was idly flicking through it.

"I didn't know you'd been out," he said. "You should have asked me to get the shopping."

"I picked this up in the surgery," she said.

"What did the doc say?"

"Just gave me some more pills." She shrugged and turned a page. Suddenly she gasped, the magazine fluttering to the floor.

"What is it? Are you all right?" Harry grabbed her hand, which was icy-cold.

She pushed him away. "It's OK. I just had a bit of a shock, that's all. But it couldn't be — I must have been seeing things."

"Something must have upset you," Harry said.

Mary picked up the magazine, folding it back to reveal a coloured photograph. "I was just being silly," she said with a little laugh. She thrust it at him. "I thought for a moment — it looks just like her."

Just a quick glance was enough. There was no mistaking that smile. Harry felt the colour drain from his face as he held the picture up to the light for a closer look.

The article was spread across the centre pages and Harry waited until he'd read every word before speaking. It could have been a coincidence — a girl who looked like Ellie and just happened to be good at design. But by the time he got to the end, he was convinced. In addition to the girl's looks, there was the name — Helen Scott Cameron. And she worked from a studio in Essex, not far from where they'd had the first postcard. What really convinced him was the picture of the butterfly-and-flower design. He'd seen something very similar not long ago, when he'd gone into Ellie's old room and been disturbed by the sight of her early paintings still pinned to the walls.

"It is her, Mum. It's our Ellie."

Mary snatched the magazine back and devoured the photograph, tears streaming down her face. "She's safe — I always knew deep down she was all right. And to think she's got her own business — and making a success of it too. She must have married as well."

Harry's stomach lurched as the significance of Ellie's name change hit him. He could understand her calling herself Scott and Helen was only a different version of Ellen. Cameron must be her husband's name. But that didn't matter, they'd be able to find her now. He put his arm round Mary. "Don't cry, Mum. We'll get in touch with the magazine — that's if you want to."

"Want to? Of course I do — she's my daughter. I have to see her." Mary leaned back in the chair and closed her eyes. "Why hasn't she been in touch with us?"

Harry patted her arm. "She probably thinks we're still angry with her for running away."

"Her father is," Mary said. "He'll never forgive her. You know he won't have her name mentioned. Perhaps we should let well alone."

"But, Mum —"

"No. She knows where we are. She's the one who should write to us." Mary picked up the magazine, staring for a few moments at the spread of words and pictures. Then she screwed it up, threw it down and without another word got up and stumbled out of the room.

Ellie carefully folded the last of the scarves and placed it in the box. "All ready for delivery tomorrow," she murmured.

She glanced at her watch. Time to get on with her latest painting before Alex got home. She went across to her easel and studied the design critically.

She was finding it harder to come up with something new. Perhaps she should never have embarked on these abstract designs. But for Carnaby Street it had to be "new", the next big fashion. So different from those for Sylvia — she knew just what her customers wanted.

She needed a change of scene — fresh sights to inspire her. Ellie fondled her bump. Already she felt like the side of a house and had little energy for anything besides her painting — and there was ages to go yet. Ellie sighed. Alex now seemed resigned to her carrying on her "little cottage industry" as he called it — at least until the baby came. Although she'd nodded agreement, she was determined not to give up. Alex still didn't know about her contract with the printing firm in Chelmsford or her dealings with the Carnaby Street shop. For weeks after the magazine article had come out she'd held her breath every time he came home, or when the phone rang.

Not that they ever had proper rows. No, Alex was always sweetly reasonable, his demands framed as requests and, she knew, prompted by his concern for her and the baby. But when he did find out, she knew he'd be furious.

She should confess, she thought, despising herself for her weakness. Why couldn't she speak up for herself, make him see that motherhood shouldn't stop her carrying on her business? Meanwhile, she must get on with this wretched design, otherwise she'd have no customers to do business with.

The flash of anger directed at herself served as a spur to her creativity and she splashed bold colour on to the paper stretched on her easel. For the original paintings, she'd started using designer's gouache, an opaque paint which came in vibrant colours more suitable for the modern designs. Then the painted design was copied on to a screen for printing on to the lengths of silk.

Soon, she was lost in her work and, as usual when things were going well, she completely lost track of time. At last, she threw down her brush and stepped back to admire the finished painting, sighing and rubbing her back.

"Darling, there you are. Have you been working in here all day? You know you shouldn't be doing so much now."

Alex's voice made her jump and she turned angrily. "Don't creep up on me like that," she said.

"Creep! A herd of elephants could walk in here when you're painting and you wouldn't even notice." He gave a little laugh and came towards her. "Seriously, though, you do look tired."

She shrugged him away. "I'm all right, Alex. Please don't fuss."

She carried on washing her brushes and cleaning her palette. When she'd finished he was waiting for her by the door and she felt a little guilty that she'd been so brusque. But as they turned out the lights and locked the studio door before going across to the house, she realized he hadn't even commented on her painting.

They had finished supper, a casserole left to cook slowly in the oven while Ellie worked, when she asked Alex if he'd take her in to Colchester the next day. "I can come back on the bus," she said. "That's if you really think I shouldn't drive myself." She had to admit that recently it had become a bit uncomfortable to get in and out of the car — not that she'd admit that to Alex.

"I'm sorry, Ellie. I have to go to Manchester tomorrow — another crisis up there, I'm afraid."

"I'll have to take the car then. I promised Sylvia I'd deliver her scarves this week."

"Didn't you say you were going to give it up?"

"This is the last lot."

Alex sighed. "That's what you said last week." He threw down his napkin and stood up. "If it's so important to you, I'll, deliver the stuff to Mrs Marshall — just this once. But no more, Ellie. I will not have you wearing yourself out like this. The baby comes first."

"I'm perfectly fit." Ellie's irritation rose again. Would he never allow her a shred of independence? "Besides, I've hardly been out of the house for days."

"I know, darling, but I worry about you. I'll be away a couple of days this time and you wouldn't want me getting in a stew, would you? Look, I'll try to get back for the weekend and we'll go up to Southwold on Sunday — a bit of sea air will do you good. You'd like that wouldn't you?"

His smile mollified her. Was it so bad that he cared? She knew he wasn't keen on visiting her friends and accepted that he was trying to please her. "I'd love it, Alex. I haven't seen Norah for ages. And thank you for offering. Tell Sylvia I'll phone her later."

It was only after she'd gone to bed that she realized she hadn't asked Alex about the crisis in Manchester. There seemed to be rather a lot of problems in their northern mill lately. He was always dashing up there these days. At one time, Alex would have discussed it with her. When she'd been his secretary he'd been pleased at her interest in the business, using her as a sounding board for his ideas and confiding any problems. Once they were married, she felt as if he had put her in a different compartment in his life. But if something was wrong, she'd rather know about it.

She could hear him moving about in the next room. It sounded as if he couldn't sleep either. If he was worried she ought to try to get him to share his problems. But, as she swung her legs over the side of the bed, another thought struck her and she sank back on the pillows. What if he'd found someone else? Suppose his frequent trips to Manchester were to see another woman?

She was surprised at the pain the thought gave her. She believed that Alex loved her, was looking forward to fatherhood. Surely he wouldn't risk what they had just for the thrill of an affair? For she was certain that's all it could be. Her stomach twisted as she realized she didn't blame him. She knew what men wanted — even a man as gentle and loving as Alex. And she hadn't been able to give it to him. It wasn't just sex either. She hadn't given him her heart — not wholly. Yes, she had tried, had told herself repeatedly that Alex was all she wanted, that she was happy. She counted her blessings daily — a lovely home, her own business, freedom from financial worry, the love of a good man. The girls she'd grown up with would be more than content with that. But it wasn't enough. Without love, it was all meaningless.

As she turned over and buried her sobs in the pillow, Ellie's only comfort was that soon she would have someone she could truly love. Her baby would grow up surrounded by love, smothered in it. He would never know the insecurities and tensions she'd had.

Let Alex have an affair, if that made him happy. Just so long as he was a good father and provided a stable home for their child.

CHAPTER
TWENTY-TWO

Harry's steps dragged as he left the building, his shoulders hunched. Had he really expected anything else? The woman in the magazine office had been sympathetic but had refused to give Ellie's address or phone number. He couldn't blame her. After all, he could be some sort of nut — a jealous boyfriend or business rival.

He ought to get back to the stall but surely there was something he could do. The magazine hadn't given the name of the shop which sold Ellie's scarves, but it should be easy enough to find. Not that he was likely to get much joy there either.

On impulse, he jumped on a bus going towards Oxford Circus. He had to try for Mary's sake, at least that's what he tried to tell himself as he found a seat and pulled the now crumpled magazine from his pocket. Ellie's clear brown-eyed gaze seemed directed just at him and a lump formed in his throat as he stared at the photo. He'd never really believed she'd run away just because he'd kissed her. It must have been something else. And whatever the trouble was, she must have known he'd help her. Was it too late? He hoped not, for he'd realized from the moment he saw her face smiling up at him from the magazine that he still loved her — always had, always would.

The bus jerked to a stop and he pushed past the other passengers, plunging into the maze of streets that made up the Soho district. Despite the cold, the Berwick Street market was crowded with shoppers and Harry fought his way past, searching for the shop featured in the article. The air was rich with spicy cooking smells and his stomach rumbled. But he couldn't stop to eat.

He walked for a long time, stopping frequently to ask directions, until he turned a corner and found himself in Carnaby Street. This was more like it. Even the people looked different — mostly young, smartly dressed in clothes that would raise eyebrows where he lived. The latest fashions took a while to reach their part of London and short dresses with knee-high boots in shiny plastic were the exception rather than the rule in Bethnal Green. Harry looked in one of the windows and gasped as he saw the price tag. No wonder he didn't see many girls in Kendall Street dressed like this. But no one here turned a hair — at the fashions or the prices, it seemed.

He stopped at an eye-catching window display. Inside the tiny shop, loud music played. Bright lights bounced off the equally bright materials of the dresses, jackets, blouses hanging in colourful array from rails which left scarcely enough room to pass between them. And, beside the door, a stand of rainbow-hued scarves fluttered in the wind.

273

There didn't seem to be a proper shop counter and he looked around for an assistant, jumping as a voice said in his ear, "Sure you're in the right shop?"

He turned to see a tall skinny girl, her height accentuated by the extremely short skirt and thigh-length boots, her eyes outlined in black, like the Egyptian wall paintings he'd seen in the British Museum.

"I'd like to speak to the owner or manager, please."

"That's me," the girl said. "Do you want a refund? We don't do refunds."

"No, no. I'm enquiring about those scarves — the *Helene* design."

"We sell a lot of those — can't get enough. There's only a few left. You want a present for someone?"

Harry thought quickly. How could he get this girl to give him the information he so desperately needed? "Actually, it's a business matter," he said. "Is there somewhere we could talk?" He glanced across the narrow space to where another girl, almost identically dressed, stood chewing gum and watching them curiously.

"Through the back." The first girl jerked her head and Harry followed her into a space even more cramped than the main shop. She pushed a pile of sweaters off the only chair and gestured him to sit, perching herself on the edge of a table.

"Business, you said. Well, what is it? If you're a salesman, where's your samples?"

"I'm not selling. Actually," he improvised. "I have a shop of my own."

The girl's eyes narrowed suspiciously.

Harry thought quickly. "I'd like to sell some of those scarves. Could you tell me . . .?"

"You trying to put me out of business?"

"I wouldn't be competing with you — my shop's up north."

"You sound like a Londoner to me." She still seemed suspicious.

"Yes — but I live in Yorkshire now. The girls up there don't want to be left behind when it comes to fashion, you know. So whenever I come down to visit the family, I have a look round, see what's goin' on in the big smoke, yer know." Harry managed a laugh. He wondered where he'd got the nerve. But it seemed to be working.

The girl slid off the table and went across to a box in the corner, holding up one of the scarves. She smoothed it out and showed him the *Helene* signature with its flowing "H". "I have to tell you, she only does a limited number of each design — that's why they're so expensive. And she told me on the phone she has more than enough orders."

"Well, it's worth a try. Could you give me her address?" Harry said, trying not to sound too eager.

"I'm not sure about that, but I'll give you her phone number."

It was more than he'd hoped for.

The girl smiled and wrote the number down on the back of an old envelope.

He grabbed it, noting the exchange. "Great Withies," he muttered. Wasn't that somewhere in Essex? He rushed out of the shop clutching the piece of paper.

★ ★ ★

Next morning, Ellie's fears seemed foolish. Alex's goodbye kiss was warm and tender and his protestations that he would miss her seemed sincere.

She knew that pregnancy brought strange fancies and imaginings and that was all it was, she told herself firmly as she watched his car back out of the garage and shoot down the gravel drive.

When he'd gone, Ellie felt a sense of relief, despite her concerns of the night before. She had two whole days to herself — Mrs Mills wasn't due till Friday and George would be gone by midday. She was quite content on her own, so long as she kept busy. She couldn't wait to get on with her painting — she had a feeling that this new design could prove to be one of her best yet.

As she crossed the lawn towards the studio, she heard the phone ringing. She hesitated, keen to get on with her work but changed her mind when she realized it might be a customer. She hurried back into the house and picked up the phone, but all she heard was the dialling tone.

Oh well, if it was something important they'd ring back, she thought. She'd have to ask Alex about putting an extension in the studio. It would save her running to and fro, or missing important calls. As she paused to pick up some fallen petals from the flower arrangement on the hall table, the phone rang again. She snatched up the receiver. "Great Withies 325," she said.

There was no reply, although she could sense someone on the line. "Who do you wish to speak to? This is Mrs Cameron."

A long silence was broken by a sharp click as the person at the other end put the phone down. Ellie shrugged. Must have been a wrong number, she thought.

But as she entered the studio a prickle of unease ran up her neck. The fear that had been her constant companion in the days following her escape from London returned. Had her father found out where she was? And if he had, why should she be scared? He couldn't hurt her now.

She uncovered her easel and contemplated the almost finished painting, methodically squeezing paint on to her palette and selecting a brush. But she couldn't settle to work and the quiet of her surroundings weighed on her.

She was being silly, she told herself. But she couldn't get the strange phone call out of her head. At last she abandoned attempts at working and went for a walk in the garden. George was still there, forking over the compost heap. At least she wasn't entirely alone.

She leaned on the fence overlooking the unkempt paddock. In the early days of their marriage Alex had suggested they keep horses and he would teach her to ride. The thought had terrified her. Turning the stables into a studio was a much better idea she'd told him. Now, he'd started talking about putting in a swimming pool.

But nothing had come of it since the increased frequency of his trips up north and once more Ellie wondered whether he was having an affair. That was it, she thought. It must have been the woman — whoever she was — phoning earlier on. Of course she wouldn't announce herself when Ellie had answered. She'd obviously been expecting Alex to pick up the phone. But he'd left early to deliver the scarves to Colchester.

Relief at solving the mystery dissolved the little lump of apprehension that had lodged in Ellie's stomach. Now it was replaced by anger. How dare she phone here?

Harry replaced the receiver and leaned against the café wall, shaking. It *was* Ellie. He'd know that voice anywhere, despite her attempt to sound posh on the phone.

Why hadn't he spoken?

Bob pushed a cup of coffee towards him. "Bad news, mate?" he asked. "'Ere, it's not Sid, is it? I 'eard he's gotta go back in 'ospital."

Harry answered with an effort. He was worried about Sid too. But Ellie was uppermost in his mind at the moment. "Tomorrow — for another operation. I'll let you know how he gets on."

He took his cup over to a table in the corner and sat down. It was half-term holidays and he'd got one of Maisie's kids minding the stall for him. He should get back, but at the moment he just didn't care about the business — about anything. All he could think of now was finding Ellie.

After talking to the Carnaby Street shop-owner, he'd dashed back to Bethnal Green to relieve Sid, sending the older man home to rest. He'd intended to ask for time off to go to Essex. It shouldn't be too hard to find Ellie with all the clues he had.

But Sid had to go in hospital again and he couldn't let his old mate down.

Finding Ellie would have to wait, although he'd given in to the impulse to phone the number he'd been given. It was almost a relief when no one answered. But a couple of minutes later he'd summoned the nerve to try again. When she'd answered he just couldn't think what to say.

Cursing himself for a fool, he swallowed his coffee and hurried between the stalls to his waiting customers. He hoped being busy would distract him but there were so many problems — Sid, Mary, and most of all Ellie.

Sid, after yet another operation, looked small and grey against the white hospital sheets. When Harry sat down beside him, he moved feebly and tried to speak.

"You've been good to me, son," he whispered hoarsely. "I don't know how to thank yer."

"You just concentrate on getting better. Your customers miss you, keep asking when you'll be back," Harry said, trying to sound cheerful.

Sid made a sound which could have been a laugh. They both knew he would never stand behind his market stall again.

Harry stayed for the whole visiting hour, holding his friend's hand while he dozed and thinking over the good times they'd had. He didn't know how he'd have got through those years before he'd gone in the army if he hadn't had Sid to run to when things got bad at home. He'd guessed a long time ago how his friend felt about Mary and wondered how things would have turned out if she'd married him instead of Bert.

As usual his thoughts turned to Ellie. The magazine article said she was married. Was she happy, or was she making the best of things too? It didn't matter either way. She would take her vows seriously, whatever her innermost feelings.

He gave himself a mental kick in the backside. How did he know how she felt? She'd kissed him a couple of times with a warmth that was far from sisterly and her letters had been full of love. He'd been longing to come home — to find out whether what he was beginning to feel for her was real. She'd been his little sister for so long and they'd always had a loving relationship. He'd always known there was something special about Ellie. Then, the last time he'd seen her, their affectionate parting had flamed into an intense passion. He'd known then that his love for Ellie was far from brotherly.

As he had so many times, he wondered what had made her run away. Perhaps, having thought of him as her brother all her life, she had been confused by the passion that had flared between them. If only he'd had time to make things right. He told himself it wasn't too late. He'd find her one day. But, looking at Sid's face creased with pain, he knew he couldn't do anything about it yet.

The bell rang for the visitors to leave and Harry leaned over and spoke softly, not sure if Sid could hear him. "I'll bring Mary next time. You'd like that, wouldn't you, mate?"

He squeezed Sid's hand and turned away, wondering if he'd ever see him again. He'd promised his old friend that he'd attend to all the formalities — after all, he was the nearest thing to family Sid had.

The funeral was one of the grandest the East End had seen for years. Sid had told Harry he wanted a good send-off with all the trimmings. And he got it too — no horses with black plumes like in the old days, but a shiny black hearse with purple satin curtains at the windows covered in flowers.

The church was crowded. Even Tommy Green came, surrounded by his minders, some of whom looked extremely uncomfortable at being in church.

Most of the market traders were there, and those who couldn't leave their stalls stood respectfully silent, paying their respects as the cortège drove slowly along Roman Road towards the Bethnal Green cemetery. Afterwards, the mourners gathered in the Red Lion opposite Bob's Café. A buffet had been laid on upstairs and the drink flowed freely.

As the afternoon progressed, the air of solemnity gave way to a party atmosphere. Sid had been well-loved, a man of warmth and humour. Harry found himself looking round more than once for his old friend. He should be here. It was his party, after all.

Harry knew most of the people in the room. But there were a few strange faces. When Sid realized he was dying, he'd given Harry a list of people to be notified, some distant cousins, old Army mates.

One of the strangers, a tall lean chap with a droopy moustache, came over to him. "You're Harry Scott, aincha?" He held out a skinny hand, its skin and nails engrained with black grease that no amount of scrubbing could remove. "I've heard a lot about you, son. Sid thought a lot of you. I'm Nobby — Norman Barnes, D Company, the Buffs. Me and Sid was together in the war."

Harry shook the outstretched hand. "Sid talked about you too — but he didn't like talking about the war. It was more the capers you got up to when you were off duty. Right pair you were by all accounts."

"Wish I'd kept in touch more. But you know how it is, when you're running yer own business, yer time ain't yer own."

"Garage, isn't it?" Harry asked politely. He would have guessed anyway from the state of the bloke's hands.

"Yeah. Sid told me you wanted to go in that line of work once? Still, I expect you'll be taking over the stall now, won't you?"

"I don't think so. It's not really my line."

"Well, I'd offer to take you on at my place, but I'm thinking of packing it in. It's all getting a bit much for me. It's hard when you've spent half your life building something up, and there's no one to pass it on to. Me son's just not interested."

Harry nodded sympathetically as Nobby drained his glass and set it down, handing him a small printed card. "If you're interested, I could have a word with whoever takes over." He stuck his hand out again.

"Nice meeting yer, son. Gotta be on me way. Give us a ring, or call in if yer ever passing — Barnes Garage on the Southend Road, just outside Grays."

"I might do that," Harry said.

When Nobby had left, Harry stared into his beer glass. He was missing Sid more than he could say.

Sheila touched his arm. "I'm taking Mum home," she said. "And then I've got to get back. The kids'll be home from school soon."

Harry leaned over to kiss her cheek. "I'm gonna miss 'im like hell, Sheila."

"I know. He thought of you like a son, you know." She patted his arm and left.

Gradually the room started to empty. But there were some, Bert among them, who would hang on till the last of the free booze was gone. These people weren't Sid's real friends. Harry had a quiet word with Stan, the landlord, telling him not to bring up any more beer.

"I know Sid said to keep it flowing, and he left the money to pay for it. But whatever's left in the kitty can go to the Victuallers' for the kids' next Christmas party," Harry said quietly.

Stan nodded understandingly. Sid hadn't been a boozer, but he'd been a good customer over the years.

When everyone had gone, Harry thankfully left the smoke-filled room, pausing in the pub doorway to take a deep breath of fresh air. Bob had left the wake earlier to reopen the café and the traders were packing up their stalls. It looked like a normal day. But Harry knew nothing would be the same again.

Now that he was free of his obligations to his mate, he didn't know what to do. Sid's licence to trade in the market had died with him, so he was out of a job now. Not that he'd planned on running the stall for ever. He took Nobby's card out of his pocket and studied it thoughtfully. Should he take up the bloke's tentative offer of a job? He was too old to do a proper apprenticeship but he'd learned enough in the Army to get by. It seemed like a chance to do what he liked best — getting his hands dirty deep in the innards of an engine. Besides, he'd never be able to save enough to start his own business. That had just been a childish dream.

He crossed the road, scarcely looking where he was going. Bob waved from behind the café counter, but Harry didn't feel like talking. He didn't want to go home either.

He supposed he ought to take a look at Sid's flat above Cook's newsagent's. There must be things to sort out before it could be let again. He hadn't got the heart to start on it now but he'd pay another week's rent to give him more time.

Mr Cook was serving a customer and Harry waited till he'd gone. He got his wallet out but the other man waved it away. "It's all paid up till the end of the month. Don't worry, Harry, mate."

"I'll come back later in the week. Gawd knows what I'm gonna do with his things. I s'pose his good clothes can go to the Sally Ann, the bedding too. They'll make good use of it," Harry said, passing a hand over his face. He'd get old Blakey, the totter from Mile End Road to clear the rest of the flat.

As he turned away, Mr Cook called after him, holding out a brown foolscap envelope. "Wait a mo, mate. Sid asked me to give this to yer."

Harry shoved it into his pocket. It was probably a note telling him what to do with his stuff. He'd look at it later.

CHAPTER
TWENTY-THREE

Alex had been away for three days this time and Ellie was sure it wasn't business that had taken him to Manchester. He phoned her each evening, his voice solicitous as usual. If he was having an affair, it was impossible to tell. But despite the lack of real evidence, Ellie was tempted to accuse him of infidelity.

But what right had she, who'd been unfaithful in thought if not in deed? She couldn't blame him, after all. And if it was just a sexual fling, she could forgive him. She wanted to keep her marriage intact — if only for the sake of the coming baby.

Surely they could make a go of things if they both tried hard enough? And if he wasn't satisfied with her performance in bed, did it really matter if he sought his pleasure with someone else?

She thought of her mother, who'd struggled to keep her marriage vows, despite her obvious unhappiness. For the first time it occurred to her that the root of that unhappiness might be the same as her own. Maybe Mary hadn't enjoyed sex with Bert, especially after being so happy with Jim Scott. It was a possible explanation for her father's behaviour. Maybe, like Alex, he'd been driven to seek satisfaction elsewhere.

286

As the probable truth of this dawned on her, Ellie felt as if a load had been lifted off her. It hadn't been her fault, she hadn't asked for it. And with the thought came a wave of hatred. She would never forgive her father for the harm he'd done, both physically and mentally.

The latest batch of London designs was ready for printing and her other customers had plenty of hand-painted scarves in stock. With nothing to occupy her, Ellie had too much time to think.

The shrill sound of the telephone broke into her introspection and she reached for the receiver reluctantly. There hadn't been any more silent calls, but she still jumped when the phone rang.

It was Alex, saying he'd be home later in the day. Perhaps she ought to cook something for him. There was plenty of time and she went upstairs, stopping in the doorway of the room which would be the nursery. She had decorated the low-ceilinged room herself in bright sunshine yellow. A hand-painted frieze of zoo animals marched round the walls and silk curtains to match hung at the windows. The furnishings had been chosen with loving care on shopping expeditions with Alex. They'd been happy then, Ellie thought, planning their new life with their baby. Surely they could be again.

As she went downstairs, a shadow fell on the glass panels of the front door and she jumped. It couldn't be Alex already. She opened the door, a polite smile hiding the nervousness she always felt when someone called at the house unexpectedly. The fear that she'd thought long conquered returned and her stomach trembled. Had Bert found out where she was?

The stranger smiled and, as she recognized him, the years rolled away and it was as if they'd never been parted. After a moment's brief hesitation, she threw her arms round his neck and hugged him as close as her distended body would allow.

Harry returned the embrace, his face buried in her hair. "Ellie, love. I've missed you," he whispered.

She pushed him gently away and led him into the drawing room. "I'll make some tea."

In the kitchen, she tried to quell the shaking of her hands, the trembling in her knees. He was here, he'd found her. Did that mean he'd left his wife?

A bubble of hysterical laughter welled up. What was she thinking — that he'd sweep her away, like a knight on a white horse? Here she was a married woman, nearly seven months pregnant. She leaned over the sink and splashed her face with cold water, willing herself to be calm. But Harry was here, he'd found her.

As her breathing steadied a cold thought stole over her. Why was he here? Something must have happened to her mother. Her knees started to shake again and she clung to the edge of the stainless-steel sink, her knuckles white. She couldn't bear it, she just couldn't.

His hand clasped her shoulder. "Ellie? Are you OK?" His voice was hesitant. "I'm sorry — I didn't think, should've phoned." He turned her gently to face him. "It's all right, love."

"Mum — is she . . .?"

"Your mother's fine. She's been ill but she's OK now." He pulled her into his arms and held her, gently rubbing her back until her sobs eased.

She pulled away, looking up into his serious blue gaze through the mist of tears. "Harry, you're not angry with me, are you?" She might have been a child again, apologizing for breaking one of his model planes.

He grinned at her, the old Harry grin. "Bloody furious."

"I don't blame you. That's why I never got in touch. I thought you and Mum would never forgive me."

He pulled her to him again and stroked her hair. "I was angry and — I blamed myself . . ."

Ellie pushed at his chest, a gesture of denial.

"I did — you know why. But then I thought there must be more to it than that. And when Mary told me about that place your dad made you work, well . . ."

Ellie sighed, her face against the rough serge of his jacket. She was safe now, safe where she'd longed to be for so many long years. Yes, they were both married and there was no future for them. But why shouldn't she stay here just for a little while, storing up these precious memories for the long lonely future? The roughness of his jacket against her cheek, the feel of his arms around her, his strong muscular body against hers — not that she could get that close to him with her bump in the way. A hysterical giggle rose in her throat, immediately suppressed as thoughts of Alex and their baby intervened.

Reluctantly she pulled away and busied herself setting a tray with her best china, filling the silver teapot. She needed these few moments of busyness to calm herself.

Harry watched her silently then followed her down the hall into the drawing room. He stood for a moment in the middle of the room, taking in the polished parquet floor, the Persian rugs, the French windows looking out on to the expanse of garden.

"You've done well for yourself, Ellie," he said, as she set the tray on a small table between them.

"Not me — Alex," she said simply.

"Your husband . . .?"

"He's away at the moment — on business. But he'll be back later this afternoon. You'll be able to meet him." She didn't really want Alex and Harry to meet. What she wanted was to leave this house and go with Harry — wherever he wanted. She didn't care. Seeing him again, feeling his arms round her, had simply confirmed what her heart had always known. She loved him.

But Alex was her husband and she was expecting his child. Despite her suspicions, she knew how important she and the coming baby were to him. How could she hurt him after he'd been so good to her? Besides, wasn't Harry married too and with a child of his own?

He sat on the edge of a chair facing her, leaning forward, his hands loosely between his knees. His thoughts seemed to echo hers for he sighed and said, "What are we going to do, love?"

"You can go home and tell Mum and the rest of them that I'm fine, that I've got a good life. You can leave me to get on with my life — and you can get on

290

with yours." He would never know what an effort it was to say those words.

"I want you to come home, Ellie. Your mum's not well. She needs to see for herself that you're OK. She's been out of her mind with worry."

Ellie realized how selfish she'd been. Why hadn't she written, especially after she'd got married? That would've set her mind at rest. And Harry wouldn't have felt the need to find her. He wouldn't be sitting here now, gazing at her with his blue eyes full of love, reminding her of everything she'd tried to forget over the past few years.

"I can't explain, Harry. At the time I thought running away was the only option. I felt I couldn't come home — Mum would never forgive me."

"Can you imagine what we went through, wondering what happened to you?"

"I'm sorry, so sorry." Ellie began to sob again. "I was in such a state — I didn't think anyone would care —"

"How could you think that?" Harry's voice rose. "You must have known you could confide in me — if not in your mum."

"But you weren't there, were you? You were in Sheerness."

Harry pulled her towards him and, once more she let herself cry in his arms. She could never tell him what had made her so desperate. What would he do to Bert if he found out?

When her sobs eased and she tried to pull away from him, he wouldn't let her go. His lips were on her face, her eyes, her hair, then on her lips, fierce, burning. For a moment she responded, her body weak with feelings she had denied for so long. But it was no good. They shouldn't be doing this. She pushed him away.

His eyes burned into hers. "Ellie, that last time — just before I went to Sheerness . . ."

She shook her head but he persisted.

"You did feel something too? You do now, don't you? I didn't imagine it?"

Her smile shone through her tears. "No, darling Harry, you didn't imagine it. I love you — I always have. And when I realized . . ." She shook her head again. "But I convinced myself I was just being a silly kid."

"And now?" His grip on her hands tightened.

"I don't have to tell you, do I?" She pulled away and dried her eyes, sat back in her chair. She looked at him seriously. "Harry, we can't always do what our hearts tell us to. You know that. We have responsibilities now." Her hand went protectively to her swelling stomach and a little smile touched her lips.

Harry sighed and stood up. "You're right of course. But, Gawd, it's hard. How can I go home and just carry on as normal?" He paced the room restlessly. "Come with me," he said, turning to her.

"I can't."

He sat down again. "At least come back and see your mother. She needs you, Ellie. I promise I won't try to talk you into anything. I've got Sid's old van outside — it's only an hour's run. I could have you back here by teatime."

"I don't know — I'm not sure I can face everyone." Ellie looked out of the window. She didn't want Harry to see how frightened the thought made her. She longed to see her mother but that longing was overridden by her dread of coming face to face with Bert. Wasn't that the reason she'd stayed away so long?

"Your mother wants to see you, Ellie. She seems OK now. But I'm still worried about her. Seeing you could be just the tonic she needs."

"Why didn't you bring her with you then?" Ellie asked.

"She doesn't know I've come. I wanted to check things out first — see how you felt. For all I knew, you might have shown me the door. And I couldn't bear the thought of Mary being hurt any more than she has been already."

His voice was bitter and Ellie's throat closed at the realization of how much she'd hurt them; so wrapped up in her own pain, she hadn't thought about anyone else.

She made up her mind. "Come on then — but I won't be able to stay long." She clutched Harry's arm. "I won't have to see Dad, will I?"

"Don't worry, he's hardly ever there," he told her.

She grabbed her handbag and a coat from the closet. At the door she turned and took one of her scarves out of a drawer, folding it carefully into her bag.

The van was parked in the lane and she smiled when she saw the lettering on the side — "Varney's Fruit and Veg — always fresh." Dear Sid, it would be good to see him too.

That was when Harry told her that Sid was dead.

Her sobs didn't stop until the van was on the outskirts of London. The green fields had given way to rows of terraces, then parades of shops, behind them the towering cliffs of multistorey flats.

She turned to Harry. "How did you find me?" she asked.

He told her about seeing the magazine article and the detective work that had led him to Great Withies and Withies Farm. "I had your phone number — I tried to ring several times, but when I heard your voice I couldn't speak," he confessed.

"It was you, then. I thought . . ." Ellie paused. She couldn't tell Harry about her suspicions. She eased her aching back against the lumpy seat of the old van, dried her eyes and looked around with a sense of homecoming. She was all cried out now — her tears not just for Sid Varney but for all her lost childhood.

"Poor Sid," she said. "He must have been so lonely — no family to look after him when he was ill."

"I don't think he was lonely. He was a big-hearted man, Ellie. He might not have had a family as such, but the market people were his family. He treated me like a son, you know — gave me a job when I came out of the army."

"Sid always liked you, Harry. I remember how much he missed you when you went away."

Harry took his eyes off the road, grinning and Ellie saw that he was seething with an inner excitement. "What? There's something you haven't told me," she said, returning his infectious grin.

"You're right, Ellie. Sid did like me — in fact he loved me." Harry's face flushed a little. "Like a son, I mean. Do you know what the sentimental old beggar did?

"Tell me — please," Ellie begged.

"He left everything to me — everything he owned." Harry's eyes had misted over and Ellie realized how much it meant to him. Not in a material way of course. After all, what did Sid have to leave — the stall, a clapped-out old van, maybe a few pounds in the bank?

"That's wonderful, Harry. Will you carry on in the market then?"

Harry pulled up at a junction and turned to her. "You don't understand, Ellie — Sid had quite a bit of money stashed away. No one guessed — least of all me. I still can't take it in."

His jaw was tight as he tried to clamp down on his emotions and Ellie realized it wasn't the money he was thrilled about, but the fact that Sid had cared for him.

"What will you do now, then?" she asked.

"I can do what I've always wanted to do — set up my own business. Not greengrocery. I can't get excited about spuds and caulis." He grinned at her, his old self again. "I've always wanted to work with cars. Maybe I'll set up a repair business. I learnt how in the army."

"That's wonderful, Harry. I'm so pleased for you." Ellie fell silent. She was pleased for him. She wanted him to be happy, didn't she? It should be the most exciting thing in the world — both of them achieving their childhood dreams. But what good did it do if there was no one to share it with? Alex didn't understand her need to succeed on her own terms, treating her art merely as a hobby. And Harry would be sharing his success with his wife and child — not with her.

As the van drove deeper into the heart of the East End, familiar landmarks began to appear and Ellie looked out of the window, marking their progress by her childhood memories. She'd been back to London with Alex several times and, of course, she'd visited the Carnaby Street shop where her scarves were sold. But that was a different London.

Now, as she passed the red-brick primary school with its tarmac playground, the bus stop where she and Judith had waited for the grammar school bus each morning, she realized it hadn't all been bad.

As they reached the corner of Kendall Street, she saw that old Solly's shop was still boarded up and the whole street had a dingy abandoned look. Old cigarette packets and chip-wrappers whirled in the chill wind, collecting in the doorways of the empty shops.

She turned to Harry in surprise when the van stopped. "Mum's still living here?"

He nodded and leaned across to open the van door. "Best if you see her on your own," he said, lighting a cigarette. "I've got a few things to do. I'll come back later and take you home."

She got out, pulling the collar of her coat closer around her neck. Of course he had things to do. He had a wife to go home to — a wife who was probably wondering what her husband was up to.

296

As she turned away and reached the door to the flat, she realized that Harry hadn't mentioned Gerda or his child.

CHAPTER
TWENTY-FOUR

As Harry drove away, Ellie hesitated before reaching out a tentative hand and pushing the door open. She entered the narrow passage, noting the peeling wallpaper, the patches of damp. Poor Mum never did get her council house, she thought.

The mingled smells of cooking and polish returned her to childhood days when she'd leapt the stairs two at a time, longing to tell Mum something that had happened at school. Now she mounted slowly, her heart beating faster, haunted by other times when she crept indoors, desperate to reach the sanctuary of her attic room.

She caught her breath, willing herself to be calm as she opened the door to the kitchen. Nothing seemed to have changed. A fire still glowed in the old-fashioned range, although a modern cream-painted electric cooker now stood against the wall next to the sink. Bert's chair still occupied its place near the range. Even the little wooden stool where she had crouched as a child was still in its place by the brass fender.

Tears welled as she gazed round the familiar room. Lost in memories, she jumped when a voice came from the room across the landing.

"Is that you, Harry? Have you brought my medicine?"

Ellie opened the door quietly. The woman on the bed was pale, thinner than she remembered, the wavy chestnut hair, once so like Ellie's own, now lank and streaked with grey. She was facing the window, her eyes on a golden shaft of sun which had found its way through the partly-drawn curtains. At the sound of the door opening, she turned her head. "Where have you been, Harry? I expected you back ages ago . . ."

"Mum?" Ellie approached the bed hesitantly.

Mary gasped. "Am I dreaming?"

"No, Mum, it's really me. Harry found me and brought me home." Ellie's voice choked with tears and she sank to her knees beside the bed. "Oh, Mum — if only I'd known you were ill."

She reached out to clasp Mary's hand and buried her face in the candlewick bedspread, soaking it with tears, surprised she still had any left to shed. She felt her mother's hand on her head, stroking her hair and murmuring.

"No need for 'sorries', love. You're here — that's all that matters." She struggled upright and took Ellie in her arms. For a long time they clung together, their sobs saying more than words.

At last Ellie drew away, fumbling for a handkerchief. Mary took her hand. "Were you really so unhappy, love?"

Perhaps now was the time to explain why she'd really run away. But it would kill her mother to know what Bert had done, especially as she seemed so frail.

Ellie kissed her cheek. "It's all in the past, Mum. I was just a silly kid. Just tell me I'm forgiven, please."

"There's nothing to forgive. I never blamed you — just worried myself sick that something awful had happened to you. But you've made a good life for yourself. I couldn't believe it when I picked up that magazine." She patted the side of the bed. "I want you to tell me all about it — how you met your husband, and how you started your business, everything." She pointed to Ellie's swollen body. "And you're expecting! I'm going to be a grandma again — and pretty soon, judging by the look of you."

"In a couple of months, Mum. Now, that's enough about me — I want to hear about you — why are you still living here? I thought you were on the council list."

"Well, they said we didn't qualify for a house, only a flat. I didn't want to go in one of those tower blocks. Your dad didn't want to move either. Still, we're going to have to find somewhere soon — the new owner wants us out. The whole street's coming down to make way for a new parade of shops."

Ellie wished she could persuade her to move to Essex. But she'd never leave Bert. "You'll find somewhere," she said. "Now, tell me about the family."

"Well, Harry must have told you he was working for Sid until he died."

"Yes, but where's he living now? There was so much to talk about on the way down — I didn't get round to asking him."

"He's living here, love — didn't you know?"

300

Seeing her puzzled look, Mary's lips tightened. "There wasn't any baby, she just pretended to be pregnant," she said.

Anger flared. How could Gerda do such a thing? Ellie could see her mother was upset so she changed the subject, asking about Sheila. Mary's voice grew stronger as she spoke of her two little granddaughters. Vicky and Debbie were both now at school but visited at weekends and holidays. Sheila was still married to Tommy and, although she spoke disparagingly of her son-in-law and the source of his wealth, Mary seemed to have accepted her daughter's choice of husband.

"She seems happy enough — and Tommy absolutely dotes on the girls," she said.

Ellie, worried that her mother was getting tired, forced a laugh. "I've been here ages and not even put the kettle on. But first, here's a present for you." She pulled the silk scarf out of her bag and arranged it tenderly round her mother's shoulders.

Mary smiled and fingered the soft material. "It's lovely, Ellie," she said. "Did you really make this yourself?"

"It's my latest design," Ellie told her.

She turned the scarf round, reading the signature across the corner. "*Helene*," she said. "Is that what you call yourself now?"

"I'm still Ellie, Mum. Helene is sort of like a trademark." How could she tell her mother she'd rejected her name when she'd run away, determined to make a new life for herself?

As she laid a tray, Ellie knew that she'd have to ask after her father. She hoped he wouldn't come home before she'd made the tea and taken it into her mother. Then she'd make her escape.

She helped Mary to sit up and adjusted the pillows behind her. As she handed the cup to her she said as calmly as she could, "How's Dad? Is he working these days?"

"He's at the Club." Mary glanced towards the door. "He won't be home yet. But I think it'd be best if you weren't here."

"It's OK — I'll go soon. Besides, I only came to see you."

"He was furious when you ran off. He'll go mad if he sees you."

Seeing her mother's nervousness, eyes constantly flickering towards the door, Ellie found the courage she'd never had before. She had a right to visit her own mother, didn't she? How many times over the past few years had she convinced herself that Bert could no longer scare her? But since entering the flat the old apprehension had returned and she'd found herself listening for his steps on the stairs with the same dread she'd felt in childhood. Now, her protective instincts towards her mother made her brave.

"He doesn't scare me. I'm not a kid any more," she said.

Mary nervously smoothed the sheet between her fingers. "You know I can't stand rows and arguments, Ellie. Please — don't upset him."

"It's OK, Mum. I'll go soon, but I'll come again. Maybe you can come and visit me when you're feeling

302

better." She smiled. "I want my baby to have a proper family — a grandma and aunts and uncles and cousins."

"We were a proper family once upon a time," Mary said wistfully.

"Oh, Mum." Ellie hugged her close, unable to voice what was really on her mind. Had Mum forgotten the rows, the money squandered on drink and gambling, the fact that Bert had wanted Harry put in a children's home? Maybe she was thinking back to an earlier time, before Ellie had been born, when she'd been happily married to Jim Scott.

She sighed. Nothing had changed and, despite her promise to keep in touch, Ellie knew she couldn't face coming again. Her mother was getting better. Hadn't she said she would soon be "good as new"?

"I still get tired though. Don't know what I'd've done without Harry. He's been so good to me," she said.

"You need a holiday, Mum," Ellie said. "When I've had the baby, you must come up to Essex and stay."

"We'll see, love." But Mary's voice was tired.

Ellie noticed the lines of pain etched on the dear face. She had to go — but how could she leave her like this?

The downstairs door slammed and Ellie jumped. She hoped it was only Harry. But she bit her lip as stumbling footsteps and muttered curses told her Dad was home and she knew the fear was still there. The door opened and there he was, swaying slightly, his eyes bloodshot, face flushed with rage and booze, just as it had been the last time she saw him.

As he registered her presence, he glared and raised his clenched fists. "So, the whore returns. I'm surprised you dare show your face here after the grief you caused your mother," he said.

"I've told her it's all right, Bert. I'm glad she's here," Mary protested weakly.

Bert's fist slammed against the doorjamb. "It's not all right. I said I wouldn't have her in the house and I meant it." He looked Ellie up and down, a sneer on his face. "Look at 'er, all dolled up in 'er posh clothes — and with a bun in the oven, too. 'Oo does she think she is?"

He paced the room, muttering incoherently. Ellie longed to flee, but she summoned up her courage and faced him. And as she looked him in the eye she wondered how she could ever have been frightened of this pathetic blustering bully.

She spoke calmly. "Look, Dad, I don't blame you for being upset. But I've told Mum I'm sorry. And I'm a married woman now, expecting your first grandchild."

Bert turned to her viciously. "That don't alter the fact that you ran off and left me a laughing stock. You would've 'ad it made if yer'd stayed at the club — meeting all sorts, famous film stars and that."

"Oh yes. The likes of Philip Devereux, you mean. I'm not a naïve little girl any more, Dad. I know what you had planned for me."

Bert's eyes flickered nervously towards his wife, but Mary had her face in her hands. "I don't know what yer talkin' about," he said.

"Don't worry, Dad — I won't say anything. But you know why I ran away." She held out a placatory hand. "Look, I'm only here because I heard Mum was ill." She didn't say that Harry had brought her home. "I'll go now — but I'll come back and see her — and you can't stop me."

Bert looked at her with loathing. "I'm master in my own house — I say who comes and goes."

Ellie's lips twisted in a semblance of a smile. "I'm not scared any more, Dad. You're all bluster."

"I'll show you . . ." He stepped towards her but a cry from the bed stopped him.

"Leave her alone. You drove her away once — I won't let you do it again."

Bert gave a short laugh. "*You* won't let me? We'll see about that."

Mary started to cry. "What's wrong with you, Bert? Don't you remember how you doted on her when she was little? How you used to play games with her and call her your little Angel."

At the mention of the old pet name Ellie felt the rage rise in her throat and she couldn't stop the words from tumbling out. "It was his *little games* that caused all the trouble, Mum. When I didn't want to play any more, he forced me — and threatened he'd do worse if I ever told. He hurt me, Mum — that's why I ran away."

Her mother's face was chalk-white, her eyes wide with disbelief and a dawning horror as she turned to her husband.

"Bert, please tell me it's not true," she gasped.

"Of course it ain't true. She'll say anything to justify the way she treated you. She's just like her sister — always was a little tart, leadin' blokes on. Look at the way she used to fawn over that so-called brother of hers."

The pain in her mother's eyes made Ellie wish she could retract her hasty words. She took a step towards the bed. "Mum, I didn't want you to know. That's why I stayed away — I couldn't face you, or him."

But her mother turned her face away and tears slid down her cheeks. Ellie looked at Bert and saw her own loathing reflected in his eyes. She picked up her handbag and turned towards the door.

"I'm sorry, Mum — I can't tell you how sorry." Blinded with tears, she stepped on to the landing as her father's hand shot out and gripped her arm.

"I told you what I'd do to you," he hissed, his face close to hers.

Ellie managed not to flinch. "You can't hurt me any more than I've been hurt already," she told him, pulling her arm away.

"Oh, can't I?" he said, aiming a vicious punch at her stomach.

Ellie gasped and clutched the newel post. His fist clenched for another blow and all the pent-up rage and humiliation of years exploded as she swung her handbag at his head. The metal clasp caught his temple and he raised a hand in disbelief. Then with a roar of rage he rushed at her. She stepped to one side and watched in horror as he tumbled down, to lie in a crumpled heap at the bottom of the stairs.

★　★　★

Harry signed his name with a flourish, a huge grin on his face. He was now the proud owner of Barnes Garage on the Southend road — owner of a mortgage at least. Now it was up to him to rebuild the business that Sid's old mate had sadly let go. As he leaned across the desk and shook hands with the solicitor he was confident that hard work and the skills he'd learned in the army would ensure his success. Nobby had faith in him anyway, and had promised to help him get started.

He left the office and rushed out into the street, hurrying through the market, waving to his stallholder friends. Anxious to get home and tell Mary and Ellie, he didn't stop to chat.

Still grinning he pushed open the side door into the passage. The grin vanished when he caught sight of the still form slumped at the foot of the stairs. Stupid, drunken fool. Served him right, he thought, prodding the body with his foot.

There was a muffled groan and Bert moved. He was still alive then, more's the pity. Bending down, Harry quickly examined him. There was a cut on his head, the blood already congealing, and one arm was twisted awkwardly beneath him.

Harry supposed he ought to help, but it was tempting to leave him there. With a sigh, he eased Bert into a sitting position. "You oughter take more water with it," he said with a laugh.

Bert groaned again and opened his eyes. "Where is she — the little cow? I'll teach her —"

Harry gasped. "Ellie," he shouted. Leaving the injured man propped against the wall, he rushed up the stairs into Mary's room. "Where's Ellie? If he's hurt her . . ."

Mary turned a tear-stained face towards him. "She's gone, love. He hit her and she pushed him. I heard him fall. Then she screamed and ran downstairs. I heard the door slam, then it all went quiet." She started to cry and Harry went to comfort her.

"Don't worry, Mum, I'll find her. We won't lose her again."

"Is he . . .? I was frightened to look." Mary clutched at him, hope and fear at war in her eyes.

"No, he's not dead — unfortunately. He's got a nasty cut on his head and I think his arm's broken — but he'll live." Harry stood up. "I wish I'd stayed now. But I thought he wouldn't be back. And I had some business to attend to." Suddenly his news didn't seem so important any more.

"Go after Ellie, love. She probably thinks she's killed him. It all went so quiet, I thought he was dead myself."

"I told her I'd drive her back to Essex," Harry said. "Why didn't she wait?"

"I expect she was frightened. She didn't even say goodbye to me," Mary sobbed. "Find her, Harry, please."

"I don't like to leave you alone with him," Harry said.

"Don't worry about me. Just go after her."

Harry kissed Mary's cheek and went downstairs. Bert was still propped against the wall, looking dazed. "I can't believe the little cow hit me," he said.

"You probably asked for it," Harry's voice was filled with contempt.

"Well, she 'asn't 'eard the last of it. She needn't think she can come back 'ere throwin' 'er weight around with her lah-di-dah ways." Bert got up, staggering a little.

Outside, he crossed the road towards the Red Lion, clutching his arm to his chest. "I suppose you'll go runnin' after her. Well, tell 'er from me, she don't show 'er face again or I'll 'ave her for assault," he shouted over his shoulder.

Harry ignored the threat and made his way to the railway arches where he'd parked the van. Where would she go? She shouldn't be wandering the streets in her condition. Perhaps she'd gone to the station. The Chelmsford train left from Liverpool Street and he drove there as fast as he could. But the station was crowded with commuters. He left the van, not bothering to find a parking meter, and raced up the stairs leading to the walkway connecting the platforms. From here he had a good view of the departing passengers. But there was no sign of a pregnant woman in a blue, fur-collared coat.

He turned away in despair, not knowing what else to do.

Back at the flat Mary was sitting at the kitchen table in her dressing-gown. She looked up expectantly as Harry came in, her face falling as she saw he was alone. "You didn't catch up with her, then?"

"She's probably home by now. I've got her phone number — we won't lose her again. Now, tell me what happened."

"I knew there'd be trouble if he saw her. He'd been drinking, of course." Mary's face twisted in pain. "I was so happy for those few minutes. Then he turned up and everything went wrong." She started to cry. "Oh, Harry, I can't believe the things they said to each other . . ."

He put his arm round her. "People say things when they're angry. It'll all blow over in time." But he was speaking more to comfort her than from any real conviction.

When Mary hesitantly told him what Ellie had revealed about her relationship with her father, it was all he could do to stop himself rushing out of the house and dragging Bert out of the Red Lion. He'd like to beat him to a pulp. He'd seen the fear in Ellie's eyes when she'd opened the door to him that morning — until she realized who it was. And he'd sensed her apprehension as they neared home. Now he understood why she'd cut herself off from her family.

Mary sobbed as she berated herself. "I should have realized. I had my suspicions about what he was doing to Sheila. God forgive me, I blamed her. But his own daughter . . ." She bit her knuckles, stifling her sobs.

Harry comforted her, blaming himself for being the cause of stirring up so much grief. But when he tried to say so, Mary insisted it had been worth it, just to see Ellie for those brief few minutes. "I can't thank you enough for making her come," she said. "How did you know where to find her?"

He told Mary how he'd managed to track her to the lovely old farmhouse and how she'd nearly fainted when she opened the door and saw him standing there.

310

"I nearly fainted too — when she walked in the room. I had no idea you were trying to trace her. Why didn't you tell me?" Mary asked.

"I thought of it as soon as I recognized her from that magazine. But it wasn't easy. And I didn't want to raise your hopes. Suppose she'd refused to see you?"

Mary nodded, imagining how she'd have felt. "If I'd known where she was I'd have jumped on a train straight away — however bad I was feeling," she said.

"Yes — and you were in no fit state to do that, or to have the worry of it. Anyway, I would have gone sooner, but what with Sid being ill — and then having all his business to sort out after the funeral. Today was the first chance I had."

"Thank you, Harry. You can't imagine how much it meant to me, being with her just for that little time. After today's upset, she might not come again — and I wouldn't blame her. But at least I can picture her in her nice house with a good husband and her baby. All I ever wanted was to know she was well and happy."

Harry smiled at her. "She might not come here again, Mary. But I'm going to make sure she visits us in our new place — even if I have to drag her by the hair."

"You mean, you've found somewhere — we won't have to go in one of those awful council flats?" Mary had always dreaded being stuck ten floors up in a block miles away from the people she'd known all her life.

Harry took the papers from his jacket pocket and passed them to her, smiling at her shocked expression.

"You've actually bought this place? It's yours?" she asked.

"All signed and sealed. I told you I'd put Sid's money to good use, didn't I? And I've done his old mate a favour into the bargain." Harry leaned forward and took her hand. "You will come with us won't you, Mary? I can't bear to leave you here with *him*."

Mary looked confused. "You mean — move out of London? Leave Bert?" For a moment she looked frightened. Her hands shook and she bit her lip. Then she looked up and smiled. "Why not? I've done my best by him all these years — and after today I don't think I owe him anything."

"We'll keep it between ourselves for now, shall we?" Harry said.

"I don't relish when the time comes to tell him I'm going," Mary confessed.

"You let me worry about that. Now, sit by the fire and get comfortable and I'll go and get some fish and chips. I don't know about you, but I'm starving. While I'm out I'll try phoning Ellie, make sure she got home all right."

He went straight to the phone box on the corner. But there was no reply. When he'd bought their supper, he tried again. Still no answer. He let it ring for a long time before giving up and going back to the flat, wondering what to tell Mary. He didn't want her to worry, although he could feel the knot of apprehension growing in his stomach. Even if Ellie hadn't reached home yet, her husband should have answered the phone. Hadn't she told him Alex was due back later that afternoon?

CHAPTER
TWENTY-FIVE

Alex turned the car into the lane leading to Withies Farm, whistling under his breath. The last flush of sunset skimmed the tops of the trees bordering the lane and he realized he was later than he'd promised. Ellie would forgive him. She always did. He pictured her in the kitchen, bending awkwardly to get a dish from the oven, and smiled at the imagined domestic scene. Despite the way he had spent the past few days his heart rose as he neared home.

He wasn't ashamed of his relationship with Barbara. She knew the score and was only too happy to supply what was lacking in his marriage. Any man would do the same, he told himself. But he couldn't bear the thought of Ellie finding out. She hadn't told him everything about her past, but from hints dropped by Norah and Trevor, he knew she'd had an unhappy childhood. Something had made her the way she was and he didn't want to hurt her any more by pressing the matter.

Everything would be all right once she'd had the baby. He was eagerly anticipating fatherhood, picturing himself taking his son to the mill, teaching him everything he knew. Somehow, he was sure it would be a boy. That would make everything right. And if things with Ellie didn't change, he could still carry on seeing Barbara. It wouldn't make any difference to his marriage.

He swung the wheel and skidded to a stop on the gravel drive. Without stopping to take his case out of the car, he banged open the side gate and crossed the flagged terrace to the back door.

The kitchen was in darkness and there was no evidence of a meal in preparation. Damn it — she knew he was coming home today. Still in that damned studio, he thought with a little burst of irritation. He peered out of the window across the yard, but the outbuildings were in darkness.

He stood in the middle of the kitchen, his keys still in his hand, a hollow feeling in his stomach. Had she found out about Barbara? Had she left him? Worse — was there someone else?

He went into the hall, looking for a note. He was being irrational. She couldn't possibly know he'd been unfaithful. She'd probably gone shopping.

Still feeling unreasonably annoyed at her absence, he strode down the hall and threw open the drawing room door. The silver tea tray stood on a small table between two chairs, a film of milk congealing on the cold tea in the bone china cups. An ashtray filled with stubs was beside the tray. Someone had been here.

Alarmed, Alex rushed through the house and ran across the yard, his feet throwing up spurts of gravel. Ellie's car was still in the garage, the studio empty and silent.

Really worried now, he wondered if she'd gone into early labour. But surely she'd have left a note or someone would have phoned him. Had she found out about his affair and just taken off? Without a word, without waiting to talk it through with him.

Alex's confused, guilt-ridden mind could think of no other explanation. He walked slowly back to the house and poured himself a large glass of Glenlivet. Carrying glass and bottle, he stumbled into the drawing room and threw himself down on the sofa. Three glasses later a shrill ringing pierced the fog of his despair. It was probably Barbara, he thought.

He couldn't talk to her now. Ignoring the phone, he took another swig from his glass. The phone was still ringing when he sank into a troubled doze.

Several hours later he clutched his aching head and rolled off the sofa on to the floor. The empty glass rolled with him and came to rest by his left cheek. He forced his eyes open, squinting against the harsh overhead light. The shrill ringing of the telephone made a discordant counterpoint to the hammering in his head. He'd been aware of it earlier but hadn't managed to get to the phone before the caller hung up.

He definitely shouldn't have had that last whisky, he thought as he crawled towards the door. His head thumped and his stomach heaved as he remembered coming home to an empty house and the reason for his present sorry state.

He snatched at the phone, praying it was Ellie. Apprehension made his voice rough with anger. "Ellie, where the hell have you been?"

"Is that Mr Alexander Cameron?" a brisk female voice broke in.

"Yes. Who is this?" Alex wished she'd get off the phone. Ellie might be trying to get in touch with him. He glanced at his watch, amazed at how late it was. Surely she should be back by now — if she was coming home, that was. His thoughts skittered here and there as he tried to take in what the other person was saying.

Hospital. The word pierced his consciousness. "What hospital, where?" he demanded. "Is my wife all right?"

"Chelmsford General — Maternity Wing," the woman said. "We've been trying to contact you for hours. The baby . . ."

"I'm on my way," Alex said, slamming the phone down.

He shouldn't be driving with the amount of alcohol he'd drunk. But he had to get to her — apologize for his suspicions. No, he amended, he couldn't admit what his first reaction had been. There *had* been a man at the house today although there was probably an innocent explanation. It was his own guilt that had provoked his angry suspicions.

As he skidded out of the drive and accelerated through the narrow lanes, he vowed he'd give Barbara up. If only Ellie and the baby were all right, he'd make it up to them.

The lights of the hospital loomed towards him and he swung the wheel sharply, skidding to a stop and leaping out of the car.

"Maternity," he gasped and a grinning orderly pointed him in the right direction. He pushed through the swing doors at the end of a glassed-in corridor.

316

"Cameron," he said to the nurse at the desk. "My wife."

"Wait here, Mr Cameron," she said calmly. "The doctor would like to speak to you."

He ignored the chair she indicated and paced the corridor until a young woman in a white coat approached briskly. "Where's the doctor? Why won't they let me see my wife?" he asked.

"I'm Doctor Bastow," she said. "Your wife is resting now, Mr Cameron. She's been through rather an ordeal. I think it best you let her sleep." She took Alex's arm leading him into a small partitioned cubicle, forcing him into a chair. She sat opposite and gazed at him compassionately.

"What is it? She *is* all right, isn't she?"

"Mrs Cameron will be fine. The baby . . ." She touched his hand. "I'm sorry, your son was still-born. He was a few weeks premature, of course. There was nothing we could do."

"I don't understand. Everything was fine. Ellie was perfectly healthy. What went wrong?"

"As I said, Mr Cameron, your wife had rather an unpleasant time of it. She had a fall apparently. She should have seen a doctor or gone to a hospital for treatment in London. But somehow, she managed to get on the train —"

Alex stood up, running his hands wildly through his hair. "London? What the hell are you talking about? My wife was at home when I phoned this morning. I told her I'd be home later today. She wasn't planning to

317

leave the house." But she had left, hadn't she, without leaving a note? What was she doing in London?

"Sit down, Mr Cameron," Dr Bastow said, putting her hand firmly on his arm. "As you said, she was in good health and the baby wasn't due for several weeks. There's no reason why she shouldn't have gone out for a day's shopping. But she was hurrying for the train and had a fall. Despite being in pain, her only thought was to get home." She smiled sympathetically. "I'm so sorry. We did everything we could."

While Alex paced the confined space the doctor explained that Ellie had gone to London on impulse and, anxious to be back before her husband returned home, was hurrying for the train when she tripped. The pains had started on the journey home and when the train stopped at Chelmsford, someone had telephoned for an ambulance.

"I kept telling her to be careful — not to overdo things. Why didn't she listen to me?" Alex asked, his despair turning to anger. It was his son too.

"It could just as easily have happened at home, Mr Cameron," Doctor Bastow tried to reassure him. "But your wife is a healthy young woman. When she recovers there's no reason why —"

Alex turned on her. "That doesn't alter the fact that my son's dead," he snapped.

Doctor Bastow held his gaze. "Yes — but your wife is all right. And she'll need your help to get through this. I suggest you go home and get some sleep. Come back in the morning."

"At least let me see her," he asked.

The doctor showed him into the tiny room, hardly more than a cubicle. He crossed the room and looked down at Ellie. Her greenish pallor, the purple shadows beneath her eyes, made her look young and vulnerable, and Alex felt the ice in his heart begin to melt. He hadn't realized until the doctor had broken the news to him, how much this child had meant to him. But he knew Ellie had been just as eager for parenthood. She wouldn't have intentionally put her baby at risk.

He touched her hair briefly and left the room, his thoughts in turmoil. Grief mingled with guilt as he realized that, if he'd come home a day earlier instead of staying with Barbara, he'd have been able to stop Ellie going off to London.

As he drove homewards, he remembered the unknown visitor. Whoever it was had either driven Ellie to London or taken her to the station. Later, when she was feeling stronger, he'd tackle her about it. The suspicion that Ellie might have another man in her life fuelled his anger once more. He felt better having someone to blame for the tragedy.

Ellie opened her eyes in the dimly lit room. Where was she? The light came through the open door and she saw that she was in a small cubicle of a room. She turned her head towards the uncurtained window and saw herself reflected in the darkened panes, a small figure on a high, white hospital bed.

Confused, she tried to sit up, wincing as she became aware of her bruised, torn body. She whimpered softly, screwing her eyes shut in pain. What had happened to

319

her? All she could remember was raised voices, her father's hand tight on her arm, his eyes flashing hatred as he spat words into her face.

She lay back on the pillows and blackness descended once more.

When she woke again, the room was full of sunshine. A nurse was holding her wrist, smiling down at her. "Well, Mrs Cameron, you're looking a lot better, I must say. Here, let me sit you up and tidy your hair. Your husband will be here in a moment."

She was still confused. But as she let the nurse fuss round her, everything came flooding back — Harry's unexpected arrival, her mother's joy, the row with her father. She closed her eyes against the memory of those last few moments in her old home. She wouldn't think about it, must pretend it had never happened, for Alex's sake — and her baby's.

"The baby," she gasped and, as the nurse patted her hand the doctor's words came rushing back, and she sank back on the pillows, sobbing.

Gradually she became aware that Alex was standing by the window. As she stopped crying and wiped her eyes he turned to her and she flinched away from the bleak expression in his eyes.

"I'm sorry, Alex," she whispered.

"Sorry — that you killed our son?" he said. "I told you — I begged you — to take care. But you took no notice. How could you put your own pleasure before the welfare of our child?"

Ellie looked at him aghast. Surely he would comfort her, take her in his arms and tell her everything would be all right. He was grieving, true, but surely he must realize that her grief was just as overwhelming. But he kept his distance and continued to look coldly at her.

"It wasn't like that at all," she said.

"Oh no, what was it then — a new customer you couldn't turn away, a brilliant new design? What could be more important than our baby?" His voice was bitter and he turned to the window again.

Ellie wanted to put her arms round him and reassure him. But what could she say? The habit of silence was now so ingrained that she found it impossible to find the words to tell him what had happened yesterday. How could she explain how her father had ended up in a crumpled heap at the bottom of the stairs? There was no excuse for what she'd done.

She turned her face to the wall and let the tears slide down her cheeks. Guilt gripped her heart. If only she had resisted Harry's pleas to return to London. Her father would still be alive and she would be at home with Alex, her baby still safely in the womb.

CHAPTER
TWENTY-SIX

Ellie shifted in the deckchair, squinting against the sun. She breathed in the scents of early summer but it did nothing to lift her depression. She'd gone into the garden, taking her sketchpad and pencils, determined to shake off this awful lethargy and start working again. As she'd told herself countless times since returning from the nursing home, she couldn't carry on like this. But as usual, after a few minutes, the pencil had slipped from her hand and she had closed her eyes, reliving once more that awful day and indulging in the fruitless game of "if only".

Her recovery had been slow. Physically, she was well, so the doctors said. But she still couldn't speak without dissolving into tears — in fact she hardly spoke at all.

When Doctor Bastow had expressed concern that she was not coping with her grief, Alex had moved her to a private nursing home. The doctors there had poked and probed, telling her that if she could only talk about it, her heart would start to heal.

But how could she? Once she started it would all come out. Alex hadn't forgiven her for the loss of his son. How would he feel if he knew she'd killed her father too? Her mind clamped down on the thought, but she knew the memory of that lifeless body at the foot of the stairs would never be erased. Horrified at what she'd done, she'd fled the house, not stopping till she reached the main road and flagged down a taxi to Liverpool Street station. Slumping into a seat, the pain had washed over her and she became aware of the warm dampness between her legs.

As she lay in the hospital, she started every time the door to her private room opened. Surely the police would question her when they discovered she'd visited her parents. She didn't care for herself but Alex didn't deserve to be hurt any more.

Back home she started to relax a little. Maybe they thought it was an accident. Bert had been drinking as usual and, even if Mary had seen what happened, Ellie was sure she'd keep quiet for her daughter's sake, especially after what she'd learned.

A shadow fell across her face. It was Mrs Mills. "Mrs Ridley telephoned. They'll be over to see you tomorrow."

Ellie didn't know how she'd have coped without Norah and Trevor. They had visited often, offering their uncritical support and sympathy. But the busy season was starting and they couldn't come so often now.

She stood up, gathering her drawing things together and folding the deckchair. She must try to make an effort for them this time. She'd bake a cake. It wouldn't be anywhere near Norah's standard but it would show them that she was on the mend.

In a sudden burst of enthusiasm she sifted the flour, beat eggs into a bowl. Then, as if a shadow had passed over the sun, she started to shiver. The whisk fell from her hand to clatter on to the worktop. She sat down and put her head in her hands, waiting for the spasm to pass, as she knew from experience it soon would.

Alex found her there when he returned from the mill. She looked up at him, scarcely recognizing him as he gazed coldly at her.

"You've got to snap out of it, Ellie," he said. "Otherwise you'll end up back in the nursing home."

"No, Alex, I'm all right. Really, I am." She was anxious to reassure him. The idea of returning to the nursing home filled her with horror. She wasn't ill — just tired.

"Look, I was making a cake for Norah and I started to feel giddy." She pointed to the bowl of beaten eggs, the ready-greased cake tins, forcing a smile. "Why don't you have a drink while I get dinner ready?"

"I've already eaten," he said. "Don't you realize it's past midnight?" He left the room abruptly.

Ellie couldn't believe she'd lost so many hours. She cleared away the debris of her cake-making efforts, before going upstairs to her lonely room. Since her return from hospital, Alex had slept in the guest room. Resuming marital relations was the last thing on Ellie's mind, but she missed the comforting warmth of his body against hers. Not that he was here that much these days — business seemed to take him to Manchester more often. His frequent absences, together with his continued coldness, served to confirm what she'd only suspected — he was having an affair.

As she undressed and brushed her hair, Ellie wondered why she minded so much. She was still fond of Alex and was truly sorry she'd hurt him, but she'd never really loved him as she felt he deserved to be loved.

In the early days, determined to make her marriage work, she'd tried to please him, tried to prove herself deserving of his love. They had been happy — for a while. But it was too late now. He'd never forgive her for the loss of their child.

Ellie got into bed and switched off the bedside light. The darkness couldn't hide the images that paraded before her closed eyes as she relived the row with her father, his vicious blow and her enraged response; his lifeless body at the foot of the stairs. She lived again her headlong flight through the streets; the pain, the blood running down her legs, and the agonizing ambulance trip which ended at the hospital.

She sat up and swung her legs out of the bed. It was no good — much as she hated them, she'd have to take one of her tablets. At least her sleep would be dreamless. She went to the bathroom cabinet and swallowed a pill with a mouthful of water. Back in bed, she schooled herself to think of Norah's visit the next day.

But, at last, she spiralled down into drug-induced oblivion, her last thought was a despairing cry from the heart — why hadn't she heard from Harry or her mother? Had they deserted her? Did they too blame her for the death of her father?

★ ★ ★

Alex was also sleepless that night. His anger with Ellie had cooled. How could he continue to blame her for the loss of their baby when she was so obviously suffering too? But try as he might, he found it impossible to make the first move to comfort her. It was easier to find solace in Barbara's arms.

The nursing home doctor had reinforced Dr Bastow's opinion — Ellie was young and healthy; there was no reason why she shouldn't have another baby — and the sooner the better.

The trouble was, Alex knew how his wife felt about sex, although she'd tried not to let him see what an ordeal it was. He'd been patient. But his patience had worn thin — that was why he'd taken up with the eager and enthusiastic Barbara.

Now, after spending so much time with his mistress, the idea of forcing himself on Ellie just to make her pregnant was totally repugnant to him. And would a baby really save their marriage? Wouldn't it be better to end it now?

As he tossed and turned in the narrow guest-room bed, Alex admitted that that was what he really wanted — a clean break and a fresh start. He'd believed his love for Ellie would last for ever and he sighed as he recalled their early days together. From the moment he first saw her, he'd been entranced by her unselfconscious beauty. But it was her enthusiasm and determination to succeed that had won his heart.

In retrospect he knew that his marriage had been a mistake. The very things he'd loved about her — her independence and hard work — were not what he wanted from his wife. But it was too late now. He could hardly desert her until she recovered from what the doctors were calling a nervous breakdown.

Resolving to make the best of things for the time being, he turned over in bed, punching his pillow to try and get comfortable, and resisting the temptation to get up and take one of his wife's sleeping pills.

The next morning, eyes gritty and sore from his sleepless night, Alex went down to the kitchen and made his own coffee. He wasn't surprised that Ellie was still in bed. The effect of the pills the doctor had prescribed seemed to make her tired and lethargic by day as well as helping her sleep at night. Maybe it was time she stopped taking them and tried to return to a semblance of normal life.

He took her a cup of coffee and reminded her that the Ridleys were due for lunch. "I'm sorry I won't be here. I simply must go and sort out a few things at the mill. I've spent so much time in Manchester lately that I've been neglecting this end of the business."

Ellie sat up in bed and rubbed her eyes. Her face was pale and puffy, dark shadows under her eyes. "I wish I'd phoned and put them off," she said. "I don't feel like visitors today."

Alex felt a spurt of irritation. "They're not just 'visitors' — they're the nearest thing you have to a family, for God's sake," he snapped. In the early days of their marriage Alex had resented the couple's place in Ellie's affections. But he acknowledged that if anyone could help his wife now, it was the practical down-to-earth Norah.

Ellie's eyes filled with tears, as they did so often these days. But this time he wasn't moved, just exasperated. Despite his earlier resolve his voice was rough as he urged her to snap out of it. Even as he spoke the words he knew it wasn't the answer. She just needed more time.

He left the room abruptly and picked up his briefcase, calling out a goodbye from the foot of the stairs. As he opened the front door the phone rang and he snatched it up quickly, worried it might be Barbara.

He tensed as he recognized the man's voice — the same man who'd phoned often over the past few weeks asking to speak to Ellie.

"I'm afraid my wife is still in the nursing home. She's too ill for visitors, and she certainly won't be taking any orders for a long time yet — if at all," he said.

"I'm sorry to hear that. Please pass on my good wishes," the other man said.

Alex put the phone down and glanced towards the stairs. It was for Ellie's own good, he told himself, justifying his lies. He couldn't have her bothering her head about making scarves until she was better. As he left the house and got in the car, he wondered whether the mysterious caller really was a potential customer. He'd gone through Ellie's papers and been shocked when he realized how many customers she had, but had found no reference to the name Barnes. Was he the unknown visitor on the day of his wife's accident, and was he a former lover?

CHAPTER
TWENTY-SEVEN

Harry was beginning to get to grips with the business end of running the garage and despite his earlier apprehension, it wasn't as complicated as he'd feared. Looking after Sid's small business had helped and he'd always been quick with figures. He preferred the practical side though, getting down in the pit under the cars, breathing in the smell of oil and getting his hands dirty.

He'd been delighted when, a few days after the move, Mary had declared the house "straight" and asked if she could help in the office. Now she spent the best part of the day answering the phone, booking cars in for their service and dealing with the official forms demanded by the new MOT tests.

Mary looked fitter than she had for years. She'd been understandably nervous at the thought of leaving Bert, as well as making a new life away from the place she'd lived all her life. But now she'd stopped looking over her shoulder, thinking that he was going to come after her.

Sometimes though, Harry caught a distant look in her eyes, a drawing down of the corners of her mouth. It only echoed his feelings. Ellie hadn't been in touch since her flight from Kendall Street, the second time she had run away.

They now had a phone number and address, but, apart from learning from her husband that Ellie had lost the baby, there was no further news.

Harry put down the phone, his eyes bleak. There must be something seriously wrong. This latest phone call had convinced Harry that Alex hadn't passed on his messages. There had been something evasive in his voice. He stood up, decision made. He'd go and see for himself. Never mind the business. It would all mean nothing if anything had happened to Ellie.

Mary came in with two mugs of coffee and nodded towards the phone. "Any joy?" she asked.

"I spoke to her husband again. He says she's still in the nursing home — no visitors allowed."

"Did you say you were a relative? Perhaps if he knew her mother wanted to see her, he'd change his tune?"

"I can't do that, Mary. You know why," Harry said, knowing how much it would hurt her. He'd explained already that Ellie's husband thought she had no family. That was why, when he'd first spoken to Cameron and he'd assumed Harry was one of Ellie's clients, he'd given the name Barnes.

"She obviously didn't get a chance to say anything when she got home that night. From what I can gather she was taken straight to hospital and lost the baby — and she's been ill ever since."

Mary gave a strangled sob. "My poor baby. If only there was something I could do."

"Well, I'm going to do something. I'm going up there and I'm going to make Cameron tell me the name of the nursing home. I want to see for myself what's wrong."

"I've been hoping you'd say that," Mary said, brightening.

"I couldn't before but now things are up and running, I can take a day off."

After the front door closed and the sound of Alex's car faded away, Ellie sat up in bed. Her face was swollen with tears. She couldn't let Norah and Trevor see her like this. Alex was right, she thought miserably. She should snap out of it.

She'd always been strong. Hadn't she survived her father's assaults, coped with her grandmother's death? Even running away and making a new life had taken courage. And she'd stood up to Michael Turner when he'd tried to ruin Alex's business. She'd built up her own business too and made a success of it.

She swung her legs out of bed and forced her unsteady legs to carry her to the bathroom. The bottle of pills on the glass shelf caught her eye. Were they really doing her any good? But if they were, why did she feel so much worse these days? She picked the bottle up, then replaced it firmly. Doctors didn't always know best.

Her friends would be here soon and she wanted to be clear-headed when they arrived. Norah was really worried about her and she wanted to reassure her friend that she was on the mend at last — even if she still felt as if a black cloud hovered over her head most of the time. She would smile and join in the conversation if it killed her.

It took an age to wash and dress and the effort of doing her hair and make-up left her drained. She sat on the bed, longing to lie back and pull the covers over her head. But she wouldn't be beaten. She pushed herself up and went downstairs on unsteady legs.

In the kitchen she looked in the larder and the fridge. What on earth could she give them for lunch? She was still trying to decide when the door bell pealed.

Norah gave her a hug, while Trevor hovered behind, beaming his usual wide smile.

It was another warm day and Ellie led them out to the garden where a table and chairs were set out under a flowering cherry. Norah went back into the house to make drinks. Like most men Trevor was uncomfortable with illness and they sat in awkward silence until Norah rejoined them with a tray of iced tea.

The older woman looked at Ellie critically. "Well, love, you're certainly looking better but you could do with bucking up, though. How about a little sea air, get the roses back in your cheeks?" she suggested.

"That's just what I said to Mum," Ellie said before she could stop herself. Her hand flew to her mouth as Norah looked her in the eye.

"What do you mean?" her friend asked, then flapped a hand at her. "No — don't feel you have to tell us, not if you don't want to."

Ellie gazed at her two dearest friends and her eyes filled with tears. It would be such a relief to confide in them. But, although she hoped they'd understand, she couldn't tell them everything.

332

As she hesitated, Norah smiled encouragingly and flapped a hand at Trevor. "I've got a feeling this is girl's talk, love. Why don't you go and talk plants with that gardener bloke?"

Trevor gave an embarrassed laugh and patted Ellie's shoulder awkwardly, before ambling across the lawn into the kitchen garden. When he'd gone Norah took Ellie's hand.

"You know Trev and me love you like you were our own, don't you?" she said. "And we've been so worried about you. It's not just the baby is it?"

Ellie shook her head and her bottom lip quivered.

"I thought there was something else on your mind. If there's anything I can do to help . . ."

"There's nothing anyone can do," Ellie cried. And then it all came out — running away from home and cutting herself off from her family, her love for Harry and her despair when he wrote to say he was getting married, and, last of all, her visit to her old home and the row with her father. But she left out her reasons for running away and she certainly couldn't tell Norah that her last sight of her father had been his body at the foot of the stairs.

When she'd finished she leaned against Norah's comforting arm and wiped her eyes. "I should have told you before — not let you think I was an orphan," she said. "Do you think it was very bad of me?"

"You had your reasons, love," Norah said. "But I don't understand. Your mum must have been relieved to see you — I'm sure she forgave you."

"She did."

"Well, then?"

"I haven't heard a thing since I got home from the hospital. They've got my address and phone number and I wrote to them as soon as I was feeling well enough." Ellie wiped away a stray tear. "I can only think it's because of the row with my dad."

How could she tell Norah she'd killed him? Maybe Harry and her mother were protecting her by not getting in touch — or maybe they blamed her for the accident. She hadn't meant to hurt him, had she? Remembering the hatred and anger she'd felt as she lashed out, Ellie wasn't so sure.

"Maybe losing the baby was a punishment," she whispered.

"Don't talk nonsense, Ellie. Losing the baby was a tragic accident. It could happen to anybody." Norah poured a glass of iced tea and handed it to Ellie with an encouraging smile. "There's no reason why you shouldn't have another baby," she said.

"I'm not so sure about that," Ellie said, sipping the cool drink.

Norah gave her a sharp look. "Is everything all right between you and Alex?"

"I don't know. One minute he's behaving quite normally, the next it's as if he hates me. I know he blames me —"

"That's nonsense too," Norah declared.

"I didn't tell him why I went to London that day. He thinks I went to see a customer and he's furious that I put my business before the baby."

"But surely if you explained about your mother being ill, he'd understand."

"I lied to him — and it's very hard to find a way to tell the truth once you start lying. Besides, I'd have to explain about Harry."

"You still feel the same way about him?"

"Oh, Norah. I know it's stupid. I kept telling myself it was just a childish infatuation. When he came home on leave that last time I realized he felt the same. But he was already married by then . . ."

"So you married Alex."

"I knew I'd lost Harry for ever. And Alex loved me. I tried to make it work." Ellie went to lean on the fence, gazing across the paddock. She turned to her friend. "I had everything a girl could wish for. I even convinced myself I was happy, especially when I got pregnant."

"And now it's all gone wrong," Norah said softly.

"I don't think things will ever be right again," Ellie said. She looked up and saw Trevor coming towards them. Giving a little wave and a forced smile, she took Norah's arm and they went to meet him. "I don't mind Trevor knowing what I've told you but you won't say anything to Alex, will you?"

Norah agreed. "It's none of my business, Ellie — although I do think you should tell him. And you must get in touch with your family. They might not know about the baby and I'm sure your mother at least would want to be told."

"I'll think about it," Ellie promised.

"And think about talking to Alex, too," Norah advised.

"I will," Ellie said. But she knew it would be hard.

After a sandwich lunch, which they ate in the garden, Ellie's friends left, promising to come again soon, provided their assistant had managed the café all right in their absence. Now they were getting busy they didn't like to close for even one day a week.

When they'd gone, Ellie bathed her face, still blotchy from the tears she'd shed. To her surprise she did feel a lot better. Although she hadn't told Norah the whole story, it had relieved some of the burden.

Now, all she had to do was try and regain Alex's trust and affection. She'd been so wrapped in her own misery that she'd hardly given a thought to his feelings. He had said some harsh things, spilling out his grief and hurt. But, if they were to have a future together, they had to break down the barriers, grieve together and move on from the tragedy.

Ignoring the bottle of pills once more, and with a lighter step, Ellie ransacked her wardrobe for something special to wear. She brushed her hair and put on more make-up, then slipped the pale-blue cotton dress over her head. It was one that Alex had always admired, tight over the bodice and with a wide belt cinched at the waist, accentuating her regained figure.

She looked at herself in the mirror and practised a smile. The old Ellie might not have all her sparkle back yet — but she'd put on a convincing act. She owed it to her husband.

Just for a second she allowed herself to think of Harry. Those few moments in his arms had been enough to tell her that her feelings hadn't changed. Ever since their childhood there'd been a bond between them, strengthening into love as they grew up. Despite the mess they'd both made of their lives, the thread that bound them together was even stronger. They both knew it although they'd tried to deny it.

With a sigh she stood up and began tidying the room. It was too late. After what had happened she didn't think he'd ever want to see her again. She didn't really blame him for not getting in touch.

She wouldn't cry, she told herself as she threw things into a drawer. She'd made her decision — a new beginning with Alex. And she'd make a start by moving his things back into their room. In the spare room, his open suitcase, still not unpacked, stood on a chest at the foot of the bed. Ellie hung his suit in the wardrobe and put the dirty shirts and socks in the laundry hamper on the landing. There were a couple of magazines and a book in the bottom of the case and she idly flicked through them. As she did so a little cellophane packet fell on to the floor.

At first she didn't realize what it was. She and Alex had never used contraception.

When he returned from the mill she was sitting on the bed in the spare room. He paused in the doorway and she held her hand out. In it was the damning evidence of his infidelity.

She didn't have to say anything. She could see the truth in his stricken expression.

"Who is she?" she whispered.

"Does it matter?" Alex's shoulders slumped and he moved towards her, his hand outstretched. "Ellie, I'm truly sorry —"

"The question is, Alex — what are we going to do about it?" She couldn't believe how calm her voice was. But she'd had time to absorb the shock, to sort out her conflicting emotions. And in a way, it was a relief. It meant that she could blame someone else for the failure of her marriage. But it was up to Alex now. She was prepared to forgive, if not to forget, and have one last try at patching up their shaky relationship.

But Alex had gone on the offensive. "What are *you* going to do about it, you mean. What did you expect? I wanted a proper wife, not a career woman — and a frigid one at that."

Her eyes widened in shock. It was the first time he'd accused her so blatantly.

He was immediately contrite. "That was unforgivable. Whatever the problem is, I'm sure it's not your fault." He turned and paced the room. "I wanted things to work out, Ellie, and I thought that given time —"

"That's what I wanted too, Alex, truly."

He turned to face her, his eyes bleak. "If only . . ." His voice trailed away.

"If only our child had lived, you mean. Don't you think I've thought the same thing over and over these past months? But, Alex — we have to move on. We've got to decide what we both want in the future." Or even if we have a future together, she thought.

Alex paced the room, struggling for words while she sat on the bed watching him. Then he turned to face her. "I think it would be best if I moved out for a while — give us time to think things over," he said.

Ellie didn't try to dissuade him. "Will you go to her?" she asked calmly.

"She's in Manchester," he said.

"It's late, you don't have to go tonight. We'll sort it out in the morning." Suddenly Ellie felt worn out by her emotions. She wouldn't need any pills tonight.

When she woke it was almost daylight, the birds outside chattering their dawn chorus. She felt surprisingly refreshed especially when she realized how early it was.

The door to Alex's room was closed and she wondered whether he'd packed and left during the night. Suddenly she just didn't care any more. He could go or stay — she would be the one to leave.

She showered and dressed in a light summer dress and sandals. Packing a small case, she decided to leave behind the expensive silk underwear, the mink coat and the jewellery that Alex had lavished on her in the early days of her marriage.

It was still early, the sun scarcely showing above the hedgerows. Trevor and Norah wouldn't mind her turning up unannounced, but she couldn't arrive at this unearthly hour — they would scarcely be out of bed. She went across the yard to the studio and gathered up her paints and brushes, her book of sketches and a few lengths of silk. She would need something to keep her busy, maybe even to earn money. She had no intention of asking Alex for help.

Taking a last look round the studio, the place she'd been happiest during her life at Withies Farm, she realized guiltily that she'd neglected her clients over the past few months. It would take time to regain their confidence.

She hadn't driven her Morris Minor for months. But Alex had always made sure it was regularly serviced and the petrol tank topped up. She drove down the lane and through the village towards Chelmsford, intending to turn on to the A12 and make for Southwold. But when she reached the main road she changed her mind. Turning right, she was soon speeding in the direction of London.

As she drove slowly along Roman Road and turned into Kendall Street, she gasped in shock. Her old home was just a pile of dusty bricks, surrounded by a sagging wooden fence. Bulldozers roared and, above the noise of the machinery, men shouted. A group of children screamed in delight as the wrecking ball ploughed into the next house.

Where were her mother and Harry? Still dreading repercussions from the fight with Bert — not for herself, but for the distress it would cause her mother — she was reluctant to ask the neighbours.

Seeing the wreck of her former home, she realized that Mum had probably never received her letter. But why had neither she nor Harry tried to communicate? Perhaps they didn't want to know her any more.

Should she just turn round and drive back to East Anglia? No. She had to find them.

In the old days she'd have run to Sid Varney and she swallowed a sob as the reality of his death struck home. The other market-traders might be able to help, but suppose they thought she was responsible for her father's death? She could try the council office, but there might be questions there too.

The smell of brick-and-mortar dust from the demolition reached her, bringing back memories of playing on the bombsite near Gran's house. Thinking of Gran brought another muffled sob, but it also reminded her of Auntie Vi. Surely she'd know Mum's new address. The blocks of flats all looked the same, gleaming white and pale gold in the spring sunshine, some of them with brightly painted balconies. Which one was Auntie Vi's? In the old days, everyone had known everyone else. But things had changed and no one remembered her. With a resigned sigh Ellie knew she'd have to give up. At least she'd tried. Now, all she could do was make the long trip to Southwold — or go home to Withies Farm and try to patch things up with Alex.

As she drove back towards the market, the smell of frying bacon drifted through the open car window, reminding her that she'd had nothing to eat or drink today. But, hungry as she was, she couldn't go in Bob's café or Al's pie-and-mash shop; she'd be unable to face the inevitable questions if anyone recognized her.

Regretfully passing the scenes of childhood treats, Ellie drove towards Victoria Park. She remembered a pub on the corner near the park — far enough away for her to be reasonably sure she would meet no one she knew.

Harry stopped the car at the entrance to Withies Farm and turned to Mary. "There's a car in the drive. Someone must be in."

Mary gripped her handbag, her face strained. "I'll wait here, if you don't mind." She'd been very quiet on the long drive and Harry wondered whether she was regretting her impulse to come with him.

"I won't be long," Harry assured her. "When I find out what hospital she's in, we'll go straight there. I won't let him fob me off any more."

He marched up the drive and rang the bell, keeping his finger on it until he saw a shadow moving behind the glass panels. As the door opened, he glanced back and gave Mary a reassuring wave.

"Well, what do you want?" The voice was slurred.

"Mr Cameron, I'm here to see Ellie — er, Helen, your wife." He cleared his throat. "You see, I'm her brother and we're worried about her. When I spoke to you on the telephone you said she'd been ill . . ."

"My wife has no family," Alex said. "I don't know what you're playing at —" He made to shut the door but Harry stuck his foot out. "I'm sorry, Mr Cameron. I must insist on seeing her — to reassure Ellie's mother that she's all right."

"What are you implying?" Alex leaned towards Harry and pushed him in the chest. His eyes were bloodshot and Harry smelt alcohol on his breath.

342

He stood firm. "I demand to see Ellie."

"She's not here," Alex said.

"Well, tell me what hospital she's in. We'll go and see her there. Despite you telling me she's not allowed visitors, which I don't believe for one minute, I'm sure they'll let her mother in."

Alex looked bewildered. "I keep telling you — my wife has no family. I don't understand." His shoulders slumped and he sighed. "When I say she's not here, I mean she's gone — left me. Didn't even leave a note. We had words . . ."

"Well, do you have any idea where she is?"

"How would I know?" Alex snapped, slamming the door in Harry's face.

Harry stood for a moment, wondering whether it was worth ringing the bell again. But the man had obviously been drinking — he wouldn't get any sense out of him. He trudged down the drive, wondering what to tell Mary. She'd been determined to see Ellie and reassure her that she wasn't to blame for Bert's injury.

CHAPTER
TWENTY-EIGHT

The inside of the pub was cool and dim. They'd only just opened and Ellie was the only customer. The barman looked her up and down and finished polishing the glass in his hand before getting the shandy and the ham sandwich she ordered.

She took her food and drink to a table in the corner and, as she sat down, a man came in. The barman jerked his head in Ellie's direction. Perhaps a woman alone was a rare sight in this pub. She tried to concentrate on her food, until she noticed the man staring. He got up and walked over to the table.

"Don't I know you?" he said.

"I don't think so. I don't live round here."

The man snapped his fingers. "I know — you're Bert Tyler's gel, ain't yer?"

Ellie froze, the glass halfway to her lips. She didn't know him and she was surprised he'd recognized her. Should she deny it — or brazen things out? She took a sip of her drink and put the glass down carefully.

The man pulled out a chair and sat down. "I remember — right little looker you was — still are." He grinned and Ellie stared coldly at him. "You worked at that club of Tommy's up West. Bert was mad as hell when you took off. Said you'd had a better offer up north." He swigged his beer, laughing. "I could make you an offer."

Raging inwardly at the suggestiveness in his voice, Ellie kept her voice steady, even managing a small smile. "I doubt it," she said.

He laughed again. "Yeah, Bert always said you fancied yourself too good for the likes of us round 'ere. Oh well, can't blame me for trying."

Ellie pushed the plate away and drained her glass. As she stood up he leered at her. "Well, nice meetin' you again. I expect you're off to see the old man now. Shame about him an' Mary splittin' up. Still, I expect she's well settled in her new place. And knowin' Bert, he couldn't 'ave bin easy to live with."

Ellie's heart began to thump and her palms were wet. Bert was alive, the fall hadn't killed him. All these months she'd blamed herself for his death — told herself losing her baby was a just punishment. Now, all the old hatred welled up. She still wasn't free of him. She sat down again and forced a smile. "I'd like another shandy, please," she said.

He grinned and went over to the bar. She took a few deep breaths, watching as he and the barman sniggered together. He obviously thought she was a pushover and, once she'd found out what she wanted to know, she'd have to get rid of him.

When he came back and put the drinks on the table she smiled up at him and took a sip of shandy. "If you're mates with my dad I expect you know we fell out. He said I'd let him down," she said.

"I gathered something of the kind. Well, yer can't blame him really. He was so sure you'd come up with the goods and Tommy had a lot of money invested in that club. He was bankin' on you to bring the punters in."

Ellie nodded as if in agreement. "I felt really bad about it — that's why I've come back. I want to make it up with him. But the old house is gone and I don't have a new address. Maybe you can help?" She smiled at him over her glass.

Leering, he leaned across the table and patted her hand. "Always glad to help a lady in distress," he said. "Well, as I said, your mum and dad split up. Mary's gone down to Grays with young 'Arry. You must've 'eard that Sid Varney died and left him some money. Doin' well for 'imself, 'e is — got his own car-repair business." There was a trace of envy in his voice.

"So where is my father living then?"

"He moved in with yer sister fer a while, then Tommy found him a little flat. Not sure of the address but you can ask Tommy. 'E'll be in later."

Ellie forced herself to stay calm. She had no wish to confront her brother-in-law but she had to find out a bit more before she made her escape.

"And how is my dad these days? Fit and well?" she asked.

"Well, 'e was a bit brassed off having to walk around with 'is arm in plaster. It took weeks to heal and he couldn't drive or nothin'. But 'e's OK now."

"What happened?" Ellie held her breath for his answer.

"Silly sod fell downstairs — drunk as usual, I dare say." Bert's mate laughed. "Serve 'im right, I say."

Ellie couldn't agree more, but her relief that she hadn't killed him far outweighed any other emotion.

Someone came into the bar and she ducked her head, hoping Tommy Green hadn't turned up already. She'd have to get away, but how? Her companion wouldn't let her go so easily after buying her a drink.

She picked up her handbag. "Where's the ladies?" she asked.

He nodded to a door in the corner. She crossed the room and turned to smile at him. Let him think she was coming back. She ignored the two toilet doors and opened one marked private at the end of the passage. It gave on to a small storeroom and, as she'd guessed there was an exit into the yard at the side of the pub.

Slipping quickly through the gate, she crossed the road and jumped into the Morris. Bert's mate would probably relay their meeting to Tommy and word was sure to get back to her father that she was back in London. But she didn't care. She had all the clues she needed to find her mother and Harry.

With the burden of guilt over her father's fate removed, Ellie felt almost light-hearted. Her earlier despair had vanished and she was confident that she and her mother would be reunited before the day was out. She was also sure they'd have an explanation for why they hadn't been in touch. Her main worry now was how she'd hide her feelings for Harry when at last she came face to face with his wife.

On the outskirts of Grays, she was bewildered by the profusion of busy main roads, the signs for the new Dartford tunnel and new houses going up everywhere. She'd never find them, she thought with a sob, as she stopped at yet another set of traffic lights.

Well, she wasn't going to give up now. She drove back along the main road towards Southend, passing a small parade of shops built in mock Tudor style. At the end of the row she saw an Esso sign and a petrol pump with a large workshop behind it. Next door to the garage was a bay-windowed thirties-style house set back off the road.

Was this it? As Ellie drove on to the forecourt and parked near the pump, her mouth was dry, her hands perspiring on the wheel. A thin elderly man with a drooping moustache came out of the workshop, wiping his hands on a dirty rag. Ellie let out her breath in disappointment. As the old man replaced the petrol cap and took her money, she summoned up her courage. "Does Mr Scott own this place now?" she asked.

"Yeah, Nobby Barnes retired a few months ago."

It *was* the right place. Taking a deep breath Ellie asked if she could speak to Mr Scott.

"He's gone out somewhere — said he might be gone all day. But if yer car needs something doing I can get Stan to have a look." He gave her change and, without waiting for a reply, shouted over his shoulder.

"Put yer car over there," he said, pointing. "Stan'll be out in half a mo."

A car behind her tooted and Ellie drove across the forecourt, parking near the entrance to the workshop.

Stan, a stocky middle-aged man came out, blinking in the sunshine. "What's the trouble?" he asked.

Ellie smiled, a little embarrassed. "I'm afraid the other man misunderstood. There's nothing wrong with my car. I wanted to see Mr Scott."

"Well, you can wait if you like — but I don't know when he'll be back." He made to turn away but she detained him.

"It looks as if you're busy," she said.

Too busy to stand talking to you, Stan's look said, and Ellie quickly apologized. "I didn't mean to keep you from your work, but I really do need to see Harry — Mrs Tyler too. I went to their old house in London and was told they'd moved out here."

Stan looked at her sharply. "You wouldn't be Ellie by any chance?"

She held her breath.

"Well, blow me. Mary's been real worried about you, my girl. Why 'aven't you bin in touch?" he asked.

"I've been ill," Ellie said. She didn't feel up to giving a detailed explanation.

"I knew it. Well, they'll be chuffed to bits when they get back." Stan beckoned her inside. "You'd better come and wait in the office."

Ellie followed him into the dim interior, Stan warning her to be careful and steering her round the piles of old tyres and boxes of tools and spares. She stepped over a pair of legs clad in an oily blue boiler suit projecting from beneath a car. Harry must be doing all right if he was employing three people and could afford to take a day off in the middle of the week.

349

Stan showed her into the cluttered cubicle which served as an office and she wandered round, running her hands over the filing cabinet, the scuffed wooden desk, feeling a little thrill at the thought of Harry being here.

Stan returned with a mug of tea and told her they shouldn't be long. She was surprised Mary had gone with Harry and his wife. She'd understood they didn't get on.

"Does Harry's wife help in the office?" she asked.

Stan looked puzzled. "Harry ain't got a wife — leastways he didn't 'ave when he moved in 'ere." He gave a little chuckle and went back to his work.

Ellie's heart started a slow thick thumping, as if her blood had stopped moving round her veins. No wife? That couldn't be right. Maybe she'd gone back to Germany on a visit.

While she waited she poked around on Harry's desk, suddenly spotting her own phone number on a scrap of paper. The numbers were surrounded by doodles as if he'd sat here for some time waiting for an answer.

Her heart lifted and her lips curved in a smile. So he had been trying to get in touch. She wondered when he'd phoned and the suspicion that Alex hadn't been passing on messages returned. She sighed, trying not to think of Alex and their confrontation the previous evening.

Noises from the workshop told her that Stan and the denim-clad youth were busy and, reluctant to disturb them, she wandered outside, walking down the narrow alley between the garage and the house next door. Stan had told her that that was where Harry and her mother now lived. It was a pleasant-looking house with French windows giving on to the tangled back garden, and a bay window at the front. Compared with Withies Farm with its unused rooms, outbuildings and well-tended grounds, this house seemed quite ordinary. But, reflected Ellie, it was probably more of a home than the farmhouse would ever be.

She leaned on the fence, lost in thought, until the sound of an old van clanking to a halt outside the garage brought her round the side of the workshop in a rush.

They didn't see her and she stopped, suddenly shy. What was she going to say to them, how to explain her silence over the past few weeks? She could hardly tell them she'd thought Bert was dead.

Harry spotted the Morris Minor and called out to Stan, "Got a new customer?"

As Stan came out of the garage, Mary caught sight of Ellie. She gave a little gasp and took a few uncertain steps towards her. As Ellie flew into her arms, Harry realized who it was and rushed over to hug her as well, the three of them holding each other as if they'd never let go. Mary sobbed incoherently and Ellie only just managed to make out what she was saying — "Drove all that way for nothing. You were here all the time."

She looked at Harry and he grinned, that old infectious smile. "We've been all over Essex looking for you." He let her go and turned to Mary. "You'd better take her indoors and get that kettle on. I'll just give

Stan a hand with locking up and make sure Joe's OK to man the pump for a bit longer."

"You're not thinking of driving back to Essex tonight, are you, love?" Mary asked as she ushered Ellie into the house.

"I'm not going back at all," she said, although until this moment she hadn't really been sure.

"You mean you'll stay?"

"If you'll have me."

"Oh, Ellie — if we'll have you!" Mary sat down at the kitchen table and Ellie realized her mother was shaking.

She sat down too and took hold of her hands. "Mum, what can I say? I didn't mean to upset you. I'm sorry for all those things I said last time I saw you."

Mary's eyes filled with tears. "I didn't want to believe you — I thought you'd blame me for not protecting you. But after you'd gone I started remembering little things. I should've realized what was going on — with Sheila too."

Ellie nodded. "Mum — it wasn't your fault. Besides, what could you do?" She shook her head. "I shouldn't have told you."

"Is that why you ran away again? Did you feel I might blame you?"

Ellie hastened to reassure her. "I was so scared, Mum. I thought I'd killed him. And then I lost the baby and I was ill for ages. Then, when I didn't hear from you, I thought . . ."

"It doesn't matter — you're here now," Mary said.

Ellie hesitated. "What about Gerda? Why isn't she here?"

"Didn't you know, love? She wasn't really pregnant — tried to trap him until someone better came along. Good job Harry found out in time."

Ellie's heart was pounding. Not married? If only she'd known when he came home on leave that time. Was it too late now?

She steadied her breathing and smiled, trying not to let Mary see how the news had affected her. "It's a miracle I found you," she said, as the door opened and Harry came in.

"Maybe," he said, "but I would have gone on searching till I found you. And now you're here, I'll never let you run away again."

Mary laughed. "Don't worry, she said she's going to stay, Harry. Are you pleased?"

"Chuffed to bits, love." He bent and kissed her cheek. "You look tired, love. Why don't you go to bed. Plenty of time to talk tomorrow."

When she'd left the room, he came and put his hands on Ellie's shoulders. "Are you really going to stay?"

"Only if you want me to," she said.

"Of course I want you to — you don't know how much."

Ellie smiled hesitantly. Was he saying what she hoped he was? He pulled her towards him, holding her close. His hand stroked her hair and she turned her face up to his. The kiss was sweet and tender and it was as if a block of ice around her heart had started to melt. She moulded her body to his and there was no holding back. She knew — as she'd always known — that when two people really love each other everything else follows as naturally as a rainbow follows a summer shower. But not just yet.

She pulled away, gently, and gave a shaky laugh. "Is this really happening?" she asked, her eyes misty as she gazed into his rugged open face.

"We've waited long enough, haven't we?" Harry said, pulling her towards him again. "But do you think we could wait a little longer? I'd feel better if we sorted everything out first — you know?"

Ellie nodded, smiling. "I want things to be just right this time," she said.

"Are you really sure this is what you want?" Harry kissed her again.

Ellie returned his kiss. "I'm sure," she said simply.

"And you don't have any regrets about leaving that lovely house and your studio and everything?"

"No regrets at all." She gave a little giggle. "Who needs a studio? I can paint anywhere — a garden shed will do me."

"So — you mean to keep up this painting lark then, being a famous designer and all?"

Ellie's smile faded. Surely he wasn't going to be like Alex, denying her the right to a career of her own? "You don't mind, do you?" she asked.

"Well, I do have one condition." He tried to keep his face straight but she realized he was teasing. He wagged his finger sternly. "You've got to change your trademark. It's not *Helene*, it's 'Ellen'. You know we

Londoners don't sound our aitches. And just because we've moved out to Essex doesn't mean we have to abandon our roots."

"Anything you say, my love," she said, going back into his arms.

As she clung to him, breathing in his dear familiar scent, at last she knew she'd really come home. And there would be no more running away.